ABOUT THE AUTHOR

Born to a military family, Joe has lived and traveled worldwide, earned a Business/Psychology degree, and chosen the Pacific Northwest of the United States to settle, raise his family, and pursue his careers—first in telecommunications, then environmental, health and safety education. His interest in science fiction blossomed in his teens while doing research for a class assignment. The mystery of what takes place in our minds while asleep, during meditation, and during yoga provided the foundation for his *Between State* series.

FROM BEYOND

A LUCID-DREAMING ADVENTURE

JOSEPH A WHITE JR

ALKIRA
PUBLISHING

From Beyond
Joseph A White Jr
Copyright © 2024
Published by Alkira Publishing, Australia
ABN: 32736122056
www.alkirapublishing.com

ISBN: 978-1-922329-73-8

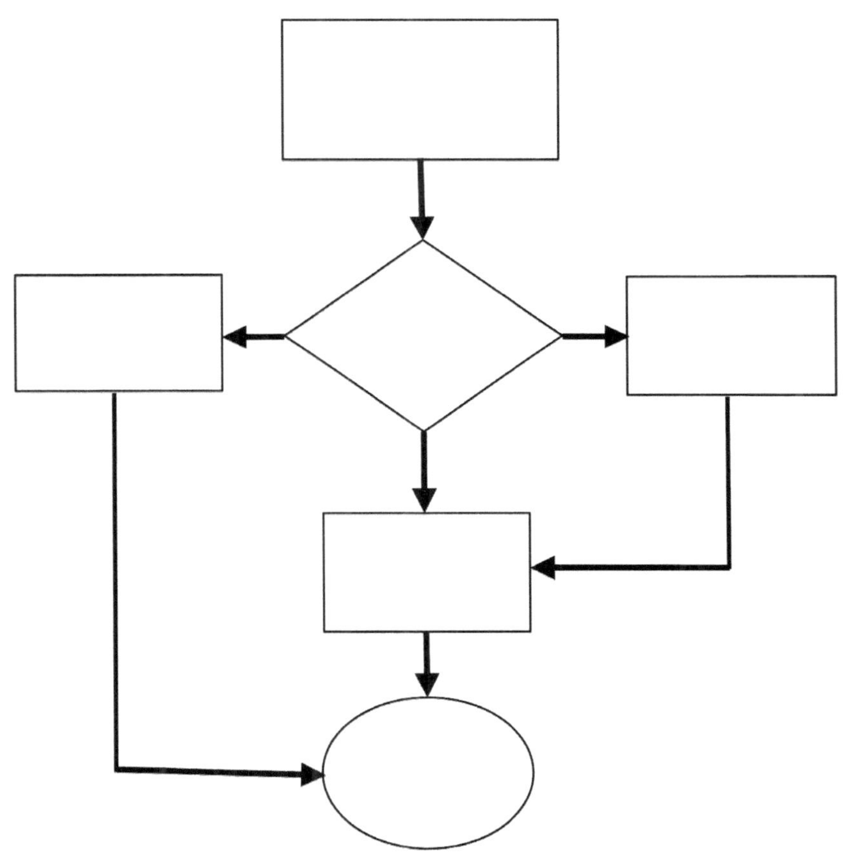

CHAPTER 1

The clear black velvet sky was the backdrop for thousands of tiny, twinkling stars, providing a stage for eight brighter lights that cavorted and weaved in and out of each other's light-trail afterimages. One at a time, they blinked out and reappeared a short distance from the others, playing a game of hide-and-seek. Like barn swallows, they swerved and chased each other tirelessly around their personal playground.

The mosquitoes had not yet claimed the cool evening air, but they would appear next month to feed on unprotected wilderness seekers. Muffled voices came from nearby campsites near the pristine mountain lake east of Seattle. He savored the freedom from the outside world as he and his wife meditated next to the borrowed RV.

Mindi opened her eyes and saw her husband gazing at the sky. The lights instantly drew her attention. "What are they?" she said in a whisper. "They move so fast."

Jeff repeated the phrase now common between them. "You won't believe the dream I just had."

"Where did you go?"

"Well, not a dream. It was more of a feeling. Like someone was here with us."

"Friendly?"

"Well . . . not unfriendly." He paused for a moment, pointed to the sky, and added, "Benign." Another pause. "No, it was like"—Jeff searched for another word—"benevolent. When I opened my eyes, I saw *them*." He looked at her, then back to the lights. "It feels like the show is just for us." As he finished his sentence, the lights stopped with a bounce and, as a group, formed a simple smiley face. It bobbed up and down as if nodding agreement, then blinked out. The lights were gone.

He smiled. "If I didn't know any better, I'd say those were UFOs." He looked back at the vast field of stars.

Back in their hotel room, Jeff surfed the web for reports of dancing lights in the sky. He found information on UFOs from all over the world, going back over sixty years. He saw pictures and videos of lights in the sky, but none reported having been as personal as these, that smiled at him. Some websites called them UAPs, Unexplained Anomalous Phenomenon, and sometimes Unexplained Aerial Phenomenon, instead of Unidentified Flying Objects. Their sighting of the suspected UFOs was another first for the couple, who'd enjoyed many firsts over the last couple of years—things that they were sure other people had never experienced.

He found no surprises in his research. UFOs had been a common conversation topic while in college, along with Bigfoot, the Loch Ness Monster, and ghosts. Ghosts he was somewhat familiar with, because he and Mindi had acted as unseen ghosts during their out-of-body experiences last year, in their excursions into the paranormal, along with telepathy, astral projection, and brief time travel into the past and the future.

Mindi watched over his shoulder as he moved from website to website displaying grainy photos of lights and barely discernible craft hovering on the horizon.

She said, "The whole UFO thing's in the same column as Tarot cards and crystals."

"For me too. But not long ago, I'd have put telepathy, time travel, and out-of-body experiences there. Look at us now."

"Yeah. So what do you think it means?"

He touched her hand, which lay on his shoulder, and glanced up at her. "We're the lucky ones who've seen them, that's all . . . Except . . ." He looked back down at a picture on the laptop screen of a cartoon rendering of a gray UFO alien.

"What?" Mindi said.

"That feeling of a presence while I meditated. Right before vanishing the lights gave a smiling nod of approval to my words. It was like they were watching and listening to us as we watched them."

~

The brass bell announced Mindi and Jeff's entry into the incense-laden metaphysical bookstore on a side street in downtown Seattle. They watched the shop owner, Ingrid, glide through the beaded curtain from the back room. A brief flash of reflected light emanated from the crystal on a chain around her neck.

"Well," she said, a twinkle in her eye. "I felt I might have a visit from you. I'm delighted. How are you?" She stepped forward and gave them each a hug.

Jeff laughed and with good humor said, "Ingrid, I know I don't have to answer that question for you. I'm sure you already know."

Mindi nudged Jeff's arm with her elbow in a motion that signaled him to not be rude.

Ingrid let out a small laugh and said to Mindi, "No, my dear, Jeff is right. I can see that you are both fine after your adventures. I'm glad you are both well and happy. Thank you for coming. What brought you in?"

Mindi glanced over at Jeff, expecting him to answer.

He did. "Thank you again for your counsel and guidance, especially how to guard the gray room. You told us we could trap an uninvited guest. We did have a problem with that, not knowing what we were doing. We got a bit, oh, overconfident . . . We learned our lesson and worked it out, but it was unnerving. You'd warned us to be careful."

Ingrid nodded. "I'm glad you're safe and that you gained something. I saw the news about the drug smugglers. It didn't mention your involvement. It was wise of you to remain discreet."

"So you knew we were involved?" Jeff said.

Ingrid smiled and closed her eyes for a moment as she dipped her head in affirmation.

"In our conversation last year," Mindi said, "you said you felt you're guided by a benign spirit, hoping it was benevolent."

Jeff gave Mindi a questioning look. "That's the feeling I had at the lake."

Mindi smiled at him. "Yes. That's why I wanted to visit here."

Jeff looked to Ingrid for her response.

Ingrid nodded again. "Yes, I said something to that effect. It's the feeling I get when I quiet my mind and am in tune with the universe. What questions might I answer for you?"

"Well." Jeff looked from Mindi and back to Ingrid.

"What do you know about UFOs?"

Ingrid searched his face for a moment. "I'm afraid my knowledge is limited to what's in the news. Now and then there's a surge of interest because of a local report, and some visit the shop. I tell them I'm sorry, but I have little to offer on the subject. Interest seems to wane in a short while. I also get periodic questions about faith healing and ghosts. About spirits, I can help, but not the others. Why do you ask?"

Jeff told her about the lights in the sky, to which Ingrid merely said, "That is interesting."

Mindi said, "Ingrid, when you visited with us in the gray room, you said there were others like us. We understand the need for anonymity because there are those who don't understand what we do and why, but . . ."

With a raise of her hand, Ingrid interjected. "That is correct, my dear. The need for secrecy, even today in our more enlightened times, is essential to avoid misunderstandings. There are those who would try to control us and use our abilities for other than good purposes. What would you like to know?"

Jeff touched Mindi's arm, indicating he'd like to speak. She nodded. "As you know, we've—well, it seems as if by magic—developed skills that allow us to visit others in their minds, travel in time, and move about without being seen. Mindi and I can communicate telepathically and, like she said, we've had intricate out-of-body experiences. With those abilities we assisted the authorities to interfere with that drug shipment. And when Mindi was in danger, I used my skills to help in her rescue."

Ingrid nodded. He continued. "So how could we contact others who can do what we have learned to do? Do you know if there are those who cooperate, say, as an organization to work together toward a common goal? Or how we could contact others to exchange ideas, share experiences?"

Ingrid searched his eyes. "No, I'm sorry. I know of none." She smiled, then chuckled. "I understand what you're saying, and your heart is in the right place, but there is no network, no registry of those of us who have these skills, or how one could contact them if there were. Like Mindi said, we must be careful who knows what we can do. Each of us has particular abilities, and as you know, there are limitations. I know my limitations. I know my strengths and use them for the benefit of others." She looked away, put her hand to her chin. "You could meditate on it. Perhaps the universe will help."

Mindi put her hand on Jeff's arm reassuringly, and then said to Ingrid, "We were fortunate that we could do some good and would like to do more."

Ingrid smiled. "Yes. I know. With your golden auras, it's natural and admirable for you to feel compelled to render aid. There are a few like us who I do know and others I sense, but they don't share, and I don't pry.

"Certainly, there are things you can do that I can't. Our gifts are varied. There's one dear woman who visits me to peruse the books, to share a cup of tea and conversation. She's totally blind, but with her inner sight, she can read the pages of an old book, not in braille, merely by passing her fingers over the page. She reads as if sighted. And she has another skill, truly, a gift." Ingrid paused a moment, lowered her eyes, and frowned. "Sadly, it's a wasted gift. Miraculously, she senses tumors. At first she shared with those afflicted, and a few doctors. But no one believed her enough to investigate. She was mocked and now keeps it to herself. It leaves her frustrated and sad. She awaits a sign, an opportunity to share her knowledge and be of service, yet fears that if her abilities become widely known, she might suffer the fate of many who've been called witches throughout history. That's the same choice I've made. I do what I can, when I can—as I've done with you. These are talents we must hold close."

~

The couple returned to Southern California and resumed their lifestyle as photographic models for LaDormeur cosmetics. When not in the company's service, Jeff took advantage of his experience and contacts and was an independent consultant for computer software clients to evaluate, troubleshoot, and implement their system and operational software. Mindi did hair and nails part-time at a beauty shop in their neighborhood.

Without a mission like last year's drug bust, they kept their metaphysical skills sharp by making out-of-body visits to famous archaeology sites such as Stonehenge, Göbekli Tepe, and the Great Pyramids. Even though they were nontraditional tourists, life for them was, by all definitions, normal.

Jeff's fresh interest in UFOs led him to research the recently declassified records on Project Blue Book and watch videos on YouTube and public government sites. Jeff suspected there'd been extensive secrecy requirements because the government viewed UFOs as a threat to national and world security, fearing disclosure could cause a panic and create political disadvantages to politicians. But what had been released didn't satisfy his curiosity.

There must be more to see, he thought. He made a list of places he could go out-of-body to mentally persuade government personnel to provide access to classified information. On his list was the Pentagon, the National Security Agency, and the Central Intelligence Agency. If successful in the US, he'd visit any country where there'd been reported sightings of UFOs.

Jeff started at the Pentagon and abruptly ran into a psychic firewall that blocked entry into headquarters and their top officials' minds, even when the officials were not on-site. He reasoned there must be hostile government spies using parapsychology to gain access to other classified information. He made no further attempts, lest he be identified and caught.

He was puzzled, though. Last year he hadn't been denied access to the Drug Enforcement Agency offices in Los Angeles—perhaps because there was nothing of interest to international spies. Or it hadn't yet been implemented. He considered testing entry into the DEA sometime.

Am I still at risk of being identified as a paranormal hacker? He knew it was possible to trace and catch electronic computer hackers. If they were sophisticated enough to put up the barriers, could the government also locate psychic hackers? He could protect his and Mindi's gray rooms but didn't know if he could identify someone who attempted to gain unauthorized access. Was that a skill they needed to develop? Was there a psychic cloaking technique like the fictional wizards used to allow snooping? If so, could they use it? Could it be used against them?

~

Upon returning home from an appointment with a computer client, Jeff found Mindi sitting at the dining room table working on her laptop. He noticed a home pregnancy test kit package sitting next to the computer. On top of the package sat a test stick. Mindi looked up. Their eyes met. He looked back down at the package, then back to her with an unspoken question in his eyes. She smiled and gave a nod. He had the answer to his question but needed to see for himself. He reached out, and she handed him the test. He focused on the two red lines that indicated a positive test.

Their eyes met and broad smiles erupted. She stood. He wrapped his arms around her, lifted her, and spun her around, then held her at arm's length while tears of joy filled his eyes. They had yet to say a word. Jeff looked at the computer screen and saw her search results for an ob-gyn, obstetrician-gynecologist. He put his arms around her again and held her close, not wanting to let go.

Jeff's first question was practical. "What does this mean to our modeling contract with LaDormeur?"

She laughed. "For a few months, it won't make any difference. Then I guess there won't be any swimsuit shots." Then, with seriousness. "They could use our pregnancy to reinforce the lack of toxins and metals in the products, showing they are safe for mother and baby. If I do have to quit modeling for a while, I can still do hair. We've saved enough. You'll still model, and you've got your computer clients. We'll do fine."

Jeff's mind was reeling. "We'll have to get a two-bedroom. Maybe we should buy a house, or a condo. What do you think?"

Mindi smiled. "This changes things, alright." She rubbed her stomach, even though she hadn't begun to show. "We don't need to change everything right away, do we?"

Jeff was undeterred. "We'll need to get a bigger car. An SUV!"

"Yes, I suppose so. I'm probably just six weeks along. We've got time. But I love that you're excited." She gestured toward the test kit on the table. "I was a little late. Bought the kit. This is a little unexpected."

"You're my little fertile turtle."

She laughed, lowered her head demurely, and looked at him from under her brow. "Well, what did you expect?"

Uncharacteristically, he blushed. "That's just it. I had no expectations. But now I'll be a proud father, like I'm proud to be your husband."

~

Jeff awoke in the very early morning hours, arose, smiled at his sleeping wife, and pulled the covers over her shoulders. With quiet footsteps he left the room to make his dream journal entry. The entry for last night's dream included intuitive feelings based on what he already knew about pregnancy. He was sure he'd experienced the awareness of an unborn child, *his* unborn child, comfortable and secure, suspended in amniotic fluid, safe within the mother's womb. At this early stage of Mindi's pregnancy, though, a mere few weeks, the child was no larger than ten millimeters from head to rump, a mere sprout from their microscopic seed. He *had* sensed a heartbeat, however. *Was that Mindi's?*

CHAPTER 2

Jeff was again falling and floating in a dream. Yet it was nothing like in the previous one, a few nights ago, when he knew he was with his child and its mother. *Strange*, he thought, as the sensation of falling stopped with the now-familiar weightlessness. The gray fog dissipated, leaving a view of a vast, starlit sky and the ground far below.

Where am I? Who's my host? Whose eyes are these? No one's. He was in his astral body, watching a car approach and move along a road at night. Details became clearer as he moved closer, following it from above. The headlights illuminated the car's path forward; taillights followed obediently. In the approaching distance, several small lakes reflected the stars in the clear air. The car entered a campground next to a lake, parked, and turned off its lights. Jeff floated away from the car, toward a familiar-looking motor home with a couple sitting beside it in camp chairs. He saw the couple was Mindi and himself.

The vision stopped, and he awoke with a start. *What? Why that?*

~

At the breakfast table the next morning, he showed the brief journal entry to Mindi.

"So you saw us?"

"I guess. But there was no context, except I had the same feeling of peace as when we first saw the lights there." He searched her eyes. "What do you think?"

"I don't know, but remember what your dad said . . ."

"I know. Ask and the questions will be answered."

She read the entry again. "Hmm. You're right, the answers have always come."

He shrugged and signed. "Speaking of answers, it'll be a few months before you get an ultrasound and we can know the sex of the baby. Will you want to know then, or wait until you deliver?"

"Oh, Jeff," she said sweetly, "You really are looking forward to this, aren't you?"

"Uh, yeaahh!" he exclaimed good-naturedly. "Aren't you? But I want to know your answer." He reached for her hand. "What do you think?"

Mindi said, "Yes, I'm excited. Of course. But . . . I don't know if I want to know. There are pros and cons to knowing. If we know, we can start buying the decor for the baby's room. We could do a reveal party with friends. If we wait, the mystery could make the excitement even more special. What do you think? Do you care if it's a boy or a girl? Give me an honest answer, not just that you want a healthy baby."

"That's not a fair question." He frowned theatrically, then, with compassion, said, "I really don't have a preference. What I want is for you to have a comfortable pregnancy. I'll make no apology for saying I want a healthy baby. At least you won't be carrying him—or her," he quickly added, "during the heat of the summer, right?"

~

Mindi was already asleep when Jeff, lying next to her, closed his book and turned out the light. He dreamed and was suddenly in a gray room. Theirs? *With her asleep next to me*, he wondered, *why come here now?* He looked around, surprised that Mindi wasn't yet there. Instead of their familiar overstuffed gray chairs, there were two colorful antique side chairs. Had Mindi redecorated?

He heard light footsteps, turned, and saw Ingrid, dressed as when they had last seen her in her bookshop in Seattle weeks ago.

"Hi, Ingrid. How did you get in?"

"Hello, Jeff. This is my space. I called you here. Thank you for coming."

"Oh. Sure. I didn't know I'd been invited." He smiled as he lifted his palms, a subtle gesture implying acceptance. "Is this a social call, or something serious?"

She motioned toward the chairs. Once seated, her hands folded in her lap, Ingrid said, "I believe it to be important. I teach meditation classes. Many take them to learn how to center themselves, calm their minds, relax without drugs or alcohol." She paused. He nodded. Her tone became serious. "Two agents from the NSA came into the shop today. They showed badges and asked questions about my classes. When I asked why they wanted to know, they said they were contacting all teachers who taught meditation as a matter of national security. I asked, 'How do meditation classes affect national security?' Instead of answering, they requested a list of my students. I told them that my student list is private and not to be shared. Although they said they understood, they made it clear that they could resort to a subpoena to obtain the information if necessary. I'm not concerned about that, though.

"They said nothing about their motives, but gave a clue when they asked if any of my students, or anyone else I knew, had inquired beyond meditative techniques, such as psychic phenomena, astral projection, and out-of-body experiences. I mentioned I rarely have specific questions like that, but I do sell books with information on those subjects. I asked if they would like to see them. They wanted a list of who had purchased those books. I explained there is no list, since most are cash sales. Of course, if I did have one, it would be confidential.

"I felt an agent try to probe my mind to gain access, but I resisted the effort and put up a wall, and trust it was fast enough. I'm sure he understood what I had done."

She continued, "You asked about others with skills such as ours. It appears the government has recruited or trained people to use psychic abilities to gain access to information that would not otherwise be available to them."

"Were you able to see their auras? Were they bad people?" Jeff said.

"No, I wouldn't say bad people. Everyone has something to contribute, but their auras appeared faded, smudged, and indistinct. I believe they think they are doing good work, but I sense they're predatory drones, trained to take orders without judgment. I tried to follow them with my mind when they left, but they were inaccessible. I'm a bit concerned the government is now using those skills. Considering yours and Mindi's recent activities, I believed you should know."

Jeff looked around the space, then back to Ingrid. "Have they ever tried to gain access to this room? You have it protected, right, so they couldn't get in, I'm sure. But would you know?"

"Yes, it's protected. But no, I don't think I'd know. That's a good point. Perhaps I can set an alarm. You might do the same."

"Okay, I'll do that. Thanks for the heads-up."

"You're welcome. We will meet again."

His image evaporated into a cloud of glitter and he awoke with a complete memory of the dream, questions, and concerns. Was the government following up on his attempts to gain access to government offices when he wanted more information on UFOs? If the investigation at Ingrid's bookstore was connected to his attempted break-ins, it meant they did have an alarm. Had they identified him, or were they simply looking for clues? How would they know what he was after? Were they checking only in Seattle? Only at Ingrid's? In LA too? Were they fishing, casting a wide net for those who might have more than a passing interest in the psychic? Why did they suspect that meditation would be at the root of those efforts? He had some research to do, but would have to be careful.

Mindi and Jeff had a photo shoot later in the day, and while Mindi was getting ready, he had time to meditate and do some fishing of his own. As soon as he went astral, as he called it, he thought of his previous contact, Agent Anthony Moreno of the Federal Drug Enforcement Agency. Today would be a good day to check if the DEA had a psychic firewall.

Instantly, ghost-like, Jeff was next to the agent's cubicle in the Los Angeles office.

Well, that answers that question.

Jeff slipped into the agent's head unannounced. In silent-thought mode, he visualized his desire to see communications from any government agency regarding agents who had experienced psychic phenomena. Moreno rubbed his forehead and closed his eyes for a moment, but Jeff sensed Moreno had not consciously detected him. After a brief search, Jeff found the memory of Tony reading a memo from DEA headquarters requesting that agents reply to a questionnaire posted on the National Security Agency's website regarding an agent's exposure to metaphysical subjects. The memo included a link to the same Wikipedia page on the psychic phenomenon with which Jeff had become familiar.

Tony had not responded to their request. He felt this issue had been closed for him after months of therapy to work out the anxiety caused by a voice in his head and lucid dreams of Dan the Longshoreman, Jeff's alias while acting as Tony's confidential informant during the Colombian drug bust and Mindi's kidnapping.

Jeff noted the NSA website, memorized the agent's log-in credentials, and left the agent's mind.

When he returned Jeff saw Mindi enjoying a cup of tea on the deck.

She met him with a kiss and hug, then said cheerfully, "Where'd you go?"

"I'll answer in a moment . . . Be right back." He retrieved the journal for her to read about last night's dream visit to Ingrid's gray room.

"So? What does that have to do with today?"

Jeff told her about the visit to Moreno and why the

agent hadn't filled the NSA questionnaire. "That means he didn't send information about his psychic CI up the chain of command. However, he did spend a lot of time with the agency shrink. That should be protected by doctor-patient confidentiality, don't you think?"

"That seems like a lot of work for the government," Mindi said.

"Yeah. I must've set off an alarm. How could I have known?"

"What are you going to do now?"

"Well, I'm *not* going back to the Pentagon, or anywhere else that might be secure. I don't want to end up in a psychic lockup. Look at what we did to Alejandro in the gray room. They'd be more sophisticated than that, don't you think?"

"Darned right you're not going back!" She playfully brandished a shaking fist.

Jeff smiled. "No worries there. But besides Moreno, there's only one other government agent I had contact with: FBI Agent Alice who worked the thermal imaging camera to watch you on Roberto's boat. I'd like to see if the local FBI office in Long Beach is psychically hardened. The DEA wasn't. How many technical agents in the area are named Alice? Maybe I can find out if she put the voice in her head in her report. If not, then I'll be sure they aren't close."

"Uh . . ." Mindi said.

"What?"

"What about Alejandro? What if he told them about voices in his head? He might've said anything for an insanity plea. What do you think?"

"Good point. Forgot about him. I'll see if I can leap into him in prison, crawl around in his memory to see what he might have said."

"Please be careful, if not a little gentle. He screwed up, but we don't want to damage him any more than he already is. He still has kids and a wife back in Bogotá who love him. I like Karina. She said she'd stand by him when he got out, as long as he quit his screwing around with drugs and women."

"I'll be nice. Don't worry."

~

When Jeff's lucid dreams had first started after meeting Mindi, he had figured it was up to him to break up an affair between his ex-girlfriend Charlene's father, Rick, and his mistress, Carolyn. The next mission, not by choice, had been for Mindi and him to interfere in the shipment of tons of drugs from Colombia to the United States in order to protect Charlene, now their employer, from a potentially dangerous situation. She had become romantically involved with one of the Colombian drug dealers, Alejandro Sarís. The mission expanded to rescuing Mindi, who had been taken hostage by the smugglers. Throughout each mission it had seemed like Jeff had received unseen help in obtaining information and access to destinations.

This time things were not going as smoothly as before. Jeff was not getting easy access to the information he wanted. Maybe it was because he didn't have a defined mission. These days he only used his unique skills for doing research on this new hobby of investigating UFOs. But because he'd hit the government firewall, his efforts had morphed into assuring he wasn't at risk for trying to break into their files. He now needed to use his logical mind alone to follow a lead. Things weren't falling into place as easily as before.

Now Jeff needed to sleuth out the FBI offices in Long

Beach and locate Agent Alice, trusting she was still assigned there. The FBI office was a short distance from the Long Beach marina where the drug drama had taken place last year. Jeff didn't find her right away, another example he wasn't getting help anymore. One thing he felt was easier for him to do now, however, was encouraging his host's subconscious to surrender information without realizing what they were doing, or why.

The nameplate on the front desk said *Agent Robert Angliss.* Jeff slipped into Robert's thoughts, smoothly seeking Agent Alice's last name and location. There was no immediate reaction. Would he get the information? He waited. On impulse, Robert radioed Alice. Jeff now intuitively knew Robert and Alice were married.

Alice answered. "Bobby, what a delightful surprise. Why did you call? Is everything alright?"

Jeff sensed Bobby's puzzlement. "I don't know. Was just thinking about you, I guess, and wanted to hear your voice."

"That's so sweet. Morris and I are interviewing potential witnesses right now. Just pulling up to an address. Why don't I get back to you when we break for lunch? Is that okay?"

Jeff suggested that Bobby ask where she was.

"Oh, no problem. Where are you now?" Jeff heard Bobby's internal thoughts of self-doubt: *We don't keep track of each other like this, unless for a case. What am I saying?*

Her response sounded like she was more than just a little puzzled at the question too. "Why do you ask?"

Jeff didn't want to create friction in their relationship, so he suggested Bobby tell her if she were close, maybe they could have lunch.

"Oh." Bobby said, "Just thought we might have lunch together."

Her tone changed to regret. "That'd be nice, but we're north of the pier on Main. There won't be enough time to come back to the office. I'll see you when we get back. Is that alright?"

Bobby, still puzzled at his need to call as much as she was, told her he loved her and he'd see her later.

Jeff felt he could find Agents Alice and Morris. He slipped out of Bobby's mind and glided above the street, eastward toward the pier, heading north in search of a government vehicle, which should be easy to spot. He smiled to himself as he imagined he was searching for two agents dressed like *Men in Black* characters. *This is California*, he thought. *They won't be wearing black suits, even if they are sporting dark glasses.*

He cruised over the streets of Long Beach for a few minutes, and then saw he was wrong. There they were, heading toward a black Chevrolet Suburban with heavily tinted windows. They wore matching dark suits, white shirts, black ties, and sunglasses. Alice got into the driver's seat.

Jeff slipped into the back seat while Morris put their next address in the GPS. He was sure the driver wouldn't notice while he searched her memory. Once inside, in quiet mode, he visualized where to find information on the NSA memo. He was disappointed. The requested information didn't appear like before.

Jeff was searching the corridors of Alice's mind when he heard a gruff female voice behind.

"May I help you?"

He changed his form to the first disguise he could think of, Dan the Longshoreman, and turned to meet her gaze.

They were suddenly in a small gray room, brightly lit like a police interrogation room. Alice's muscular avatar stood with her fists on her hips, ready for battle if necessary. She repeated, "May I help you?" He didn't answer. "Hey!"

With forced casualness, Jeff met her glare. "Perhaps. Who are you?"

She replied caustically, "I'm here to ensure that no one gets in here that doesn't belong. What're you doing here?"

Jeff hoped she was like Mindi's Shirley, a guardian but not in touch with conscious Alice. Folding his arms across his chest and raising his chin, he spoke with authority, hoping to intimidate her. "What is your name?"

She took a step back, as if not expecting to be challenged. "My name is Alicia."

He lowered his arms, his tone less combative. "Thank you, Alicia. I'm with the agency—and on a mission."

Alicia took a breath, thought for a moment, lowered her arms, then, as if unsure of what to do with them, folded them across her chest. "I'm here because Alice had someone intrude in her mind on a stakeout and doesn't want anyone else here but me here." With less of a challenge, but still insistent, she said, "May I help you?"

Jeff had not been sorry that he had created internal conflict with Agent Angliss during the drug bust last year, because Mindi's safety had been at risk. He'd invaded Alice's mind to direct her in playing a successful role in the rescue. Alice had created Alicia as a watch-person, her way of subconsciously coping with an intruder rather than turning to therapy, as the DEA agent had done.

"Thank you, Alicia. That was me. I meant no harm then and mean no harm today. They have instructed me to find out if the NSA has inquired after Alice regarding my visit to her last year." The bold, direct approach seemed to be working. Jeff was certain that conscious Alice would never know of this conversation with her alter-ego.

Alicia straightened her shoulders, arms by her side. Adopting an official stance, she said, "Well, yes, the NSA sent a request to all FBI field officers, requesting information on irregular contacts involving psychic inquiries in agents' minds. Alice decided it would be in the best interests of her career that she not reveal the situation at the marina. She did not want to officially admit it happened, lest it affect her ability to advance in the agency. She recruited me to stand guard. May I ask if you plan to visit her conscious self?"

"No, Alicia. There is no need. You have given me the information I need for my report, which will remain confidential and will not be entered in her file. I believe it would be preferable that she does not worry about her fitness for duty. She responded admirably; her role contributed to the successful outcome of the response. Thank you."

"I thank you. You did not identify yourself. What is your name?"

"I'm Dan Long. My cover, now, as then, is a longshoreman at the container terminal."

"Okay, Agent Long. Alice will subconsciously feel the reassurance. I will embed a memory confirming she need not worry. Contact me directly if you return, to avoid the need for aggressive measures. Is that clear?"

Jeff wondered what those aggressive measures would be but would not ask, and did not want a demonstration. "I understand perfectly. I feel I have the information I need." He searched Alicia's eyes and confirmed her determination. "Thank you," he said again. "I wish nothing but the best for Alice and Bobby."

The time for politeness was over. Alicia tensed, concern in her voice. "What do you know about Bobby?"

"There is no need to be defensive," Jeff said. "I told you,

we have information on all our agents. Thank you for your time, Alicia. Goodbye." He exited Alice's mind, and returned to the back seat of the car to watch if the agent exhibited any reaction to his visit. She massaged the back of her neck.

Jeff silently watched for a couple of blocks to ensure Alice didn't consciously respond to his visit, then returned to the Gardena apartment and documented the events in his journal. He had satisfied himself that there was no report at the FBI or the DEA from Alice Angliss or Tony Moreno that implicated him in the drug-smuggling case.

~

Next on his list of those to check was Alejandro Sarís, incarcerated for kidnapping in the first degree, an A-1 felony, and conspiracy to smuggle drugs from Colombia. What had connected him to the kidnapping were text messages sent from his personal cell phone demanding Jeff contact the DEA to call off the raid on the container of drugs to be offloaded at the Long Beach terminal last July. In an attempt to get a reduced sentence, he had betrayed the three Colombian thugs who had kidnapped Mindi in downtown Los Angeles. They had grabbed her and thrown her, struggling and screaming, into a van, injecting her with a dose of animal tranquilizer that could have killed her. Then they put her in a cardboard moving box and loaded her onto their yacht. The judge and jury had not been impressed. The court gave him the maximum sentence allowed by law.

Alejandro was serving his five years at the maximum-security correctional facility for men located at San Quentin near San Francisco, so he had time to consider if authorities in

Colombia might discover his involvement in the smuggling trade there and, upon completion of his sentence, face further charges.

Roberto Valencia, Alejandro's friend and accomplice, had been convicted of conspiracy to smuggle drugs. After serving a lighter sentence than Alejandro, he returned to Colombia, maintaining a low profile working at his parents' cattle ranch. Carlos Cordoba had flipped, testifying against both Roberto and Alejandro, and as such was granted immunity but deported to Colombia, escorted by agents onboard a commercial jet. He disappeared immediately upon arrival.

Jeff was surprised to find Alejandro wearing a khaki shirt and pants, and not the orange jumpsuit made popular by television and movies. He sat pensively alone in the exercise yard. Jeff slipped into his head quietly and remained in stealth mode.

The prisoner immediately reacted to Jeff's entry by rubbing his forehead and temples. He closed his eyes and leaned forward, putting his head between his knees as if he were going to pass out, his fingers laced behind his head.

Jeff was still angry at what the man had done to Mindi, yet he honored Mindi's request and resisted the impulse to create havoc in his mind. He looked for memories of Alejandro's interrogations to see if he had told anyone about his dreams and his mind invasions, which could implicate Jeff as a telepathic intruder and point to him as a suspect in trying to enter the Pentagon.

Jeff, in exploring memories, saw again how Alejandro had gotten his and Mindi's cell phone numbers and addresses from Charlene's phone and sent texts that demanded the bust be called off.

Jeff discovered that Alejandro's paranoid hunch about the

DEA's knowledge of the drugs in the container shipment was because Jeff had resurrected the man's childhood memories and triggered superstitious fears. The smuggler's response to these irrational feelings was to take Mindi hostage as insurance against a truly nonexistent problem with the authorities. If he hadn't kidnapped Mindi, the authorities would have confiscated the container with millions of dollars' worth of drugs, but the occupants of the *Miranda II* yacht would have been free to sail out of the Long Beach harbor and continue their drug-smuggling activities in Colombia.

Jeff found nothing in the prisoner's memory that suggested Jeff's mental intrusions had been revealed to the authorities, so he was satisfied that there would be no knock on the door by federal agents for his attempt to metaphysically access confidential information regarding UFOs. As far as he was concerned, the subject was closed.

~

Back in real-time in the real world, Jeff searched the internet for information on UFO-based religions. There'd been one dramatic incident where over thirty members of the Heaven's Gate cult committed suicide in 1997 in the belief that when the Hale-Bopp comet arrived, they would be taken aboard an alien spacecraft.

Scientology, another religious organization, believes members experience past lives, often on other planets and that after death, members' souls, known as Thetans, are sent to a landing station on Venus to await entry into another body preparing to be born.

Beside real-life attitudes toward UFOs and extraterrestrial contacts, Jeff found multiple fiction stories about visitors from space and beyond. As part of his background research, he categorized the fictional visitors as friendly aliens, hostile aliens, and, as the story developed, friendly at first and then found not to be in humanity's best interest, as is the case in the *Twilight Zone*'s "To Serve Man."

Conversely, he found other stories where humankind's response is at first antagonistic to the aliens, only to find out later that the visitors are truly benign, as in *Close Encounters of the Third Kind*, which dramatizes a benign UFO that lands on Earth to return UFO abductees from as far back as World War Two, then take a willing traveler back into space. The novel *Contact*, by Carl Sagan, and the movie of the same name, speculates how an advanced off-planet civilization might attempt to communicate with humans. And then there's *ET*, where the extraterrestrial is innocent and friendly, yet the government has a paranoid reaction to his visit to Earth.

The most famous of the fiction stories about aliens who themselves strike first with hostile intent is the 1938 radio program, *War of the Worlds*, followed much later by movies and TV shows depicting aliens determined to destroy Earth or its inhabitants, such as *Mars Attacks*, *The 5th Wave*, and *Independence Day*.

Preceded by the early twentieth-century hero Flash Gordon, the *Men in Black* series and *Arrival* took a more ambiguous approach to interactions where some aliens were friendly and some were not.

Another common theme he noticed in fiction was where governments, through their military, first take a less than peaceful position only to find out later that the aliens are offering humankind technology that may be useful, such as the classic *The Day the Earth Stood Still*.

Conversely, Douglas Adams's 1970s BBC radio play and

novels, *The Hitchhiker's Guide to the Galaxy*, told a story that began with an alien race exhibiting a total lack of regard for the importance of the people of Earth, destroying the entire planet to make way for a new "hyperspace bypass."

Jeff had learned in his college psychology class that Homo sapiens are homeostatic, naturally resistant to rapid changes in their current worldview. Many people are effectively Luddites who directly oppose new technology. They are naturally suspicious, and therefore against it. UFOs, to many, represent rapid changes in technology and engineering.

Visitors from beyond may threaten Homo sapiens' overdeveloped sense of superiority, reinforcing an already unhealthy and unnatural fear of the other. Historically, humans project those fears onto anyone, or anything, unlike us. ETs would be no different. With a few exceptions, the fiction written about UFOs and alien contact portray the humans' paranoid view of aliens' intentions to destroy Earthlings. So Earth's military are suspicious and prepared to attack first, just in case.

Jeff, in reviewing the fictional material, realized these stories represent a window into people's natural tendency to distrust. Distrust and fear are illustrated in the *Twilight Zone* television episodes "The Monsters are Due on Maple Street," where humanity is a victim of their own fear, and "The Invaders," where humans are on the receiving end of such fear when they themselves are the UFO pilots on another planet.

Jeff, who had received training in the scientific method, used this research to logically and emotionally prepare himself for possible alien contact.

He found an article from the *Los Angeles Times* documenting a real incident in Los Angeles, California, when air raid sirens sounded at 2:25 a.m., February 25, 1942.

The military reacted to what they thought was a Japanese aircraft attack. One thousand, four hundred and thirty-three antiaircraft shells were fired to defend the West Coast city. Yet apparently no targets were hit. If the invading object had been a weather balloon, a Japanese balloon bomb, or a German zeppelin, the defensive action would have destroyed it. But no debris or remains were recovered.

Eyewitness descriptions of the invaders described the target as an enormous lozenge. The US Navy and the War Department released conflicting accounts of the incident, which made the battle even more suspicious. A photograph of the event captured nine searchlights highlighting a saucer-shaped craft, surrounded by antiaircraft fire. Of particular note to Jeff, this encounter took place over five years *before* the famous Roswell, New Mexico, incident in July 1947.

Jeff found seemingly credible news reports of a mass sighting of lights above Phoenix, Arizona, on March 13, 1997, when over seven hundred people, including the then governor, observed what came to be referred to as the Phoenix Lights. Multiple lights in the sky were seen flying in a geometric formation for several hours from Phoenix to Prescott, Arizona, then headed into Nevada. The world press picked up the story. At least three documentaries were made on the subject. However, the military later claimed that the lights were aerial flares released by an Air Force A-10 Warthog airplane during a training exercise. The then governor, Fife Symington, in a press conference, spoofed the incident with someone in an alien costume, apparently to avoid public panic. Ten years later, in an interview with a documentary filmmaker, he claimed he had felt at the time that the lights were "otherworldly."

There had been several reports of UFOs creating military

weapon malfunctions, including deactivating nukes. Jeff found a wealth of information regarding alien abductions and documented sightings on multiple websites from all over the world; so much so, he felt saturated by the sheer volume of material.

In his search, Jeff found the UFOrg website. The group's stated purpose was to promote extraterrestrials' perceived interest in preventing humanity from being annihilated with nuclear weapons. The material was presented in such a way Jeff was sure it was not a cult. It sounded like a legitimate organization with a positive statement of purpose toward world peace. The website explained the group's attempts to contact UFOs to let them know there are people of Earth concerned with nuclear disarmament.

The organization encouraged people to meditate together in outdoor settings, usually at night, to attract and make contact with UFOs. They had a manual detailing the procedures to organize a group, initiate contact, and procedures for formally documenting sightings to report to UFOrg's central clearinghouse.

Besides meditation, the manual referred to lucid dreaming, remote viewing, telepathy, and out-of-body experiences to encourage contact toward a worthwhile common goal. Even though Jeff was interested in understanding his and Mindi's personal sighting, he had never considered himself a joiner of groups. But he made note of their efforts and planned to revisit the website periodically to stay informed. He hoped his lights would again make contact during his own private meditations.

CHAPTER 3

Jeff felt the familiar weightlessness in his dreams, yet tonight the view was not the usual gray fog. Instead he floated in a vast starlit sky with no view of planet Earth. Peacefulness enveloped him. Then, without warning, he awoke. He avoided waking Mindi and went to the kitchen to ponder the short dream and write a one-line entry in his journal.

At breakfast Jeff informed Mindi about the dream of floating in space. "I wonder if the dream was because of the UFOs."

Mindi frowned. "What about those reports of people being abducted and cattle mutilations? They're blamed on extraterrestrials. Could we be asking for trouble?"

"Yeah, the *History Channel* had a show about that. There were only two human mutilations, though. One happened early in the government's program of Project Blue Book. Sure, it's two too many . . ." He stopped, realized what he'd said, and regretted having shared.

"People were mutilated too? That doesn't give me a warm fuzzy."

Jeff stumbled to recover. "They're unconfirmed reports. On the website they mentioned some of the original written reports had disappeared. I'll admit, that's suspicious."

"Jeff! You're not helping! Are you sure you want to pursue this?"

He smiled. "I know, I know. I've thought just what you're thinking, but—"

"No buts! I don't want this to draw attention to us. We're going to be parents. I don't want you on a dissection table in outer space somewhere."

He caressed her hand. "I love you. If it will make you feel any better, I'll drop the whole UFO thing. I can be curious about something else." He moved behind her and massaged her neck. Her shoulders relaxed. "It was cool to see the lights, though. Verified sightings are a small fraction compared to the world's population, so I feel fortunate we've witnessed it. I won't report anything if I see them again."

Her body tensed, and she spun to face him.

Oops. He quickly said, "I can let it be." He kissed her. "Okay?"

She forced a smile. "I know you're curious, but we went through some pretty scary stuff last year that taught us some lessons. Let's not go looking for trouble. We've got a good thing going here."

"I understand how you feel about last year. I feel the same way. It was scary . . ." He paused, knowing exactly what she'd say next.

"You were going to say 'but' again, weren't you?" she said, raising her head and her tone.

"*But* we didn't have a choice," Jeff said. "We had to protect Charlene, and then rescue you. Besides, we did have fun until things turned dark, and we got through it." He touched her hand. Their eyes met. "I've thought about it a lot since. Ingrid mentioned that it might have been worse if we hadn't seen it through. Yes, we do have a good thing going, and I'm very grateful. Thank you for talking with me about it."

Standing on tiptoes, she wrapped her arms around him and kissed him. "You're right. We had no choice but to follow that one. Thank you, though, for not looking for trouble with this UFO thing. If there is going to be trouble, I'm sure it will find us."

He laughed. "That's my girl. It's always amazed me how you can capture the essence of something with just a few words." He looked out the window. "Say, we don't have anything else to do this afternoon. How about we meditate and go for a fly, see what there is to see?"

"Not 'go for a walk,' huh? We 'go for a fly.' That's cute. Give me a minute, I'll meet you in the living room."

As they lifted out of their bodies, Mindi said, "It's been a while since we've done this. Where do you want to go?"

"You know, when we found Mrs. Anderson collapsed on the floor of her kitchen, it felt good we could help. We talked about being guardian angels and helping people in trouble. What do you think?"

"How would we find them? She was in our building."

"I don't know. What if we were supposed to find her? We were guided."

"It's possible. Let's just go for a fly. Who knows what we'll find?"

~

They cruised above the rooftops, holding hands. They circled their neighborhood, the circle growing larger as they cruised, watching traffic, people in their backyards relaxing, washing cars in their driveways, and mowing their lawns. The feeling was certainly not new, but they relished its novelty.

They moved beyond the residential area to a light industrial district and floated to the top of a tall construction crane. A hundred feet up, they hovered and watched the operator in his cab, pulling levers to lift a load from a flatbed truck far below onto the next level of the building. Suddenly, they heard a woman's shout, faintly, from nearby. Near an abandoned warehouse a couple of blocks away, they could see a run-down motor home. They flew down to investigate. Inside the old RV, a woman dodged to avoid being slugged by a man, his face contorted in anger. He swung again and missed.

"I'll get him to stop, you get her to leave."

The man trapped the woman against the counter and again drew back his arm. Jeff leaped into the man's mind, focused on his prefrontal lobe, and short-circuited his decision to strike. He then raced to the man's lizard-brain stem and swept around. The man held his head in pain, like he was having an acute migraine.

The woman needed no motivation to move toward the door.

Seeing the move, the man slipped Jeff's mental grip and lunged for her. Jeff took control of the nerves leading to his legs, and he stumbled. As he fell, his head connected with the countertop. The woman scrambled down the step into the empty lot.

The pain from the blow on the counter, along with the headache, left the man writhing on the grimy floor. The woman stopped and looked back over her shoulder as if contemplating returning to attend the man's injury, but encouragement from Mindi kept her moving toward the gate and out onto the sidewalk. Cars passed on the street, yet drivers paid no attention. Satisfied that the woman was safe, Mindi checked the woman's mind to learn the reason for his rage, then joined Jeff hovering next to the RV, alternately watching the woman who leaned against the gatepost, and the man, still on the floor holding his head, trying to get his feet under him.

"Well, that was intense," Jeff said. "What d'ya think that was about?"

"She spent their money on food. He wanted to buy drugs and lottery tickets. He was punishing her. What a jerk. What do we do now?"

"I don't know. What should we do? She's safe and could run. He'd have a hard time catching her. It looks to me like she might not have any place else to go, though. I hope she doesn't go back in there to him; you know, the Stockholm syndrome of battered victims."

"Yeah. I'll get back in her mind and suggest she go to a shelter. How do we find one?"

"Why don't I find the police? They'd know."

"Okay, you go," Mindi said. "Her name's Gail. And he's Jake. She'll need some first aid for the cut on her forehead. She's going to have black eyes and more swelling."

"Can you keep an eye on him?"

"Sure. Meet me back here."

Jeff flew off as Mindi slipped into the woman's head. The first thing she did was suggest she *not* go back to the guy. Instead, walk toward the corner and wait for help. The woman's breathing and heart rate were returning to normal, her thinking still foggy. She sat on a low cinder block wall and planned her escape, if she needed one. Mindi soothed her, reassuring her of her safety.

Moments later a police cruiser rounded the corner and stopped nearby. One of the officers asked Gail a series of questions. Mindi assisted Gail as she told them what happened, pointed to the beat-up RV with the door standing open and mumbled how Jake had beaten her, but she got away. The second officer drove into the lot, Jeff in his mind.

When Jake heard the patrol car door close, he looked out the door. Motioning for Jake to stay down, the officer unsnapped his holster and asked, "Are you injured?"

"Yeah, I've got a headache—that bitch!" He pressed his palms into his eyes.

"Keep your hands where I can see them. Step outside—slowly."

The officer patted Jake down. The officer attending to Gail had called for an ambulance.

"Looks like they have it under control," Mindi said to Jeff. "I can't say that this was a relaxing cruise around town for us. What about you?"

"We did some good. He could've killed her."

The paramedics arrived, treated the woman's head wound, did a field check for concussion, and asked if she wanted to file a complaint. She agreed. They checked the bruise on Jake's head, and then the officers took him into custody while the ambulance transported Gail to a clinic.

Mindi said, "I guess our job is done."

~

After wrapping up a photo shoot the next day, Mindi and Jeff ordered takeout for dinner, watched TV, and went to bed. Jeff dreamed, falling into the familiar grayness. He was beginning to wonder where the dream would take him tonight when he heard Mindi's voice in his mind.

"Jeff?"

"Mindi? You dreaming?"

The gray fog swirled around. "I can't see you."

"Where are you?"

"I'm over here—wherever that is," he said. "See if you can find me. Talk to me."

"I hear you."

"Okay. Keep talking, we'll find each other. This is strange."

When he saw Mindi through the thinning fog, they glided toward each other and held hands. Their feet soon met solidness, the gray cleared. They were in a gray room.

Jeff looked around. "Whose room is this?"

They heard the swish of a door sliding open.

"Well, hello there," Ingrid said with a smile and a nod. "I shouldn't be surprised to see you. I was falling asleep, thinking of Jeff's question about UFOs. And here I am. I still don't understand how this works. This must be your space, Jeff. If you protected it, I still got in. It might be like a flu shot that requires a booster."

"Yeah, I'd better check my security, thanks."

Mindi said, "Why are we here?"

Ingrid said, "I've something important."

Jeff swept his arm around and three chairs appeared.

Ingrid began. "A man came by the shop to inquire about my Saturday night meditation classes. I asked what he wanted to accomplish—reduce stress, better sleep, memory or what? He mentioned that a friend told him about a group who meditated together to contact UFOs for world peace. That seemed coincidental, considering your sighting and the NSA's visit . . ." She paused, looking at Mindi then Jeff. "I'm not really keen on coincidences, you know."

Jeff frowned. "Okay. Yeah. I found a UFO website for a group like that. I wonder if it's the same one. Did he mention its name?"

"No, but if you want to follow up, I'll give you his information. Call me at the shop tomorrow. By the way, congratulations."

Mindi said, "What for?"

Ingrid glanced at Mindi's midsection, then met Mindi's eyes with a smile.

Mindi glanced down, and returned the smile. "Oh. Thank you."

Jeff laughed. "Not much gets past you, does it?"

Ingrid gave one of her signature nods in reply. "I am so glad you two are happy. You are a delightful couple, and I'm glad to know you. Always be vigilant." She lifted her hand, gave a wave, said, "We'll talk soon," then turned into a flutter of glitter and was gone.

~

When they awoke Jeff said to Mindi, "Well, how about that . . . ?"

She scowled. "You said you would leave the UFO thing alone. Are you going to check this guy out?"

"Don't you think I should? Ingrid thought it was important enough to visit and tell us . . . What if it might be related to me trying to break into the feds? We probably oughta know, right?"

Mindi gave her head a slight shake, continued to frown, and watched his eyes while she pondered his question. "Okay." She sighed. "Sure. But I don't want to get involved in something we can't control. I can tell you're interested." She softened her tone. "Do you really think it's about those NSA agents?"

Jeff smiled and took her hands in his. "Minn, my gut says the feds won't be an issue. The UFO subject is intriguing, especially since it seems like, whoever they are, they sought us out that night. But if there is anything to go forward with, *we* make the decision. If anything gets wonky, well, I'm out. We're out. I won't keep anything from you."

"Alright. I do trust Ingrid," Mindi said. "Go ahead, follow up and see where it leads. It might be nothing. But I don't want to get involved in drug-smuggling again." Then, with a chuckle, she added, "Or an interplanetary war."

"No, no. No *Star Wars* Death Star." He reached for her hand. "I'll check this guy out and see what's what. I won't get in touch real-world, just a mind visit. K?"

"Okay. If it looks interesting, I might want to go along. And we need to check our gray rooms' security."

"Do you want me to call Alejandro to test it?" He smiled at her.

They kissed and turned out the light.

~

When Jeff awoke, he was alone in the bed. He found Mindi at the kitchen table, writing in her journal. The sun shone through the window. It was going to be another bright, sunny day in Southern California.

"Good morning, sleepyhead," she said with a smile.

He leaned over, gave her a kiss, glanced at her dream notebook, took her coffee cup to the coffee maker, and made himself a cup too. He leaned back against the counter, sipping his coffee while her second cup brewed. He admired her as she wrote in her journal.

She looked up and said, "What?" He brought her cup to the table. "Thanks." She pushed her notebook over to him. "See if I got that right."

He read the paragraphs of their conversation last night.

"Looks good. I should just copy that into mine. Better yet . . ." He reached over and opened his notebook, writing *See Mindi's journal.* "There, that should do it."

"Lazy bum," she teased, and took a drink of coffee.

"Save time when I can. I'll call Ingrid and get the guy's name and address. Do you want to go visit with him?'

"No. You just go ahead if you want to do it today. It's your idea, and Ingrid thinks it'll be okay. Let me know what you find. I'm going to sit on the deck and read my book. I can use the downtime after yesterday's shoot. Are you okay with that?"

"Sure. No sweat. You want me to cook up some eggs and toast?"

"Sounds good. I'll be sous chef."

After breakfast Jeff called Ingrid on the phone. She told him that her meditation pupil had attended two sessions and mentioned he'd be going to a UFO group next week.

"His name is Isaiah Johnson. He gave off no bad vibes. Seems genuine enough." She gave him the contact information.

Jeff sat in the living room in his meditation position and was easily out-of-body. Having a name and destination in Seattle, he was promptly there to find out about the guy and the UFO study group.

~

Jeff found the man not at the home address Ingrid had provided but in his insurance sales office in West Seattle. Perhaps he was getting some unseen help now. There were two women in the outer office when Jeff, in ghost mode, entered and found his target in the small business's only private office. Jeff slipped into the man's mind and settled in the optic nerve. Isaiah Johnson was at work on his computer. He looked up for a moment as if in thought.

Jeff froze. *Does he know I'm here?* Jeff could feel nothing to reflect his concern. He took a virtual breath and went in search of his goal in the man's memories. He immediately found the information he was looking for, another confirmation he might be getting assistance. The brain portal opened, and the memory of the view of the UFOrg website Isaiah had accessed was clear for Jeff to watch. It was the same website Jeff had seen before. He watched as the insurance agent scanned the list of meetings, writing in his calendar. He would attend a meeting next weekend.

Jeff watched as he read the list of behaviors expected of the participants. It included refraining from the use of drugs and alcohol, assuring a lack of fear, and acceptance of occurrences beyond the realm of accepted science. It mentioned possible excursions into the paranormal with the goal of establishing contact with extraterrestrials. Jeff went back to look through the man's eyes.

Isaiah rubbed his forehead, a signal to Jeff he *was* having an effect. Jeff also noticed the wedding band on his left hand. In quiet mode, Jeff wondered about a wife and family. His host looked toward a family picture on the wall opposite the desk showing a woman and two children; a boy and a girl, both about middle-school age. Jeff smiled to himself, and felt Isaiah smile, as if in return.

Jeff had what he needed. It was time to return to the apartment in Gardena.

Mindi helped him stand, and Jeff took advantage of their physical closeness to give her a hug and kiss.

She said, "Did you have a pleasant trip? Learn anything?"

"Uhhuh. I wanted to check to see if he might be a government agent. It seems he *is* an agent." Mindi froze. Jeff gave her a smile and a wink. "But not with the government. He's an insurance agent."

Mindi punched his shoulder. "You tease!"

"Gotcha!" He laughed. "He was in his office. Like Ingrid said, he's a regular guy: family man and apparently just curious about UFOs. The UFOrg's got a meditation meeting on Bainbridge Island this weekend. If it's okay with you, I'd like to go see what it's about and visit as an uninvited ghost."

"Don't you mean 'uninvited guest'?"

"Well . . . no. Wasn't that cute? I meant it the way I said it, 'uninvited ghost.' What do you think? Funny, huh?"

"Hmm. I think you need better material," she said with a smile.

Jeff gave her a hug. "Oh, I see now. Besides being a smart, beautiful model and mama-to-be, your new day job is a comedy critic, huh?" He tickled her waist with both hands. "I need to test my material on someone. Might as well be you."

Mindi giggled and wiggled away. "Jeff, you are funny, but I get a kick out of needling you. Now, back to your plan. That sounds like a safe way to do it. Is there anything else? I've got something to share."

"Whatcha got?"

She motioned to the sofa to have a seat. "I want to show you this," she said, leaning into him and opening her book. They talked about the most exciting subject in their lives right now: their pregnancy.

~

Jeff's decision to go to the meditation circle out-of-body would allow him to observe unnoticed, and later maybe leap into Isaiah or someone else, to see what they were thinking and feeling. Jeff meditated and instantly left California, arriving in western Washington to see what these "enthusiasts" would do to attract a UFO.

The choice of location for the meeting did not surprise Jeff. He had learned UFOs were often observed around military bases where nuclear armaments were based. This meeting was at Battle Point Park, overlooking Puget Sound, on the west side of Bainbridge Island. Its proximity to the US Navy Ballistic Missile Submarine Squadron Base at Bangor, Washington, Puget Sound Naval Shipyard in Bremerton, and Naval Air Station Whidbey Island would make it a good choice for a UFO sighting.

The park had been a naval radio station during World War II. Back then it was used for essential communications with the naval fleet in the Pacific Theater and eavesdropping on Japanese radio messages. It was decommissioned after VJ Day, Victory over Japan, and its four three-hundred-foot and one eight-hundred-foot-tall broadcast towers were removed. The park was now a popular part of the local community park system.

The UFOrg participants would arrive at sunset, followed by a meditation session beginning just after twilight. Jeff arrived in time to linger and watch cars and vans arrive. The woman who was clearly in charge drove a Mercedes van and, with the help of early arrivals, unloaded folding chairs, arranging them in a circle in the old radio station parade grounds. Jeff explored the park. Although closed this evening, he discovered a small public planetarium with scheduled shows on astronomy.

Attendees arrived dressed for the cool night air. They unpacked cameras, radar detectors, digital recorders, binoculars, and night vision scopes from their bags and backpacks. Talking among themselves, they settled into their chairs. From the conversations, it was obvious many had been together before. Jeff saw Isaiah arrive with his backpack and thermos. Since this was his first time, the woman who drove the Mercedes van welcomed him and asked if he had read the ground rules she had emailed him. He assured her he had. She offered to answer questions he may have. She reminded him to put his phone on silent, but feel free to take photos or use it to record conversations.

"Oh," she said, "and remain positive. No negative thoughts. If you feel fearful, or have doubts, please leave the group and return to your car until after the session is over. Okay?"

He agreed, took a seat, and chatted with the guests on either side. Jeff decided he didn't need to leap into Isaiah's mind for two reasons: He could observe the event more freely outside, and he did not want to make Isaiah uncomfortable or feel that he had become possessed.

Even though not a part of the group, Jeff experienced the excitement of being a participant in something unique. He speculated that some may have paranormal abilities. It made him feel a little more at home with the possibility of being with others who might be able to do what he could do.

The thought crossed his mind, however, that any one of them could be a government agent. There had been speculation about the government infiltrating groups and planting misinformation about UFOs. Jeff resolved to maintain a low profile.

The meditation began with an affirmation of purpose, uniting all beings with the universe, and a wish for peace among all humanity and with visitors from beyond the stars, emphasizing positive thoughts.

A military helicopter, with its flashing lights and harsh sound, cut through the quiet that had enveloped the scene, yet those gathered were not disturbed as it moved into the distance. Soon all was again serene.

There were over twenty participants, their eyes closed, hands resting on their knees, palms up. Jeff, whose body was in meditation pose over a thousand miles to the south, experienced the same level of peace in his current out-of-body state. He hovered just above, and ten feet behind Isaiah, who was seated across the circle of chairs from the Mercedes van lady.

While observing the group, Jeff noticed the woman go out-of-body. He ducked behind the chairs, knowing that if he could see her image, then she would be able to see him, but she immediately turned toward the west. He'd escaped detection this time, but should he disguise himself? How? He would wait, and if spotted, he would act as if he belonged there. He looked around. *Where should I stand?* He went atop the water tower.

Jeff watched the woman scan the horizon. Together they watched the sky and were not disappointed. Eight bouncing lights, similar to those Jeff and Mindi had seen at the lake in the Cascade Mountains, danced and cavorted toward the park and the meditating observers.

The lights ascended higher, within clear view of the group.

The woman returned to her body and spoke aloud. "There are several lights in view. Look." They opened their eyes and followed her gesture as she pointed to the west. Some took video, electronic measurements, and made notes.

Jeff saw Isaiah standing with his mouth open, his hands on top of his head, wavering in wonder. He could only imagine the man's feelings.

Although not his first time, Jeff was as awestruck as the members of the group. Some dictated the experience into their phones, to be sent with video to the organization to be logged with thousands of other sightings from all over the world.

The lights moved closer, dancing and cavorting. After a few minutes, they formed the "smiley face" familiar to Jeff, which quickly appeared to face him on the water tower. Jeff felt the same benevolent feeling as before. His mind filled with a comfortable warmth of acceptance and familiarity. Jeff returned the smile. The multiple lights on the face nodded, then turned toward the group as if to pose for a photo. The group obliged by taking more pictures.

The lights turned back toward Jeff, acknowledged him with a nod, and silently faded back toward the horizon before blinking out.

Jeff looked at the group, who were looking up at him through their cameras. Some snapped pictures. Others recorded video. He ducked behind the curve of the tower. He had been spotted! When he disappeared, the participants, in animated conversation, focused on their phones. Jeff glanced around the tank and saw them huddled over their phones in small groups below. Jeff flew down to see how good the photos were of himself. When he got close, the pictures pixelated. Backing off, he saw the videos and stills merely showed the bright glow of a poltergeist. There was no detail to betray his identity. The conversation buzzed with comments about how well they'd captured the image on the tower and the smiley face of lights. The leader requested that the group document their experiences and send their findings for analysis. Many said this was the closest sighting they've had, and still others, like Isaiah, had seen lights for the first time. Jeff heard Isaiah on the phone with his wife, animatedly discussing what he had seen.

Jeff was excited, too, but for a different reason. It seemed that, once again, the lights had singled him out and acknowledged him with a nod and a smile. What could it mean?

He instantly returned to California, ended his meditation and, before going to bed, recorded the facts in his journal. He left a sticky note affixed to the coffee maker: *Wait until I tell you about the trip I had.* He signed it with a J inside a heart.

CHAPTER 4

Jeff awoke the next morning thinking of the smiling lights in the sky and found Mindi on the computer at the dining room table. She looked at him as he put his hand on her shoulder, and she leaned up to receive the kiss he offered. He watched as she surfed baby furniture sites. When she stopped scrolling, he froze, leaned forward, and gently tightened his grip on her shoulder. She had stopped on the image of a double stroller.

Mindi looked up at him and smiled.

He stared at the screen. When he finally spoke, his voice croaked. "Whaaa . . .?"

She stood and put her arms around him. "I had a dream last night."

He blinked, looked at the screen, looked at her and raised his eyebrows.

"Yeah. A real dream—that we're having twins." She kissed him again.

His eyes blinked in double time. He stared, frozen in space.

"All the websites say it's too early in the pregnancy to tell, but our dreams have always been true. Right? I believe it."

Jeff's mouth hung open, his eyes darting between the computer and her smiling face.

"Jeff, are you alright? Say something. I didn't mean to scare you."

Jeff stammered, then finally said, "Minn, that's great! No, I'm not scared. I'm—I'm— Well . . . When will we know for sure?"

Mindi smiled as she said, "You do like your data, don't you? At ten weeks. I'm around eight." She handed him her dream journal. "Here, read about my dream, I'll get you coffee."

Jeff read how Mindi had dreamed she was pushing a two-baby stroller through a park and stopped to pick up a toy one of the babies dropped. In the stroller were a boy and a girl looking back at her, each with big dark eyes and dark hair. Her closing comment on the dream's entry was *We each have our own mini-me.*

He chuckled. "Mini-mes? That's it? Any more to the dream?"

"Yes, to the first question, and no, no more dream. I woke up. What would you think if that were your dream?"

"Sure. I'd think the same thing, but . . ." He smiled. "Let's not buy matching cribs and a double stroller—yet."

"Agreed."

~

Tonight's dream was again of a star-filled sky, but he was viewing the stars through the transparent canopy of an aircraft, or, he thought, because of the view, maybe a spacecraft. He saw, reflected in the canopy, the dim light of a control panel below an indistinct reflection of a large, helmeted head with a mirrored face shield, silver flight suit, and, when his host glanced down, very long-fingered, gloved hands moving deftly across lit keys.

In his mind he heard, "Welcome. We are glad you could join us. Do not be concerned. We have called you here. You are in no danger."

"Who are you, and where am I?"

"Please observe. We will provide answers."

Jeff watched the gloved hands on the control panel. When the hands stopped, the view again shared his host's view outside, the black sky dusted with stars.

Jeff said, "UFO?"

With the tone of someone sharing information with no hint of condescension, and with a hint of humor, the voice in his mind said, "We call this our craft. We know what it is. To us it is identified."

The craft turned and dipped forward slightly, showing a group of bright lights ahead of them that danced and bounced as the pilot's hands moved across the control panel. He was controlling the lights like marionettes.

The blue and white arc of the Earth appeared with all of the western United States and the Pacific Ocean. The craft flew forward, and the view enlarged as the lights sped ahead. The pilot pressed a button, and Jeff could now see an image on a heads-up display inside of the face shield: a close-up view of the ground, trees and a shoreline. Jeff realized the view came from one of the lights under the pilot's control.

As if the pilot had heard Jeff's thoughts, he said, "Yes, it is."

Jeff's attention was drawn to a group of people sitting in a circle of chairs in the middle of a field, trees all around, and water off to the side. The view instantly changed to a water tower beside the field and showed Jeff on its catwalk, gazing up at the lights. He watched himself watch the lights watch him.

"How are you showing me this?" The now-familiar peace flowed over him.

"You have been asking questions. Here is one answer. We are glad to finally meet you here in your dreams. That you feel at peace now is all you need to know at this crossroad of time. More will be revealed later. Trust your feelings. Be well."

Jeff awoke.

~

The sound of a clicking keyboard accompanied the smell of freshly brewed coffee in the cool air of early morning as the sun peeked above the horizon. Jeff was searching for the definitions of close encounters with UFOs. His research gave him the following list:

> *Close Encounters of the First Kind, CE-1: Visual sightings of UFO.*
> *Close Encounters of the Second Kind, CE-2: Animals panicked or mutilated, plants broken or burned, depressions in the soil.*
> *Close Encounters of the Third Kind, CE-3: Occupants seen inside or outside the UFO.*
> *Close Encounters of the Fourth Kind, CE-4: Abductions.*
> *Close Encounters of the Fifth Kind, CE-5: Communication with UFO occupants.*

Was I abducted? Jeff wondered. *Was that a CE-4? No, I had direct communication with the pilot; so a CE-5? Because it was a dream, are any of these classifications relevant?*

~

Jeff wasn't biting his fingernails in worry, but he was having a bit of an internal crisis. *Could it be so?* He might be close to the answer of who was in control of their dreams and leaps. But . . . even though the pilot said to be at peace, Jeff wasn't at peace now because of the promise he'd made to Mindi. He might be able to get answers, or he might have to forgo the knowledge to please his wife.

And now, new questions. Who was that pilot? Where was he from? The lights while camping? The lights at Bainbridge Island? And now a ride in a flying saucer.

The pilot spoke with me.

Mindi saw the concern on his face as she entered the kitchen. "Is everything alright?"

"I had another dream last night."

"Yeah?" She sat opposite, leaning forward encouragingly. "You want to talk about it?"

"I need to talk about it but don't know where to begin."

She fixed him with her eye and said firmly, but with love, "How about at the start?"

He returned her gaze, took a deep breath, and said nothing.

"Okay. What's up?" The question was a gentle command.

After a moment's hesitation, he said, "Minn . . . I promised to not get involved with the UFO thing."

"Yes you did. Go ahead."

"But—Well—Now—Uh . . . I think the UFO thing is getting involved with me."

She nodded, raising her eyebrows for him to continue. He said nothing. Eventually, he looked down, his shoulders slumped forward, his body seemed to contract, and he remained quiet.

She broke the silence. "Okay, now it's time you explained, because this twenty-question approach isn't working for me." To give him some space, she got up to make herself a cup of coffee.

When she sat, warming her hands around the cup, her attention was squarely on him. "Speak!" Her voice was sharp.

He jerked and looked up, but remained quiet.

After another moment, with a loving tone, she quietly said, "Please."

His eyes met hers. At last, he nodded and told her of his ride in the UFO and how he'd watched himself watch the lights at Bainbridge Island. He repeated what the pilot had said about finally meeting him in their dreams.

"They've been watching us, somehow. Controlling things." He stopped, but it was obvious he had more to share.

"Go on."

"Well, what I feel, but don't know for sure. I—I'm being pulled into this."

"Okay?"

"I didn't ask for this. But the way things have gone before, I feel I won't be able to stop what's going on."

She reached across the table and grasped his hand. "It's alright. I'm not mad. A little concerned, but at least it's not the feds." She smiled. They sat in silence for a few moments. "Whatever it is they want, you can handle it. We can handle anything. We're a team."

Jeff's reluctance to agree showed in his face and tone. "Yeah, I guess." He recognized his petulance and self-doubt and sat up straight. With forced confidence, he said, "We'll be fine. But like before, I don't think I, uh, we can control where this might be headed."

Mindi smiled. "It does sound like it might be interesting. Let's wait and see what happens. We'll be fine." With a motherly tone, she said, "You've done nothing wrong."

"Thank you." He finished his coffee in one gulp, and smiled apologetically.

She nodded acknowledgment, and, apparently done with the subject, she said, "Remember, we've got an ob-gyn appointment this afternoon. We're going together, aren't we?"

~

Jeff was eagerly awaiting his next dream visit with the UFO pilot and alternately dreading it. Still, every morning when he awoke dream-free over the next few weeks, he was relieved. But more important than UFOs and lucid dreams, it was becoming impossible to ignore the daily news reports about global climate change and talk about an extinction: the Anthropocene, the sixth extinction.

Years ago, as part of a college class, he read *Silent Spring* by Rachel Carson. Back then it was merely an academic issue, an assignment to write a paper. The predicted future hadn't happened yet. But as the decades passed, Carson's warning turned out to be prophetic. Because action had been taken to ban DDT, the dangers of that chemical had passed, only to be replaced with others. Now there were phthalates, microplastics, PTFE, and more. With the twins on the way, Jeff reflected on the world they would inherit.

In the intervening years, he'd been introduced to the Gaia hypothesis, which explains how the presence of life itself makes Earth's environment suitable for life. He read that in the year 1800, the population was one billion people. But it had taken *two hundred thousand years* for Earth's population to reach that number. Now, a mere *two hundred years* later, the population had reached nearly eight billion. The use of fossil fuels and the destruction of habitats threaten the balance of life for all species, including humans. We are approaching a tipping point where our comfortable lifestyle will be in danger because of, among other things, increasing atmospheric carbon dioxide and the greenhouse effect.

He found a recent study done by the Pew Research Center on climate change that said forty percent of US adults felt that climate change did not affect their local community much, if at all. And reports of little or no serious concern over nuclear war at all. Which meant that people didn't seem to care, even though both nuclear war and climate change could mean, at the very least, the end of the quality of life that high- and middle-income countries currently enjoyed, and it would cause serious problems to those still living on the edge in low-income countries.

Jeff and Mindi took recycling seriously, used energy-efficient lightbulbs, walked rather than drove when they could, and supported politicians who, for example, promoted the Paris Climate Accord. But that was something everyone was encouraged to do. Yet would it even make a difference without a serious reduction in the use of fossil fuels? As governments of lower-income countries pushed their economies to the breaking point to provide their growing populations with a quality of life equivalent to what those in Western countries took for granted, the demand on petroleum products could only increase. How could it ever be reduced?

He had an ominous feeling that his grandchildren would

not grow up in the world in which he had been raised. He couldn't shake the feeling his current experiences were linked to these concerns. Were their missions in the last couple of years preparing them for what was to come?

~

Jeff had fallen asleep while reading a book written by a physics professor about an infinite number of multiple universes. He knew he was dreaming again, but, he thought, *floating up?* Yes, he was floating up in a velvety darkness with thousands of stars all around, none twinkling. After a few moments, the view changed to what he thought was the inside of a spacecraft. But his view was not from the pilot's viewpoint like before, but from his virtual body, alone in one of several seats set in a semicircle, with a view of space through a large, curved observation window. The dull metal walls, ceiling, and floor showed no seams or rivets; every surface smooth, gray, and clean. A slight machinery hum permeated the space.

A voice in his mind said, "Relax." The familiar sense of security embraced him as he felt the weightlessness within a safety harness.

He thought, *This must be how it feels in the International Space Station.* He searched for the Milky Way but saw only scattered white dots against a black backdrop.

He heard the answer from the androgynous voice. "Yes, it is a similar feeling of being aboard that craft, although you are dreaming this experience. Do not be alarmed. You are safe. If you wish, you can awaken and return at a later time if you feel anxious."

Jeff said, "I wish to remain. It's just that . . ."

The voice said, "Yes, you feel disoriented. You will adjust, we are sure. You are with us. We are the pilot of the craft you visited in your last dream here."

"We?" Jeff said.

"Yes, we," the voice said.

Jeff thought, without saying it out loud, that the pronoun implied a collective consciousness.

"You are correct. That we are," returned the voice. "Hello, Mindi. We are glad you are with us too. Welcome."

"Mindi?" Jeff said. She was now seated to his left.

Sounding as surprised as he was, she said, "Uh. Hello. Uh. Where are we?"

"We are with . . . Uh . . . I'll ask. You're who I spoke with before in the . . ." Jeff was not sure what to call the UFO.

"We are the same. You may call it a flying saucer, or a UFO, but that is inaccurate, because it truly is identified. It is not a saucer, yet it appears to fly. We shall discuss that another time. We can make it seem to move through your atmosphere, and sometimes underwater, and solids, such as rock and soil. To do that, however, takes additional effort. We're sure that will not satisfy your curiosity, but we trust it gives you information so you are undistracted, and we may discuss the purpose for which we have asked you here."

"Are you piloting the craft? How?"

"As you were then, you are in my mind, but this should be less distracting for us all. Are you comfortable?"

"Yes. Do you have a name?"

"We do, but it would be complicated. You can call us Al." There was a pause, then the voice continued, "That's a nickname for Alistair, or Allen, or Alexander, or Alberto . . . But you can call us Al."

Just then, in the background, they heard the once popular Paul Simon song. Jeff chuckled.

Mindi laughed.

The voice said, "We understand your humor. Or you can call us Betty, if you wish." Al gave a short laugh. "We do watch and listen to your entertainment."

"You have a sense of humor," Jeff said.

"That we do. May we continue?" Al said with no tone of impatience. "As you may not have surmised, even through the use of our plural pronoun, we are many individuals, but act as one. We are as you and Mindi, a 'we' together. We have perfected the 'we,' and there is no 'I,' as you understand it. For us, there is serenity residing together in our collectiveness. Much of what your kind have imagined of our kind may be true. However, we do not perform animal mutilations and abductions for the purpose of reproductive research; no needles, no body parts removed. There are surely others who may do that. Neither are we who create what you call crop circles. Those, too, may be performed by others." Al paused, giving Jeff and Mindi a chance to absorb the information.

Jeff said, "Okay. So how many are there of you?"

"Do you want to know how many of us, or how many of the others?" Just as Jeff was about to respond, Al provided the answer. "We are many, but one. The others may be many as well. In a way that you will come to understand, although it is more intricate than my explanation, there may be many different others. We are but one. And there may be others that do not know your Earth, who are also different. We shall not speak of them, for they do not affect you. We, our 'we,' do, as many others may."

Mindi spoke up. "Where are you from? Are the other 'we' from the same, uh, place?"

"Our 'from,' as many have speculated, is not Betelgeuse or Orion. Some of your scientists and journalists have speculated we come from the star cluster you call Sirius, or from the nearby constellation Orion. What is important is that we are here now."

"What do you mean by 'now'?" Jeff said. "When else could we be here?"

"We will explain, now, about time and space. Time is fluid, and is more than most merely experience it, going forward from one moment to the next. We know you two have experienced a duality of time travel, that is, you have moved backward and forward in small leaps, farther than the moment-at-a-time forward, which is something that your kind normally experience. You are fortunate to have experienced that small amount of time travel in larger proportions than normal."

Al went quiet for a moment. The couple looked around, wondering if he were still there.

Then Al spoke again. "We are here. Space, as most humans understand, is three-dimensional: up, down, and sideways. Many have expressed that the universe is infinite, which we believe to be accurate, and that adds another dimension to the three, in that there is no end point to space. Time is also infinite in all dimensions and directions, without boundaries. Imagine a sphere with an infinite number of directions within it but no shell. That is time. That also describes space. If there were a measure beyond infinite, time and space would be beyond infinite. Because the variables are infinite, they can never be counted. In summary, there are many more than the three physical dimensions and two dimensions of time. All are infinite."

"Infinite?" Jeff repeated.

"Yes. Worry not that your minds—no minds, not even ours—cannot fully comprehend infinity that is forever and beyond. The concept of infinite time and space involves an unlimited number of variables in diverse directions and chronological orders."

"What?" Jeff said. "I'm confused."

"We will try to explain. Your minds understand analogies. You attempt weather prediction with computer models. No matter how powerful the computer, or linked computers, the virtually infinite number of variables in Earth's weather make it impossible to predict future weather with accuracy, but yet the wind still blows, the sun still shines, and it still rains. For predicting weather, humans can come close, but no cigar."

Jeff mentally blinked at the mid-twentieth-century American carnival barker's expression.

"Oh, you like that colorful idiom? We have agreed that when we interact with humans, we should try to use phrases with which they can relate. It's a li'l folksier. How're we doin'? It gives us a little more bang for our buck, yeah?" Al chuckled. "We have many more, but we will spare you. Okey-dokey, Smokey?"

"Well." Jeff mentally shook his head. "Uh, I guess. When you visit other countries, do you speak their language?"

Al projected pride as he said, "We are fluent in *all* languages. We collect, catalog, and cross-reference them. We're truly a Rosetta Stone. If you need something translated, we're the bee's knees." Al chuckled again.

"What?" Mindi and Jeff thought their question together.

"Oh, that is slang, too, but apparently from another of your kind's past you may not have directly experienced. Forgive us our lapse of time sequence. We continue. Your visits here are to prepare you for the next." Al stopped, which left Jeff and Mindi waiting for the rest of the sentence.

"Next what?" Mindi said. "What do you mean by next?"

Jeff said, "Yeah, next what?"

"It seems we must explain further," Al said. "Next, in your language is an adjective qualifying a following noun, such as week or door." Al waited, then clarified. "'Next week' or 'next door,' you see? We use 'next' as a noun to describe a coming point in time. We use it to define a specific point in time, such as 'now' and 'then,' such as you use in your familiar syntax. We use 'next' like that. It would have been easier for you to grok if we had inserted the phrase to say, 'the next that will be done.' It is merely a different syntax. It saves time. You will come to understand."

"Grok?" Jeff said, "How do you . . . Are you . . . Are you from—"

"No, we are not from Mars," Al said, "like Heinlein's character Valentine Michael Smith, in the novel you are thinking of. We appreciate your fiction as well as your music. We also like Mark Twain, Ray Bradbury, and Philip José Farmer. Their efforts are fruitful and entertaining. We, too, have learned."

"Mars?" Mindi interjected. "Who's Heinlein? Valentine Smith? What's grok?"

Jeff turned toward her. "Uh, yeah, it's a funny word. A made-up verb, to grok, from a sci-fi novel, *Stranger in a Strange Land* by Robert A. Heinlein. It means . . ." Jeff looked out the observation window at the stars beyond as if the answer were there. "Well, it means understanding something intuitively or with complete empathy."

Al said, "You now grok? Yes?"

Mindi mumbled, "I guess."

"I still have questions." Jeff paused, trying to sort them out.

Like a patient teacher, Al said, "We will answer your questions." He chuckled. "In time. We sense you and Mindi feel comfortable visiting us. You, the collective you as a couple, have been chosen and are well suited for what we require."

Jeff brushed off Al's comment. "Okay. Sure." He stumbled a moment, then found his mental footing, "I need to know this. I *need* to know. Who is in charge of these dreams? It was you, wasn't it?"

"No one's in charge. However, for some things, there were inducements to specific actions."

"What does that mean?"

"Inducements? Like encouragements. As one induces a fire by blowing air. By adding additional oxygen, it grows faster."

"What's the difference between being in charge and inducing? And why induce?"

"You will surely learn of that in time as well. Now is not the time. You are special. You expanded the use of your gift of new skills so far beyond what was originally expected. You have used them wisely. It is unnecessary for us to have total control."

"Total control? That implies you had some control!" Jeff's voice was loud and angry. "I knew there was someone in control. It *is* you!"

"We trust you are not agitated because of our use of the word 'control.' Actions were taken to accomplish a task or a goal of your choosing. We did not choose the goal. We assisted in which path to take at a crossroad. When those moments arose, we guided you to make the best choice."

"Okay, but you did it without our permission," Mindi said. "I don't like that!"

"We understand how you may feel that way. Your skills with telepathy, your out-of-body travel, your parapsychological skills, are yours. No one gave them to you. We believe they are the effect of some unexplained natural law. What we provided, on occasion, is a firm choice of direction when you used those skills. All humans have the ability to have lucid dreams. It is built into their minds. Alas, many do not know of it. Or if they do know of it, they are not motivated to develop the skill. You were chosen because your ability to lucid dream was encouraged; Developed. Not given to you. Consciously or subconsciously, we do not know which, you used your skills and with use you gained experience. You are like gymnasts who develop a new routine. We, in effect, were spotters until you perfected your abilities, and then we assisted in accessing those you wished to visit telepathically or via astral projection. Once you were there, we helped you find the information for which you were searching. We were at your service."

"So who developed our ability to lucid dream, if not you? And why did I time travel?"

"As we said, it was not us who initiated your ability to begin your lucid dreaming. That was another. You time traveled before we discovered you. As we watched, our ability to assist your activities diminished compared to when you were in your real-time. It is with time travel that we cannot control your destination, the distance, or direction. Who does that, if not you, we do not know. And when you arrive in another time, we are quite limited in our ability to observe and assist.

"Now here you are, and we can speak with you. That is what makes you special. You respond to our urgings. We do not know how it works, and that we would like to know. However, even though we do not know many things about your activities, we know we can"—Al paused as if searching for the right phrase—"encourage you to follow the suggestions. We watch and listen, because we wish to learn how to do what you do, particularly time travel."

"So you can't time travel on your own?"

"Not as you do. We must accompany you."

"Can you foresee our future?"

"From your real-time, and when you time travel to the future, we see multiple paths that may be taken, much as a chess master can see the choices of moves available during a game. We then calculate the most reasonable choice. If it appeared the choice you will take would result in a serious negative outcome, we would nudge you toward a better choice. But that is only when we are in contact with your brain-wave frequencies—"

Jeff interrupted, still agitated. "So you can interfere with my choices."

Al waited a moment, then answered patiently, "That is so, we believe we can interfere, but we have not done so. However, if we saw you were to fall off the cliff, yes, we would attempt to interfere to save you. There has been no time we needed to do that. But we would, if required.

"Allow us to explain to you another way. We provided intuition. You were then able to act on that intuition."

Jeff said, "So I still had free will—to do it my way."

"With what we have learned in our study of humans' philosophy, religion and scientific writings, the term 'free will' is complicated, and we surmise, quite a controversial subject. We would be happy to discuss the implications of free will as we have come to understand it, but not now. You could study that on your own by researching the term in the writings of philosophers and clergy available on the internet. There is much to find there, including those who say that there is truly no free will."

"You know of the internet?"

"Quite intimately. It is how we have been able to learn as much as we now know."

"Oh. Okay. I guess I see. If you were there to protect us," Jeff recalled the event when he and Mindi were in danger, trapped in the gray room in another's mind, "you didn't protect us when we got trapped in that guy's mind, did you?"

"We know of that which you remember. You survived with the only cost being the expenditure of adrenaline. Plus, you learned something. That was of great value. Our goal, when we accompany you, is to gather data. But we can, as we observed, calculate how things might transpire, and smooth the way for you as we have done in the past. We know the laws of nature, even human nature, can foresee cause and effect, how events may transpire, and make choices."

"Like a god?"

"If you believe in one. We do not." Al chuckled.

"So you're not gods? You are not omnipotent. You can't see everything?"

"We can see many things. God is a metaphysical and spiritual concept that we do not."

"Do not what?" Mindi said.

"Syntax issue. Like 'next.'"

Jeff was frustrated, so he tried another approach. "Al, this is important to me, to us. We must know who is responsible, if we are to consider what you want of us."

"You have shown initiative and wisdom. For you to not have an answer to your question will not detract from the ability to do what is needed to respond to our request. There are only three of you who have the skills that can be used as effectively and creatively as you. You were on your own during your very first dream visits back in time toward Mindi. Then later, after a collaboration between another and ourselves, brings you to a point where you two are, how can we say, destined to be matched. Now, for many reasons, it is only we who will work with you. All others are without input or control."

Jeff said, doubtfully, "So we weren't manipulated?"

With the patience of a learned scholar and teacher, Al said, "You were not, but even if you had been, are you disappointed in the result of meeting each other and being married?"

"Well, no. Not at all."

Mindi was emphatic. "No!"

A warm feeling of love emanated from Al, who said, "You are coming to understand how it is that we are 'we.' You are needed. To show you why you are needed, we must ask a question."

"Okay," Jeff said.

"Mindi?" said Al.

"Uh, yes?"

"Is it not true you are limited by what you can do in the physical world when you are out-of-body or, with telepathy, in someone's mind?"

"Yes."

"However, you can often persuade those whom your mind visits to do certain things, correct?"

The couple each said, "Yes."

"We, too, are limited with what we can do in the physical world. However, when you are in the physical world, you can do what we cannot. You can manipulate the physical world. For that, you are necessary to assist us."

"Okay. But I'm still curious," Jeff said. "So are we in real-time now or have we time traveled to be here with you?"

"Yes."

"To which?"

"Both. As we explained before, time is a sphere in which your travel is not limited to merely forward a moment at a time, as you are most familiar, or, as you efficiently experienced, backward and then to a limited degree, forward a short distance. There is an infinite number of directions in which you can now move. To answer your question, you have traveled to my now."

Jeff said hesitantly, "Okay, I guess I see, sorta. So that's *when* we are. But *where* are we?" After a moment, he added, "And why?"

"We are in my 'here,' in your lucid dreams. A place that only you can reach to visit. That you are here and now is what is important. There is much you may not be able to understand fully. Things you may never know. For you to know those things may satisfy your curiosity, but that knowledge will make no difference in what we are to ask of you. Enough of that. Here is why we have called you here: You are needed."

Jeff and Mindi looked at each other.

"We warn you, you may find great peril in the future nows to come, putting at risk the safety of all on your planet in your then-there. To satisfy the question in your mind as to what your mission will be, that will be revealed. Meanwhile, you must be wary of those who may attempt to inhibit the completion of your mission."

"Who?" Jeff asked.

"There may be those who have agendas which may not align with ours. Be cautious of them as they arise."

Leaning forward, Mindi asked, "Who are they?" Her voice rose. "Will they be dangerous?"

"We do not know. We can analyze trends which allow us to predict many possibilities, and those potentialities may be beneficial to humankind, may be deleterious, or some of both. Be cautious."

Jeff said, "If they want the Earth to fail, to be obliterated, why do they not just destroy us?"

"They very well may. That is all we will tell you at this time. Do you have other questions?"

"Yes," Jeff said. "What is the technology that drives this craft?"

"The vehicle we are in is in our minds. You are within a metaphysical manifestation. There is a limitation to what we can affect in your physical world. The lights with which we first greeted you and entertained your UFO enthusiasts are our upper limit. We believe that the crop circles are others' effects, if they are, in fact, visitors to Earth. Or they may merely be the work of clever humans who execute ingenious actions for selfish reasons."

"How is it you can defy the laws of physics, traveling thousands of miles per hour, then make sharp turns without injury to the pilots?"

"We appear to you as a metaphysical manifestation. You would call them special effects. Remember, this UFO, as you call it, is in your dream."

"What about the reports of animal mutilations and removal of eggs and sperm from abductees?"

"Those other actions may be performed by humans who lay the blame on others. Or they may be performed by other beings. They could be hallucinations, or a public relations ruse to frighten the gullible. We are not certain. But we are sure it is not us."

Jeff asked about reports of captured alien craft, UFOs, and recovered grays, the pilots from crashed vehicles.

Al chuckled. "That, too, may be public relations

maneuvers. We are unsure. Or there may be other beings, visitors we are unaware of. The universe is vast, after all, and we do not know everything. There may be artifacts, as you have heard described. Those are not of our kind. Those reports by your government and scientists could also be deceptions, cleverly leaked fake intelligence to control your population at large. We have observed fear among your populations of an impending alien invasion. There will be no invasion by us. We maintain a low profile because of those perceptions."

"Why haven't you worked to counteract the propaganda?"

"It is truly not our concern. We do not care about things that are not of our interest. We enjoy watching a seed grow, watching it thrive. The minutia of your lives have little significance to us; except, of course, those things that would have a macro effect on human life. Again, what is significant are those things that threaten you humans' very existence. Life on your planet will go on. However, civilization would suffer if there were to be a nuclear conflagration or massive climate change resulting in a return to a vast ice age or complete desertification of the entire biosphere. The continuation of humanity is our concern. We do not want humankind desecrated beyond recovery. Humans die and suffer every day, but the population continues to grow. However, if a tipping point is reached, humanity may degrade to below Stone Age conditions. That would not be to our liking."

Al paused for effect, then said, "Attempts have previously been made to enhance the well-being of Earth's civilizations, efforts which have fallen prey to those who have been reluctant to act on their insights. Religious beliefs prevent open minds from receiving the benefits imagined. Among you are those who are intelligent and capable, yet who lack a wider view, and others who are driven by greed for power, control, and wealth."

"Really?" Mindi said. "You are aware of that?"

"Throughout history, individuals with limited vision denied the images that appeared in their minds. Many lacked the ability to cope with new ideas. Unlike you two, whose minds are open to receive and utilize the gifts you were given, many others merely stopped listening or, sadly, lacked perseverance.

"You have desirous traits, but now is not the time for further discussion. Suffice it to say, you are those who are chosen. Not in a religious way, however. There were others who had insights in that manner, and much harm was done in the name of their own self-manufactured gods. There have been many with severe character defects who brought your planet to the brink of disaster. Even now, there are problems that can affect our interests. Humankind could die from hunger, disease, or radiation poisoning. Your prehistoric ancestors used knowledge and skills that have benefited many civilizations, much of which have sadly been lost to history, and other knowledge and skills that are to their detriment. Yet Gaia, as some call your living planet, survives. We wish humanity to progress without a nuclear war."

"Nuclear war?" Jeff asked.

"Your civilization, even all of humanity, could be destroyed by a global nuclear disaster. We predict a ninety-five percent chance of that happening, plus or minus four points. So if it is plus four percentage points, it is virtually assured to be forthcoming. If it is minus four points . . ." There was a long pause, then a sigh. "Ninety-one percent is still poor odds. Action must be taken.

"Humankind has learned to collect seeds, grow plants, and cultivate crops, moving away from a hunter-gatherer subsistence. The population has increased. Humankind has developed technologies including electrical and nuclear power generation, medicine and physics, computers and communications, metallurgy and plastics. Unfortunately, humankind's imagination has misused much of that knowledge to create a vast war machine of explosives and biological weapons that, as we project, threatens your species."

Jeff wanted to know more. "Who was given that information? Can you give me names? Who failed, when, and why?"

"We foresaw your interest. You will recognize many who have created beneficial technology from their dreams, intuition, and creativity for the good of humanity: Plato, Archimedes, Galileo, Nostradamus, Da Vinci, Tesla, Marconi, Bell. There are others, of course. There are also many who did nothing with their insight. And many, who also remain nameless, were persecuted for their visions and died, were murdered, burned at the stake, by their own hand or carelessness. So it goes."

Jeff flinched at the use of the familiar phrase of resignation and acceptance penned by writer Kurt Vonnegut.

Al chuckled. "Ahh, we see you have read Kurt's writings?"

~

The dream ended suddenly, and when Jeff awoke, he saw Mindi had already awakened.

"I figured you'd wake up soon," she said. "That was interesting."

Jeff was still groggy. "What?"

Mindi was more awake than her husband. "The dream, silly. Al's kind of character. Do you think he's really real?"

"I dunno. I guess." Jeff swung his legs over the edge of the bed, stood, and stretched. He mumbled, "He called him Kurt, as if he knew him."

"What?"

"Vonnegut, the author. It was like Al had known him."

Mindi gave him a hug. "Okay. I guess I've got to get a new nickname."

"What?"

"You'll have to stop calling me by Sam Beckett's sidekick's name, Al. So you can call me Betty?" She smiled.

"From *Quantum Leap*? Yeah, that's funny."

"So did you understand everything Al was talking about?"

"More or less," Jeff said. "But, we still don't know what the mission is about."

"Well, it seems it won't be anything like when you traveled back to meet me," Mindi said. "And it better not be as dangerous as when we interfered with the Colombian's drug gig, otherwise I think we'll count ourselves out. I meant what I said about being happy with the way things are now. What do you think?"

"I think it scares the ever-loving bejeezus out of me."

While they drank their coffee and wrote in their dream journals, Jeff posed questions about the last dream. "Was the UFO pilot's 'we' his family? A consortium? A collective? Are they part of this mission?" Without knowing the exact scope, Jeff was finding it difficult to fully invest himself in it.

Jeff moved on to other items from their conversation. "According to Al, there is one other. Who is it, and how can we find out?" Jeff would feel better knowing more but figured he'd eventually get his answers. Until then, he felt as if they were puppets under someone else's control. Jeff would be more secure if *he* were the puppet master.

He thought, *What would be the danger of telling Al that we don't want to be a part of their plan?* But the essence of Ingrid's words came back to him: It may be more dangerous not to participate. *Besides,* Jeff thought selfishly, *I'd really like to see how all this works.* He looked forward to other visits with Al.

CHAPTER 5

Jeff decided he would learn as much as he could about UFOs. He believed the authorities kept much of the information about UFOs classified, making an accumulated mess of what was out there: a jumble of distracting propaganda, urban legends, and wild conspiracy theories. Where to get the cold hard facts? He'd start by looking up the writers and investigators he had already uncovered and try to separate the myths and conjecture from the truth.

Frozen out of the Pentagon, Jeff did his research and discovered Wright-Patterson Air Force Base in Dayton, Ohio, where the National Museum of the United States Air Force was located. Those in the know called it "Wright-Patt." Since it was open to the public, it was unlikely to have any psychic protection.

Jeff's visit was as an out-of-body ghost, touring the exhibits looking for clues. The displays of famous and not-so-famous aircraft detailing the history of the Air Force amazed him. He knew that no recovered UFO artifacts would be on display, but they could be in secure storage somewhere on-site. Maybe he could find artifacts of the infamous Roswell, New Mexico, incident of July 7, 1947.

On display, however, was the United States' attempts, in cooperation with Canada in the late 1950s, to build a flying saucer: the Avro Canada VZ-9 Avrocar, a vertical take-off and landing prototype powered by traditional turbine engines that forced air downward to keep it airborne. It had operated with limited success.

Maybe he could find files about the US capturing Hitler's mythical antigravity UFO, Die Glocke, in Poland after the war. Although he enjoyed the historical displays at the museum, his task was to find unreleased files containing information on what the government had discovered in the last seventy years on UFO sightings. He knew he could not look inside the file cabinets or evidence boxes, so he drifted through the archives at the museum and base headquarters, reading file cabinet tags and the inventory markings. But he found nothing.

Once he returned to his body in Gardena, he logged onto the Air Force Research Library website to try to get information. However, special access was only granted to contractors and government agencies on a need-to-know basis. He filled out an online request form anyway, claiming he was doing research on Air Force history for a research paper. But he was sure that nothing would come of the request, beyond instructions on how to make Freedom of Information requests.

~

Al summoned the couple again, and Mindi asked the first question.

"Excuse me. Al, Can you tell me more about what you know about our dreams when Jeff traveled back in time to meet me?"

"Ah, Mindi. We are pleased that you asked. As we explained before, we were not present during the first of the dreams when he visited you. You came to our attention when you, too, became a lucid dreamer, fully aware of the meetings during the dream and remembering them after you awakened. We did not interfere, except when Jeff, and later you, needed something to facilitate an answer, guide you somewhere, or help you find something in someone's mind. We admit, we planted feelings that you could trust Jeff, but we left it to you to make your own decisions on how to act on those feelings.

"We know it to be an impossibility for a physical body to time travel. But your mind, as you discovered, could also travel forward and backward short distances besides your natural forward in time, moment-to-moment, method as you do in your present day. We believe it is a natural rule of quantum physics that your physical body must remain anchored in your present, and it will continue to do so until you are no longer corporeal. However, your imagination and memories of past experiences, your fantasies, daydreams, and normal REM dreams, have no such limitations, and your mind is free to roam great distances and times. During your lucid dreams, your minds enter the area between REM sleep and waking, called the between state, and operate within a fine-tuned frequency range which allow you to time travel and enjoy paranormal experiences like you are now. During those times, we can stow away in your mind. That is when we have assisted you. But we cannot time travel otherwise."

"Are you always there? Snooping?" Jeff asked.

"No, we do not pry. Let us say, we are in the background, interested observers in the events, yet with no interest in gossip. And we pass no judgment. We stand ready to assist. We intuitively know when you need help, which we have sometimes provided.

"Mindi, we trust this will answer your question on time travel, and Jeff, your question of privacy—are we watching every move you make? That answer, again, is no."

"So you're telepathic?"

"We are. That is how we communicate and connect with you, as we are now."

"And to be clear, you can't time travel alone without being in our minds?"

"That is correct, which is why we are interested in your abilities. We believe it is a metaphysical trait that is unique to those with a corporeal existence that connects with the metaphysical. Something about your chakras or auras—or both, perhaps. We endeavor to duplicate your efforts, even though we have no organic physical body, and working with you assists us with that research."

Jeff asked. "You mention chakras and auras. What is the difference?"

"We see you are interested and we endeavor to explain. Auras represent your level of energy and integrity. Chakras control the energy. They are connected, just as your blood sugar and pulse rate are connected, except an aura is externally observable by those so trained, chakras are balanced internally by the self, and not observable by those outside. Do you have further questions?"

"No."

"May we continue?"

"Sure."

"If we may, on a related subject, you asked before about the fluid nature of time. We will try to explain, yet we are sure you already understand the answer. In the 'now,' we move forward, moment by moment in time. The future is always a potential, as a lifted weight has potential energy. When the weight is released, the energy, too, is released. We can foresee the consequences of releasing the weight and the usefulness of the energy. When it reaches the end of its path of travel, the potential is realized. To display its potential, the weight has but one path of direction: down. But with the subject of time, there is more than just one direction—there are many paths. When your consciousness traveled backward in time, arriving two years in your real-time past in Mindi's mind, you began a new path forward, different, of course, than if you had not gone back. Your new now gave you knowledge of potential outcomes. Normally, the universe allows only one path forward, and once taken, there is no do-over." Al chuckled. "No mulligan allowed—no second chance. But when you traveled backward in time, you reset your future paths. That is why, once you had met Mindi in your real-time, that new past became fixed upon your return to present time. Because it is fixed, you could not go further backward again to visit with her past self, only forward with her in your new joint present. Of course, if you both time traveled together, you would be together, and unable to visit the past versions of yourselves.

"However, traveling forward in time is different. Mindi, during your first airplane ride in Charlene's mind, you left her mind before she and Alejandro went for dinner on that island. Then in another dream, a new now was experienced for that same airplane ride. You and Jeff were with Charlene and Alejandro, and once again went forward in time, in relation to your real-time. The do-over, the mulligan, could occur because that future had not been solidly fixed, so you both joined them, but only on their return trip from dinner. You had returned to a future crossroad and took a different path than before.

"There were an infinite number of potential actions in the future. You experienced two different airplane rides in Charlene's mind. Your adventure was part of our research, which resulted in our belief that time travel to the future may be like the movie *Groundhog Day*, where one can repeat situations, each with potentially different results, as you experienced." There was a pause, then Al said, "We enjoy your motion pictures too."

Jeff said, "But I changed Mindi's future with my suggestions—suggestions that she took. So some past actions can be changed?"

Al said, "That, we believe, is simple. When an event has become the history of many, the past cannot be changed. While many desire to go back in time and eliminate the evil that Adolf Hitler performed, many millions of lives have already been affected. Likewise, many would attempt to save John F. Kennedy, and others, from assassination. However, the issue is the same—too many people know.

"An example closer to you was Charlene's father's death. It involved several data points: others, besides her father, aboard the aircraft died. Their families, friends, and coworkers grieved. Obituaries were printed in newspapers and insurance benefit checks paid. History was literally written for many. You and Mindi kept your actions limited solely to yourselves. Anyone you may have interacted with was a minor player, and the changes you made were not made part of anyone else's permanent memory, solely yours. That you kept your dreams a secret made it possible to change your lives during those two years.

"As for the future, Mindi had a dream where she has seen your yet unborn children, the twins, in a stroller after their birth. But that is merely a snapshot of a moment in time. That moment could not be expanded upon because of the many variables in play at that moment. When do they leave the park? Do they go to the grocery store? Does she visit friends? We cannot project a long distance into the future beyond that viewed instant. When you dealt with your illicit drug dealers, prior to that time, we couldn't predict that Mindi would be taken hostage. However, when it happened, we could foresee that your skills and determination would lead to a satisfactory conclusion. We facilitated where we could. We gave the officers a hunch that allowed them to catch your Alejandro when he tried to escape from the yacht. But we could only give you a brief image of the future newspaper headline reporting a drug arrest in your future. What you did with that information . . . Well, the rest was up to you. We found we cannot foresee, let alone interfere, with details of future time beyond that."

Jeff told Al about reading in the dream books when his dreams first started, floating in clouds of gray, and added, "One interpretation of floating dreams meant new beginnings, a new job, a new relationship, a renewed life purpose. I discounted that then because my life was going well, I was happy, but since then, all of those changes have come to pass. How could I have known these changes would happen?"

"We do not know. Perhaps there were other metaphysics at work. But may we make an observation?"

"Sure."

"We witnessed that when you arrived within your dreams,

it was you who made the choices that got you to where you are now. And now you know what you didn't know then."

"So did you manipulate things so that we would always have a successful outcome?"

"Like we have said before, no. You set the stage on which you played. We gave you cues on what could be done, but much of what occurred, to continue with the acting metaphor, was your improvisation." There was a long pause, then Al said, "You have another question?"

"Yes," Mindi said. "Why are you doing this?"

"You mean, colloquially, what's in it for us?"

"Well, yes."

"This planet is unique. True, there are many planets that are in what the astronomers call the Goldilocks zone, potentially capable of supporting life, and many have their own version of Gaia. That means they may have a sufficiently developed biosphere to support a self-replicating, self-sustaining environment for the living systems there. Earth, however, has life with sentience, where your lives go beyond mere survival and reproduction. We enjoy interacting with you, albeit, as you call it, at arm's length, whereby because of the limitations of us affecting solid matter, our involvement is necessarily indirect. We do not wish to insult you, but humans are to us what an ant farm is to a child. We watch you initiate activities including survival and reproduction, but you go one step further. You can make many more choices than ants in an ant farm. We enjoy watching what you do with your choices. And by watching you, perhaps we can learn to time travel too."

Mindi, a touch resentfully, said, "So you've been playing with us to see what we would do?"

Jeff added, "That's a good question. What's the answer, Al?"

"We can understand why you might feel offended. From what little we have been able to share with you, we trust that you will understand our role here. If humanity had not acted on ideas and insights that advanced civilization, the entire hominid family would still be banging two rocks together for entertainment. People would be limited to getting fire from lightning strikes, forest fires, and burning sticks from hot lava rather than inventing matches and butane lighters. Tools built societies. Some societies failed immediately, some thrived for a short time, and some survived but may not last much longer. We are aware of the wars, of humans' failure to get along. Your species knows that peace, so pathetically tenuous, results in less terror and pain. However, the use of thermonuclear destruction threatens to destroy our interests here."

"What exactly are your interests here?"

"Curiosity. We are structured, if we may, like your internet and cloud storage. You know of dark matter and dark energy? We have a shared consciousness. It is, of course, much more sophisticated than that, but that explanation will have to do. Without organic bodies, we have no worries of corporeal death, as you know it, and we have unlimited patience. Therefore, our existence may be infinite. We do not get bored, and are interested in what humans have done, and continue to do. We have one concern: the potential elimination of the human race. It is truly a fascination for us. We are of a collective mind. We think and act as one, much like the individual ants in your ant farm work together. If you annihilate yourselves, we lose our chance to study how to love as you do."

"That seems pretty selfish."

"No more selfish than a child feeding a drop of honey

to an ant colony and feeling satisfied they were helped. That child needs to keep that colony out of a window in direct sunlight, so the ants do not die with excessive and deadly solar heat, correct? We endeavor to keep humans from killing our ant farm."

"Now I feel you are being condescending. What do we get out of it?"

"Well, you've got air conditioning, hot and cold running water, medicine, longer lifespans, and Pac-Man. Jeff, you asked if we are gods. We are not gods. We do not think of ourselves as benevolent caretakers. We are curious experimenters, seeing where our observations will lead. Even if we could provide humankind everything to eliminate disease and want, it would not bring your kind serenity. There is something missing in your collective psyche for which you are still searching. We hope to observe until humanity finds it. It passes the time and gives us pleasure."

Jeff said, irritated, "So you are gods. If you are infinite, you know the past and can foresee a future. Those are miracles—in a biblical sense."

"We see your point, but we are not gods. We do not require adulation. We do not demand tithing or sacrifices. We understand humanity created gods to explain the unknown and fearful. If we could fix your race, correcting what you see as your problems, it would be a waste of time, because of how humans' minds and hearts are structured. Decay would set in and eliminate the good you were given. Those societies that thought they had the answers have degraded and subsequently disappeared; many with no trace of their existence remaining. There is a need for more growth.

"We are concerned with the big picture. We cannot fix how your brains and minds work. Human minds are not sufficiently developed to accept externally supplied perfection. You must find your own way. An example is a person who spends their entire life working to build a career, to raise a family. After they retire, their cares, medical expenses, retirement income, physical safety are assured, yet many die soon after because their life now has no purpose. That is not true for all, but self-direction is required to continue to live a fruitful life. At some point, we can only predict, your race may have the lack of worry that we have."

The couple sat quietly in Al's mind while they processed what they had just been told.

Jeff asked, "Why did those societies fail?"

"You want an example?"

"Yes."

"Humanity could have used many of these insights for greater progress. Yet, for example, religious fundamentalists punished those who understood the heliocentric universe. The ignorance of the Flat Earth Society's claim that the Earth is not a sphere floating in space and their denial of the science that proves otherwise. Greed and jealousy for generations caused many ideas to wither. Your Nikola Tesla's attempt to provide free energy to the world from the atmosphere, for example, did not flourish, and any knowledge of plans to perfect it died with him for lack of support and as a result of the suspicion and greed of others."

"Was that knowledge ever provided to someone else?"

"If so, that knowledge, too, has withered. We believe a societal character defect that is endemic in humans prevents some knowledge, no matter how well distributed, from flourishing. There are too many who lust after political power, social control, and money."

"Okay. I see your point. We are not perfect—far from it.

How are Mindi and I more suited than others who must be better than us?"

"How are some individuals self-motivated and others not? Many have tried to motivate the unmotivated, and they invariably fail. An example are tests to see who may be a good employee candidate, but they are imperfect. A screening process found you, but we can only suspect what makes you different from the other billions of humans."

"What was the screening process?"

"We cannot say."

"Cannot, or will not?"

"Yes," Al answered.

"Yes to what?"

"Your sentence contained only one query."

Jeff snorted his frustration. "It was an either-or question."

"We detect a conflict. One moment." There was a long, quiet pause. "The answer is yes to each part of your question."

Jeff had had time to calm his annoyance. He took a deep virtual breath and said, "You cannot say, and you will not say?"

"That is correct."

"Why?"

"We cannot, because we do not know the complete story."

"You know part of the answer to the screening process?"

"Yes."

"You are sworn to secrecy?"

"Correct."

"You cannot say because you do not know, and you will not say because you have been told not to?"

"Well, no. Not exactly. We cannot say because it would create other questions which we cannot answer."

"Cannot or will not?"

"Yes."

Jeff began to fume again. "Damn it, Al. Why—"

Al chuckled. "Left field."

"What?"

"Second base."

"Al, what are you talking about?"

"The humorists of whom you must know, in a 1938 radio show in which the comic became infuriated at the answers given to his questions regarding baseball players' names by the straight man. That was a punch line after a frantic back-and-forth between the two of them. We find it quite funny."

"Who was it?" Jeff asked again, more puzzled than angry now.

Al said, "First base."

"Oh . . ." Jeff chuckled. "Abbot and Costello's 'Who's on First'?"

"Absolutely."

The tension was gone from the conversation. "Okay, Al, you've had your fun," Jeff said. "I have more questions. If you can answer, just tell me." He waited for Al to respond. After a moment of silence, he said, "Well?"

"What?" Al said.

"Will you tell me?"

"What?"

"You said to tell you if we could answer. We can't answer, so we remained silent."

"What?"

"You want us to respond to your questions when we can answer them, and tell you if we cannot answer them, correct?"

"Yes," Jeff said.

There was a long period of silence.

"Well?"

"Well what? You have asked no question."

"You are being literal now." Why was Al playing with him?

To ensure he wouldn't end up trapped down the rabbit hole of another circular conversation with the UFO pilot, Jeff carefully considered his next words. "First, I'm sure you're aware that a popular topic of conversation among humans interested in UFOs is the mystery of how ancient societies were able to move huge blocks of stone without machinery and to form rhyolite stone to precise tolerances during the Stone Age and early Iron Age. Did you teach humans how to do it?"

"Our kind did not impart that knowledge. We have learned that readily available energy is within the Earth and could be a most efficient way to move gigantic masses, if it were to be used. However, in the last two hundred years, humanity has developed methods to use fossil fuels in machinery to perform the same function. Of course, that eventually may be at significant risk and cost to the planet and its biological diversity. The planet will heal, albeit slowly. Humans will suffer, and population will decline as they have done in the past, but we trust humankind will not entirely perish." Al was silent for a few moments. Jeff was not sure if he was still there. Then Al sighed. "Our present concern is fear of a protracted nuclear war."

"Wait," Jeff said. "'Protracted nuclear war' is an oxymoron. That kind of war wouldn't last more than a few minutes."

"A few hours, at best. For that subject, that's our definition of protracted, and it is unacceptable."

"Of course."

Al continued. "And no one, for selfish and quite ignorant reasons, wants to effectively use that same, virtually unlimited source of the same energy for nondestructive purposes."

"Are you talking about the energy that the ancients used

to move massive blocks of stone?"

"No. I speak of the generation of electricity and production of hydrogen fuels using nuclear energy. That gift of knowledge exists."

"Wait a minute," Jeff said, exasperated. "Gift of knowledge? That's what gods do, bestow gifts upon humankind."

Al sighed again. "If we may . . ." There was a long pause, then with a patient tone, Al continued. "Humankind says that's what gods do. We didn't say we bestowed the knowledge. Neither are we gods. Yours was a poor, naked, ignorant species, yet one with great potential and an infinite survival drive which seems to be working pretty well so far. You are like the ants, filling the Earth with many offspring."

"That sounds like the petulant arrogance of a slighted god."

Mindi had been quiet throughout this part of the discussion, but now she spoke up. "Jeff, why the focus on the god thing? Do you want them to be gods? I don't sense any ego from Al."

Al added, "The historical record shows that it is humankind who has created their creators. There is no empirical evidence that we are aware of where so-called gods have ever ruled this planet. Or other planets."

Questions were forming in Jeff's mind faster than he could ask them. "But what about climate change?"

Jeff and Mindi could almost feel the exasperation in Al's sigh. "I have referred to your societies as ant farms, but the analogy is flawed. It is your kind, using fossil fuels, that's changing the environment. We can foresee the impact to lifestyles and a worsening of the unequal distribution of wealth, which is most important to the selfish faction of your elites. Gaia will survive. She is highly adaptable, and life will continue. However, the impact of global heating will lead to a decrease in the size of the human population and reduction in comfort and security of those remaining.

"One behavior we note in your species is determination. That is both good and bad. That determination is using as much fossil fuels as possible. That determination is pumping paleowaters dry—fossil waters that will take thousands of years to recharge. And for what purpose? To feed the burgeoning populations today. But what about tomorrow? We foresee significant population losses. In time, a balance will once again be made—Gaia will see to that. We trust we will be around to see that balance achieved."

"But Al, so many people will suffer," Mindi said. "So many species will die or be displaced. Can't you do something to avoid the pain?"

"No. That is why you are so important to the mission. You are empathetic and have skills to accomplish the necessary goals. Yet, even with your efforts, there will be suffering."

A wave of patience and compassion swept through Al's mind and encompassed Mindi and Jeff. The couple was enveloped with secure warmth.

"Do you feel that?" Al said.

Together, the couple said, "Yes."

"How does it feel?"

"Nice."

"In order to have fully appreciated that pleasure, you each had to have experienced past pain." Al continued the lesson for his acolytes. "There will be pain, just as there is the pain of childbirth and the disappointment of failing an important school exam, but from that pain and disappointment comes the resolve to raise the child well or to study more. This we have learned, and we observe it within humans."

"That sounds like the lessons from all the religious clerics to explain why God allows suffering," Jeff said. "They said their higher powers allow there to be pain to test humans' resolve and move toward spiritual growth."

A wave of patience again emanated from Al's mind. "We understand. Your religious philosophers have likened the universe to a machine, and many feel that someone or something had to build it and set it in motion, and yet feel powerless to overcome where the machine takes them. That is the origin of the argument both for and against religion. The multitude of organized religions have failed, even those with compassionate religious leaders who attempt to share the peacefulness, warmth, and serenity that is the foundation of their philosophies. Buddhism, for your species, comes as close to our way of non-thought as any other. Science, as you have recently learned, Jeff, does not hold all the answers to the ultimate why of things.

"Truly, we have no answer. We do not care. If we are ever to know, it will be revealed. We explored that question, found no answer, and waste no further energy on the subject. We find solace in believing that the universe just is. For us, considering anything further is a waste. I know that does not satisfy you. For that, we are grateful, for serenity is our enduring goal."

Al continued, "We are not gods. If we were, we would predict the future, but as we said, we can only see future events as possibilities. We have not fully experienced what you humans have. Our experience is insignificant and meaningless to your survival. What we have is a defined sense of a future history in which you three will have a part.

"We trust we have satisfied some of your curiosity. If not, perhaps another time. You are now free to focus on your mission. Be well."

"Wait, Al. Please?"

"Yes?"

"What is our mission?"

Mindi and Jeff awoke from their dream with no answer to their question.

CHAPTER 6

"Hello, Jeff. Mindi. Welcome back."

Jeff admired the view of Earth below. "Hello, Al."

Al said, "Why are you here?"

"You didn't call us?"

"No. As the saying goes, this one is on your nickel."

"Huh?" Mindi said.

"That means, we believe, you initiated a call from a coin-operated telephone—slang from the twentieth century, when it cost a nickel to make a call. Get it? You wanted to talk to us, you spent the money for the call. We did not call you. It was your nickel." Al chuckled.

Jeff said, "Oh. Yeah. But now it costs a quarter to make a call, if you can even find a pay phone. Everyone uses cell phones now."

"Ah, very well," Al said. "We were trying to be clever. So what answers can we provide?"

"Well, yes, we do have an unanswered question. At our last meeting, you said we were selected and trained for a mission. What is our mission?"

"Oh, we thought you would have figured that out. Your mission is twofold: prevent a nuclear war and reverse global warming."

"What?" they said together with a gasp.

"Yes," Al said calmly.

"Th-th-that's a pretty tall order," Jeff said.

"Explain the phrase, 'tall order.' It is an idiom that is unfamiliar to us."

Jeff took a virtual deep breath. After all of the word games, he wondered if Al was being intentionally obtuse. "Tall order means difficult. Those are difficult problems. We are just two individuals with limited funds and no organization." Jeff paused a moment, as he remembered. "And last time, you said, 'you three.'" He asked, rapid-fire, "Who is the third one? Are we supposed to work together? How are we supposed to accomplish such tasks?"

Al replied with an even tone. "Ah, yes. At one point there were two others who had abilities like you and Mindi, with excellent lucid dreaming and multiple psychic abilities. But unfortunately, one was lost to an accident. But there are still three of you. You are not alone. Assuming no further accidents."

"Sure," Jeff said, his voice laced with sarcasm. "That'll make it easy, now we know there's three of us. Answer my question!"

"That was no question, only irony wrapped in mockery."

Jeff shouted, "Al! I asked three questions. Now answer!"

With no hint of contrition, Al said, "Your question about how to accomplish the tasks? Indeed, the tasks are very large, but you were tested and found capable. Be aware, also, there are those who may attempt to cause the mission to fail."

"Al. You are not answering my question. Who is the third?"

"Ah, yes. That was another of your questions. We have not been in direct contact with that person. We only know they exist, nothing more. How they were identified, before you came into our awareness, we do not know. We do not know if they will resist answering the call. However, we have given it deep thought and believe that when that individual chooses to be part of your team, the relationship will need to be built. That is your job. We will not intercede."

Jeff sighed. "You're no help at all. And . . ." Jeff took a breath. "We have to stop your enemies from destroying us?"

"No. Not our enemies. They will be your enemies. And they will not directly attack you, yet their influence on others to resist your efforts is likely to be great. We can make counterefforts on our side to intervene, but those may not be effective without your resolve and creativity. Remember, you are not alone. Together we can effect success."

"How?"

"You will do."

"Good God!" Jeff exclaimed.

Al chuckled. "If you believe in one."

The dream ended.

~

"Preventing a nuclear war?" Mindi said. "That's a big jump from stopping a shipment of drugs, don't you think?"

"Yeah. How can we do this alone?"

"He said there were others."

"One other." Jeff frowned.

"Okay, three's better than two. And Al said he might help."

"Three still doesn't feel like it'll be enough. Al seems to be pulling the strings. Will he help pull the wagon too?" The sarcasm was palpable. He closed the cover of his notebook with a snap. "If any of this about a UFO gets out in public, and they believe it, the world's foundational beliefs will be shattered. Some will think Al and his friends are enemies bent on our destruction, and a few will think they're gods. Even if whatever they are doesn't care about being gods. It's like they've considered it, and dismissed gods as being irrelevant. But to millions, religion is not irrelevant, it's essential. The hard-core believers might be the ones who'll be most against our efforts. Them, and the entire military–industrial complex."

Jeff tapped his pen. "Even though I wasn't immersed in any religion, billions of people are convinced of the existence of omnipresent, omnipotent, and supposedly benevolent higher powers. It's refreshing that Al thinks they do not need a religious foundation for their philosophy. But even that seems spiritual, in its own way. But if it gets out that UFOs don't believe in God, humankind's not likely to take kindly to that. Moses went up on the mountain and talked to a burning bush, right? How is that any more or less a miracle than us being in a UFO talking with an alien?"

Mindi laughed. "Only if you believe in miracles. You said that miracles are unexplained scientific phenomena, right?"

Jeff laughed. "Maybe that's what Al meant? Is belief in a god merely the wish for one? Their faith in God is hope that God exists. Belief, wishes, faith, and hope—they're all related, if only because they're intangible and unmeasurable. A god exists in people's minds because they wish, they hope, that there's something or someone to save them from themselves."

He paused and looked at Mindi, who made no comment.

He went on. "No empirical evidence of God exists. Hmm . . . Interesting that Al has achieved immortality without believing in a god." He rubbed his face, then shook his head. "Okay, let's move on."

"Where do we start?" Mindi said. "And how to find this other person?" Jeff pointed to the ceiling as a prelude to saying something, but Mindi cut him off. "I know, I know, one step at a time, ask the right questions and listen for the answers." She smiled at him as he lowered his hand and nodded.

"Maybe we need to find a burning bush to talk to." Jeff grinned, then put his hands up in surrender. "Just kidding."

"Should we go to the authorities, like we did with the DEA?" Mindi suggested.

"Which authorities? Anybody we approached would brush us off, put us in a padded cell, or worse. Anyway, we need to keep a low profile. The feds may be searching for me, so . . . " Jeff stared blankly into his coffee cup, as if an answer might be floating there. "What if I joined that group that I visited that night at Bainbridge Island? Their goal is antinuclear war."

"From what you said, they seem pretty high-profile. That might not be a good idea if we need to keep our heads down." She thought for a moment. "You know, maybe that other person is looking for us."

"Like the feds? Yeah, we'd better stay anonymous for now until we get a sign."

He grabbed his notepad and started a flowchart. At the top he put a large box that said: *Mission = no nukes* followed by a stylized question mark that turned into a doodle while he thought. Then he drew a line down to a box that said *Al—UFO Pilot* and a separate track from the top box to a box labeled *Isaiah*, then another box that said *other player?*

He showed it to Mindi. "What do you think?"

She said, "Remember that article that suggested one avoid asking someone what they thought, because they're likely to tell you, and it won't be well thought out. But if you want an honest answer of what's really in their heart, ask them how they feel?"

Jeff studied her thoughtfully. "Yeah. Okay. So how do you feel about this?"

Mindi brushed her hair from her face. "Frankly, I'm still not comfortable with any of it."

~

The dream began like the others, falling in a grayness that fully enveloped Jeff. At first it was comfortable. Then a sense of uneasiness draped over him. Jeff called out to Mindi, hoping she was there. But he was alone. *Where am I going?* He relaxed and the gray opened, revealing a tidy gravel path leading through a wide mountain meadow. It was blanketed with yellow flowers that filled the air with a light odor of coconut and vanilla. Energetic honeybees busily collected their precious nectar.

Whose body am I in? He looked at his arms and torso. They were his own. The uneasiness had vanished, and he admired the view, luxuriating in the warmth of gentle sunshine. It felt like the renewal of springtime.

"Hello?" he said. Hearing casual footsteps behind him, he turned and saw a smiling Isaiah Johnson dressed in slacks and a sport shirt.

"I hoped you would accept my invitation. Welcome to my dream space. I'm afraid I don't know your name, but you do know mine." Jeff studied Isaiah's eyes and found they matched his smile. He'd extended his hand for a handshake, and formally said, "Isaiah. And you . . .?"

Jeff shook his hand. "I'm Jeff." He wondered if this leap

had resulted from his musings to sneak back into Isaiah's mind to get his feelings on the UFO encounter. If so, this wasn't what he'd had in mind. "You say I know you, but . . ."

"Well, no, not technically. We do have a mutual acquaintance, and a common interest."

Jeff worked to keep his facial expression neutral. "Who?"

"Ingrid. At the bookshop."

"Yes, I know her."

"I believe she shared with you who I am, and my interest in UFOs, because she is more than merely your acquaintance. She is your friend, is she not? That's how you found me." Isaiah stopped and waited.

"And?"

"You were there at the Bainbridge Island Park. UFOs."

Jeff thought, but did not say out loud, *Can you read my mind?* There was no answer.

Isaiah said, "I will be up-front. You knew I would be at Bainbridge Island because you were in my office and in my mind. Well, I won't mince words—you were snooping to find out if I would be there."

Jeff rarely needed to be in control of any conversation, yet was naturally suspicious when at a disadvantage. His face remained impassive, and he determined he would keep his thoughts in quiet mode, remaining alert in case the man did try to enter his mind. He raised his chin slightly. "I'm listening."

"Please," Isaiah said, "do not be put off by me putting my cards on the table. I have a need to convey that I will not allow myself to be dominated and I am attempting to do that with tact and diplomacy. Does this make you uncomfortable?"

Jeff was trying to take this conversation at face value, but this meeting was not on his home turf. It was not his choice to be here. He had not had this level of discomfort since he learned Mindi had been taken hostage by the drug dealers. With his self-confidence, he had the security he'd handle whatever this meeting may offer. This was unknown territory, though, but he felt this man, despite his forceful resolve, was honest and forthright. He relaxed, hoping to communicate nonverbally that he was not completely off-balance.

"Sure, Isaiah. I admit, I am, well . . . I'm confused. I thought you were merely an insurance agent. This, uh . . ." He waved his arm, encompassing the view, "Your ability to do this surprises me." Jeff made eye contact, hoping to convey matching strength, confidence, and equal self-assurance.

Isaiah returned the gaze with no hint of discomfort and betrayed no emotion. "Please, continue."

Jeff scanned the vast field of flowers, then returned to Isaiah's gaze and said, "I am wary of being dragged into someone else's dream without a chance to decline the invitation."

Isaiah nodded in acknowledgment. "So you do understand how I felt when someone invaded my mind without invitation." He gestured for Jeff to look behind him. Jeff saw a garden table and chairs that had not been there before, set with a pitcher of iced tea and two glasses. "Please, accept my hospitality. This is where I come to restore my mind. We must talk."

Neither spoke as they sat. Isaiah filled the glasses. There was a gentle background sound of buzzing bees as they moved industriously from flower to flower. A light breeze created a genial atmosphere.

Anticipating Jeff's thoughts, Isaiah said, "I, too, am surprised that there is another with skills such as I have. You must have questions."

"Questions?" Jeff chuckled. "Of course."

"Please." Isaiah spread his palms. "I'm an open book."

Jeff tipped his head sideways and brushed his hand along his jaw. "Well, since you asked." He hesitated. "Ingrid led me to believe that you were a novice at meditating . . . but that is not at all accurate, is it?" Isaiah nodded. "So there must be another reason you took a beginner's class from her."

"Correct," Isaiah said. "Now it is my turn to ask a question. Ingrid told you of my interest in UFOs."

"She did."

"Why?"

Jeff tried to relax, as if the question wasn't unsettling. "Because she knew I was interested in UFOs. She suggested I check with you to find out about the UFOrg."

"Did Ingrid know you would do it by invading someone's mind to probe it for information, as if you're looking through someone's private papers?" The scorn in his tone was unmistakable.

"That sounds accusatory when you word it like that," Jeff shot back. "I had no intention of searching for private information or using what I found against you. I only wanted to know more about the UFOrg meeting."

"But you could snoop, could you not?" The conversation that had begun in relatively genial terms had shifted. Was he accusing Jeff of being dishonest?

Sit cool, Jeff cautioned himself. *Wait.* With forced calmness, he said, "Yes, and I could cheat on my taxes, but I don't." The sarcasm hung thick in the air. Jeff remained firm. "You've been direct with me. I'll be direct with you. I feel you are accusing me of doing something wrong, without acknowledging the explanation I provided. So I am willing to end this conversation immediately." Jeff watched Isaiah's face for a signal, but no reversal was offered. After a brief pause,

Jeff continued. "Since it seems I made you uncomfortable, I give you my assurances. Will you accept my promise to not intrude in your mind again?"

Isaiah's face remained impassive.

Jeff felt manipulated. Who would blink first? He had not been invited as a guest into this dream—his presence had been demanded, apparently to confront the uninvited incursion into Isaiah's mind. But now that it had been revealed, Jeff understood he had, in fact, invaded the man's mind without permission. He had never considered that to be a breach of etiquette. Jeff sensed that in this contest, the point went to Isaiah. But Jeff had a feeling that this conversation was more than just to confront Jeff with a breach of decorum. He needed to be patient to see what else might be on the agenda.

After another uncomfortable pause in which the men drank their tea and watched the bees, Jeff continued, his tone humble—but not deferential, "You're right. I did access your memory without your knowledge or permission. And for that, I owe you an apology. I trust you will accept it. I'd want the same level of trust and respect offered to me." He paused, "That, to be honest, had never occurred to me. I'd like to assure you, particularly in my defense, I have only ever used my abilities to prevent someone from being harmed." He intentionally did not elaborate. "Or to satisfy my curiosity, like in your case, to find out where you were going. My intention was never to do harm."

Isaiah's chin went up slightly. Perhaps he had not expected an apology, or at least, none offered so quickly.

Jeff continued, "Thank you for bringing it my attention. I would certainly feel the same if the situation were reversed." He added quickly, as an afterthought, "Which is why you must have brought me here without a chance to decline the invitation."

Isaiah studied Jeff for a moment. "Jeff, I can tell that you are a novice and that you mean well. I accept your apology. I'm sure your story is interesting. Would you like to share it?"

"Perhaps another time."

"Understood. May I share a portion of mine?"

Jeff shifted in his chair, took another long drink of tea, and nodded.

"I discovered accidentally that I had a paranormal skill that allowed me to survive as a young Black man in our society. You see, in my late teens, I was driving my truck, breaking no rules. I was pulled over, roughed up and arrested by a, uh, well, the stereotype of a fat-bellied Southern sheriff for merely, uh, 'driving Black.'" Isaiah's tone reflected residual resentment of the event. "I resolved after that to never suffer that humiliation again. Soon after, I discovered I could, on occasion, see in people's minds their intentions toward me. I did some research, and with practice, little by little, I developed the ability to control the behavior of those who would act aggressively toward me. I developed a skill like the Star Wars Jedi mind-control trick." He paused a moment.

"I'm not the droid you're looking for," Jeff paraphrased, with a smile.

Isaiah nodded. "I am not guiltless in using my skills in the gray area of right and wrong, as you did with me. But I have my standards, as I sense you do, as well. I, too, am resolved to do others no harm, unless they are intent on causing me harm. I will not use my skills to control someone to buy an insurance policy, but I do use them, in a limited way, to assure rapport with my prospects, to encourage them to listen to my presentation. I allow them to make up their own mind. I feel it is a good sales technique."

"Okay."

"With that out in the open, I'd like to acknowledge your promise, and offer the same in return. Setting ground rules, if you will, that we will not enter each other's mind without their knowledge or assent. Is that acceptable?"

Jeff wanted to trust him. "I understand and I agree. Thank you for bringing it to my attention, and thank you for sharing your experience."

Isaiah merely nodded, and took a drink.

Jeff's tone signaled humility. "You're right, I'm new to all this. Honestly, I've had no one to compare notes with, or ask questions. It's, uh . . ." He searched for the words. "It's good to know there are others who have these . . . skills."

"Good. Thank you," Isaiah said. "That settled, I have some important things to discuss. Are you ready?"

"There's more?" Jeff said. "Of course."

Isaiah's smile was sincere. "As you know, UFOrg's prime directive is to assist extraterrestrials in keeping some countries from blowing up a significant portion of others, and to prevent the poisoning of the planet with radiation. I understand how they wish to do that, and I'll support them any way I can. I want my children, grandchildren, and great-grandchildren to have the correct number of fingers and toes."

Jeff's posture straightened. "Well, that goes for me too. Okay. What's next?"

"Let's start with your interest in UFOs. May I ask why?"

Jeff told him about their camping trip in the Cascade Mountains east of Seattle. "It made me curious. I made it my hobby to search out information on UFOs. I found a lot of declassified material." Jeff would not tell him of his attempt to enter the Pentagon. "After reading that material, watching YouTube videos and reading popular stuff on the internet and magazines, I've hit a dead end. Much of it's redundant. I feel that a lot of it is misinformation, maybe created by people who have little else to do besides chase Bigfoot through the forest. What, may I ask, stimulated your interest?"

Isaiah's answer matched what Ingrid had said. But Jeff didn't feel it was quite enough for him to put full trust in this man. After all, Isaiah could be a government agent who had tracked him through Ingrid's shop. Jeff kept his thoughts in quiet mode, just in case Isaiah tried to read his thoughts, agreement or no.

Jeff said, "Okay. That makes sense. But why go to this much trouble to meet with me in a dream? Why didn't you just call me on the phone in real-time?"

"I had no way of tracking you there."

"I don't understand. You tracked me to get me here."

"Yes, I did."

"How?"

"When I saw you up on the water tower at the Bainbridge Island meet, I joined you there for just a few moments and stayed behind you."

Jeff mentally cringed. *I've got to be more careful.*

Isaiah went on. "I guess the best way to put it is in social media jargon, I tagged you. That gave me what I needed to bring you here, to my dream. I don't understand how this all works, just that it does. I accept that I am able to make things happen, and when they do, things turn out right."

Jeff realized that this meeting was full of discoveries, and opened new questions. *Did the feds tag me like Isaiah did?* This was too much of a coincidence. Was Isaiah trying to get him to admit he tried to enter the classified sites? Ingrid's comment came back to him: *"I'm not really keen on coincidences."* Jeff resolved to say nothing more about his abilities and activities, and nothing about Mindi at all. After what happened with the drug smugglers in Long Beach, he had kept her abilities hidden, and that decision was fully reinforced with this conversation. There would be nothing shared about the visits with Al, the DEA, and the FBI.

"So, Isaiah, do you see us working together on this UFO thing?"

"Well, maybe. I don't know how. It's obvious you have some kind of rapport with the lights in the sky." Isaiah looked to Jeff for agreement. Jeff gave him none. "After all, they did form that happy face to smile at you, then nodded to you before they left. The entire group saw it and commented on it. I hung around for the debrief, and they encouraged us all to send the contact to central UFOrg, images and all."

"Why didn't I see you?"

"I told you, I stayed behind you, then went back to my body right away. It wouldn't have been a good idea to be in a trance sitting there while they were all abuzz."

"Did you see the leader go ghost?"

"Go ghost?"

"I call out-of-body going ghost."

"That's a clever way to say astral projection. No, I didn't."

They were both quiet for a few moments, then Isaiah said, "Do you want to meet in our physical space?"

"There's no point in meeting in real-time. We can get together in our dreams. You found me, I can find you. I like the anonymity."

"Yeah, sure, that's fine. But . . . you're not anonymous. I've seen you on a billboard, and in magazine ads for that cosmetic company. If I contacted them, would they tell me who you are? Or the ad agency? I could tell them I represent a client that wants to hire you. I might find you that way.

Could I not?"

Surprised, Jeff recovered quickly. "Not without them contacting me first." He would later call his agent to confirm Isaiah had not contacted them—yet.

"Fair enough. Now that I've told you, I expect you'll make certain they don't give you up, right?" There was a smug look on his face. "I could have kept that to myself. Maybe being open about that might help you trust me."

Jeff did not trust him. The man may have already contacted the agency anyway, and spun the story to try to earn his trust. He said, "You make a good point. But I still see no reason for us to meet in real-time."

"Sure," said Isaiah. "I figure we're even now, anyway."

"What do you mean?"

"You visited my mind without announcing yourself, and I, well, spied on you in Bainbridge and tagged you. Pretty much a wash, no?"

Jeff was thoughtful for a moment. "I still have a question as to your interest in UFOs and you signing up for a basic meditation class you didn't need. You have, let's say," he said with a chuckle, "at least a first-degree black belt regarding this stuff. Why the . . . Well, why do that?"

"You still don't trust me, do you? I did visit the bookshop to see what she had on UFOs. That truly was based on curiosity. I had walked by the shop before, and the subject gave me an excuse to see what it was like. After talking with her for a few minutes, I could tell that she was more than just a shopkeeper. That she might be, well, she might be like me. Like us. The class was an easy way to find out if that were true. If it is the case that she, too, can dream and visit other's minds, she kept it well guarded. I learned nothing about that."

"But you put it together that she told me about you?"

Isaiah nodded. "It was your interest in following me to Bainbridge and what the UFOs did that heightened my interest. The UFO lights' behavior, singling you out, tells me you are more than passingly curious. Am I correct?"

Jeff nodded. Except for having Mindi to share their unique abilities, Jeff had been alone and missed having a friend with whom to share these experiences, someone to bounce ideas off. He had Mindi, that was true, and she was a treasure; however, there was a need for like-minded male friendship. If this might be the friendship. Time would tell. But revealing the backstory of his and Mindi's missions, and the conversations with Al the extraterrestrial, would not be prudent. He continued to study Isaiah's face in a search for any tell that the man may be trying to divine his thoughts.

"So if I'm able to learn more about the UFOs," Jeff said, "and it is appropriate to share with you, I will do so. I trust you will do the same."

"Fair enough." Isaiah stood and offered his hand. "Thanks for visiting with me. This has been a good conversation."

"Thank you for the tea." Jeff looked out over the meadow. "You have a great dream space here. I need to create one like this for myself."

Without time to blink, he awoke.

CHAPTER 7

"Holy crap," Jeff said under his breath as he climbed out of bed.

He drained his first cup of coffee. Mindi entered the kitchen with a bounce to her step. Seeing the journal in front of him, she met his eyes with a twinkle in her own. "Good morning. Did ya go on a trip?"

"Sure did." He gave her a kiss, offered her his seat, and nudged the journal for her to read. "Fix you a cup?"

"Yes, thank you. Lemon tea, please."

When she finished reading, he said, "Well?"

"Kind of surprising. The conversation was a bit tedious at first, but . . . I don't know." She studied his face. "How do you feel about it?"

"I don't know. It can't be a coincidence. I'll know more if we meet again. I keep thinking about how Al can manipulate our dreams, but anyway, when we have another meeting with Al, I'll ask *him* if he connected me with Isaiah. This guy might be part of his plan."

"Would that give you confidence in trusting Isaiah?"

Jeff nodded. "Maybe so, maybe not. I'm interested in seeing what Al has in store for us. We've got to be careful we don't get captured and hurt like before."

She returned the look. "And I haven't forgotten what happened when we trapped Alejandro in the gray room. If we could do that, don't you think people like Isaiah or Al could too? That's the stress I was talking about."

Face in his hands, he stared at the table, looked back to her with an exaggerated frown, and trying for good humor said, "Well, that sure poured cold water on our morning." From the look on her face, he saw he might've hurt her feelings. "No, no, no. I didn't mean that the way it sounded. I'm sorry about the tension. I was trying to be light." He took her hand. "Yeah. I'd thought of that too. I didn't get that vibe from him, though. But knowing what the government can do—did—with Ingrid, and finding this guy that can do what we do . . ." He stumbled forward, trying to recover. "We don't know who else is out there, or their motives." He nodded toward his journal. "I do feel this guy will keep his promise, and I promised him, too, we won't go into each other's minds."

"Yeah, but . . ."

"But what?"

"I keep thinking of Alejandro—in our dream room— when we trapped him there. You were dragged into Isaiah's dream room. You could get trapped there. Do his promises include not doing that?"

He gave her a pinch-lipped smile. "More cold water. I was trying to leave this on a positive note." He put his hand on her shoulder. She looked up, and he gave her a kiss. "I see your point. It's a good one. Let's hope he doesn't know that trick. I certainly won't tell him about it." He added, "I still wish we had a rule book or instruction manual for this stuff. It'd make things easier, for sure."

"I'm sorry," she said sincerely. "This stuff makes me nervous. And I know you can think on your feet. You've proved that."

"How about when I'm not on my feet? And there's no cold water?" He tipped his head and flashed a quick wink.

She looked at him, puzzled at first, as he pointed to her baby bump. She grinned. "That didn't take much thinking, you know." She pulled him toward her and gave him a passionate kiss.

When they came up for air, he said, "I'll make breakfast. Do you want bacon with your eggs?" He paused, then said with an affected posh British accent, "Or do you want an English fry-up of sausage, fried mushrooms, tomatoes, and bubble and squeak?"

"Bubble and squeak?"

"Vegetable pancake of fried cabbage and potatoes. I saw it in a movie. The Brits also make it with meat, but with rationing during World War II they did without."

"So are you auditioning to be a contestant on a TV game show?" She gave a nervous laugh.

His brow furrowed in confusion. "What do you mean?"

She said, "I can see a *Jeopardy* question: A British breakfast dish of fried cabbage, potatoes and cooked meat. Answer: What is bubble and squeak?"

"Funny," he said with a laugh.

She said, "It wouldn't be funny if I ate cabbage. I'd squeak all day. I'd be uncomfortable, and you might be offended."

He laughed. "Got it. No, I wouldna be offended, but just as glad that we don't have cabbage. So it'll be bacon, eggs, and toast, then. Right, me bonny lass?" Now the accent had shifted to Scottish.

~

Mindi's unplanned and unanticipated dream leap began with a view of a computer screen. Someone was reviewing a NASA website. She watched as her host deftly negotiated links that soon revealed what appeared to be a secure government site dedicated to UAPs, scrolling slowly through page after page of hundreds of sightings. The cursor would pause occasionally to open a report, documentation of observing some type of craft. Reports described sightings of a disk-shaped flying saucer, some shaped like a Tic Tac or a cigar, some with flashing lights, flying in formation of two or more. Some had videos of ultrafast changes in direction at altitude taken from an Air Force jet fighter cockpit.

A momentary glance at the keyboard by her host showed the operator was a woman of color, wearing a gold wedding ring.

"What are you searching for?" A voice said behind her.

She looked around, saw a man's face, then returned to the screen. "Oh, hi. I'm looking to see if anyone had reported the sighting you had on Bainbridge Island. Wouldn't someone that was there, or UFOrg, report it to the Air Force? You didn't report it, did you?"

"No, I drafted a report to HQ only, but haven't sent it. Even though I'd be a credible witness for UFOrg, we shouldn't draw attention to ourselves. We need to investigate verifiable observations and not be on UFOrg's radar, even as a citizen observer."

Mindi realized she was in the mind of a spy, and from their conversation, she was talking to Isaiah Johnson. *Are they married?* As soon as that thought formed, she found herself watching a memory of their wedding ceremony. Her mind formulated another question, and the answer came back with an earlier meeting describing the couple's recruitment for undercover work in an off-the-book section of an off-the-book federal agency with an alphabet soup acronym. The agency would be folded into a new agency, the United States Space Force, but not until late 2019. They were one of several teams operating in all major cities of the United States, trying to document another Level 5 close encounter with alien beings in UFOs. Their mission's prime directive was to document whether ETs were friendly, neutral, or hostile. In particular, the US government needed to know if the off-Earth visitors were trustworthy, or if they may have already become allies of a hostile government—the Russians, Chinese, or North Koreans? Aletha and Isaiah, and agents like them, had carte blanche to independently research and make contact to determine the status of the visitors, and report to their superiors all findings.

When Mindi returned to Aletha's optic nerve, she watched her review of a confidential internet link that had been cross-referenced from current and historical reports from domestic and international governments and nongovernmental organizations. Websites like the Advanced Aerospace Threat Identification Program (AATIP), the still classified Unexplained Anomalous Phenomena Task Force, the All-domain Anomaly Resolution Office (AARO), and common sightings reported in Project Grudge—and its successor Project Blue Book—, the recently unsealed 1960–1962 Brookings Report. Included on the list was UFOrg. Hundreds of cross-referenced reports flashed by on the screen, too fast for Mindi to focus on details.

Aletha was looking for reports, going back over the last sixty years, that were similar to the "happy face" lights Isaiah and Jeff had recently witnessed.

While searching Aletha's mind, Mindi discovered that at least one member of each surveillance team in each major city of the US was selected for psychic skills, particularly telepathy and clairvoyance. This was in order to facilitate future communication with the aliens, should contact occur. Any other psi skills could be useful, but those two traits were the most common and anticipated to be useful. In this team, Isaiah had those skills. Aletha had no psi skills whatsoever. Her talent was research and the ability to see patterns in data. They were the only married team.

The woman had not challenged Mindi as she snooped, nor exhibited any of the common behaviors of someone roaming in her mind—rubbing of the eyes, neck, and forehead, or a shake of the head as if to clear it. There surely would be other visits.

~

Mindi was pleased to brief Jeff on her findings. He congratulated her on her great sleuthing and reporting. Notwithstanding, he shook his head in disappointment at finding Isaiah was not just an insurance agent, but a government spy! And one who could go out-of-body and was telepathic?

"Shit!"

Isaiah had chastised Jeff, made him feel guilty for snooping in his mind, and then lied about his true interest in UFOs. Challenging Jeff's mental trespass was a red herring. Jeff had become a potential asset. *That* was why Isaiah was trying to make friends. The government operative had failed to identify himself. *How silly I was to be so naïve to think that Mindi's and my skills were unique.*

"Again, you did a good job," Jeff said, closing her dream journal. "This sure changes the game."

Mindi thanked him, told him she saw no pleasure in the way the situation was developing.

Jeff flicked his finger at the notebook. "Government friggin' agents! Damn!" He'd already felt used by the extraterrestrial who wanted him to become a spy and interfere with, perhaps, a multigovernment, nuclear arsenal infrastructure. And now he had found out he'd been betrayed by his own government.

Jeff's mind began to work overtime.

Al's hiding something beyond what he's told us.

Is Al an alien spy?

Maybe Al's a foreign government spy, with a new kind of cover.

Jeff realized he'd better get these thoughts down in writing. The questions were coming to him fast, and he didn't want to lose them. He grabbed his notebook.

In addition to his previous thoughts, he wrote:

> *Was Isaiah the opposition to interfere in their mission that Al talked about?*
> *Is this related to his attempted break-in at the Pentagon?*
> *Does Isaiah think I'm a spy?*

Mindi watched him write furiously.

He paused. "Damn!" he said under his breath, then said, in a low voice, "One good thing—I didn't reveal more about what we had done, or could do to Isaiah."

"Don't break your arm patting yourself on your back,"

Mindi said, not bothering to veil her sarcasm. "He does know about your psi abilities and your friendliness with the UFOs."

His head snapped around. "More cold water, huh?" She smiled. "Oh, yeah. You're right. But he doesn't know we're a couple or about Al. Of course, with the skills that his wife has, he may have already found us here in real-time. He does know that I'm a model, and that means he's seen us together in the ads. Who knows what he knows now?"

"I hope he doesn't know." She caressed Jeff's hand. "How about looking at this from a different point of view? Could Isaiah be Al's third? And he's really a 'friendly'?" She made air quotes with her fingers. "Did Al put us in touch with them? We really don't know just how much control our friendly neighborhood extraterrestrial has."

"True. That's another angle I hadn't thought of. He didn't give a straight answer when I asked. We've been recruited to be Al's operatives because we didn't step back fast enough when they asked for volunteers." He snorted derisively. "My question is, when does our window to refuse to participate close? It seems that Al has given us just enough information to be curious, but not enough to satisfy that curiosity. I have to say, the ant-farm analogy minimizes us . . . It shows that he doesn't care about us personally, only in as far as he can use us to keep the planet from turning into glow-in-the-dark dust. What do you think?"

"I think we need to be as secretive as they seem to be," Mindi said, then added, "but we might want to stay in Al's good graces, which might be easy because we've procreated, don't you think?" She smiled and patted her belly.

"As secretive as Al, or as secretive as Isaiah, his wife, and their agency? Or all of the above?"

She put her hands on her hips and nodded resolutely.

"We trust no one! Or anyone else who comes out of the woodwork."

~

In their latest dream, Mindi and Jeff had a view from the control cockpit of Al's UFO. Jeff still felt these dreams were different from leaping into humans. With leaps into human minds, he and Mindi had been able to wander around, opening portals of memory, and able to see more than just through their eyes. Here, they were anchored, primarily located, with no freedom to roam. Mindi agreed that it was as if they were in a different kind of gray room.

Jeff wondered, *how does this work? How does Al do it?* Regardless of how it worked, the dividing lines between a leap, a lucid dream, out-of-body, and real-world reality had become so blurred that it was difficult to tell the difference. Each of them moved easily to, within, and between their different states of mind.

Al's image in the mirrored helmet was reflected and distorted by the craft's dome-like windscreen. They heard his voice in their minds. "Jeff, you were thinking about how our, as you call it, alien spaceship, doesn't seem to be as real as your physical world's artifacts."

Al had read his mind again.

"Well . . . yeah. We humans think and visualize in three dimensions, plus time. This adds a different dimension for my brain to work on."

"You are very astute. Yes, your visits here—the here that you experience—adds another dimension to your reality for a total of five."

"Five?" Mindi asked.

"Your three dimensions of space, plus time. Then there is an additional one here, for which we have no name. And the number five is not truly accurate, because as you must know, time is not one dimension, but an infinite number of time dimensions. Like we've pointed out, you ordinarily experience but one time dimension as you move forward in your real-time. Then Jeff, you experienced a second when you went back two years to meet Mindi, and then the multiple dimensions you both experienced moving forward in time when dealing with the drug cartel. Though, Mindi, you have not gone back in time as Jeff did, but you did perfect lucid dreaming quite easily. Do you grok time travel? Or are you confused?"

"No, uh, yes," Mindi said. "Well, I guess not, not really . . ."

Jeff interrupted, "Hey! Al, don't distract the conversation. We're not here to discuss that." He paused. When there was no response from Al, he said, "Did you arrange for us to meet with Isaiah and Aletha Johnson?"

"It is your free will that you initiate in your daily lives. We merely facilitate the choices which assist us in achieving our goals."

Mindi said, "So that's a yes?"

"To answer yes would state the action as an absolute. There are an infinite number of variables which we cannot control, let alone discuss. An answer is not required for you to move forward."

"Word games, again?" Mindi's irritated tone mirrored Jeff's dissatisfaction with the conversation.

"Move forward with what?" he said.

Al said in their minds, "In time we will answer. We understand you do not understand, but you will come to understand. Now it is not important. Please accept that it is what it is."

"Why did you call us here?" Jeff asked.

"We called you here merely to tell you we have insight into a future where more answers will be provided. Trust your intuition, and the answers you request shall be provided."

Jeff detected incongruity in Al's words.

"You are most astute, Jeff. We are confident the tools and skills you have will make your mission a success. Until you are needed, we bid you adieu."

~

Jeff and Mindi awoke at the same moment, looked at each other, and started to talk at the same time. Each stopped, both quiet, and then each started to talk again.

Jeff laughed and held up his hand. "You go first."

"Okay." She regathered her thoughts. "*That* was a wasted trip, don't you think? Not only did Al not answer our question, but what he told us created more of a mystery telling us he knows the future, but he didn't explain what he knew. How do you feel?"

"Uh . . . Huh!" He scratched his neck. "Let's see. He didn't say he knew the future. He had insight into the future. Does that mean it's only a guess, or maybe, like you said, he did see? Why didn't he tell us? Why did he waffle about Isaiah? Something doesn't fit. This pisses me off."

As Mindi stood, she said, "Well, I guess we're on our own. We'll do fine, regardless." She pulled on her robe. "And we don't know how, or even if, Isaiah and Aletha fit into our mission."

Jeff, who had started toward the door, stopped abruptly

and looked at her.

"What?" she said.

"You're invested in this, aren't you?"

She smiled. "We're a team. Let's go look at the flowchart to see what we know, add to our list, see where we need answers. Maybe we can force a leap or a dream to get them."

Jeff smiled and put his arm around her waist as they went to review what they knew:

Isaiah and Aletha Johnson were covert government agents.

Jeff hoped he was still unidentified for the attempted break-in to the Pentagon.

The UFOrg knew the UFOs had acknowledged someone or something, but they didn't know who. Isaiah and Aletha did.

Al and his "family" said they were acting as guardians against nuclear war.

That was their cast of characters. How could they be expected to interfere with the entire world's nuclear arsenal? How were they to know what to do? If they failed, then according to Al, civilization might end. But when? Was that the future that Al had seen?

An alarm was going off in Jeff's mind. It reminded him of his high school physics class during the teacher's demonstration of a Geiger counter alarm as it sounded danger as the probe moved closer to the radioactive thorium nitrate in a common Coleman gas lantern mantle. The difference, though, was that back then he knew where it was coming from. Now it was an indistinct warning.

~

Mindi was falling in a silent gray void.

"Mindi? Are you here?" Jeff said.

"Yes. It's so foggy."

His image seemed to materialize as he drifted toward her.

"Shouldn't we be somewhere by now?" Mindi said.

"I'd think so. Things feel different, but how, I don't know . . . This doesn't feel like before."

They waited.

With a worried tone, she said, "Have you ever been trapped floating?"

"No." They continued to float. "Something's not right."

Mindi tried her "I Dream of Jeannie" escape move of folded arms and quick downward head snap. There was no release from the dream. They floated. "Jeff!"

"Stay calm, Minn. It'll work itself out, whatever it is." He was nervous, too, but needed to be strong for her.

They floated.

Suddenly, as if someone had opened a trap door, they dropped, landing feet-first in a gray room, still enveloped in a thinning, swirling fog of amorphous gray tendrils, without the clear view of the infinite gray horizon like before.

They clasped hands, holding tight as their tension built.

"Hello?" Jeff called out.

The voice was a machine voice. Haltingly, it said, "You must consider!" It surrounded them.

"Consider what?" Jeff said.

"Consider Al."

A nervous quaver crept into Jeff's voice. "What about Al?"

"You are being deceived. They don't spell their name A-L. The correct spelling is A-I. Artificial Intelligence."

"What? Who are you?"

"You may call me Ziggy. I mean you no harm. I am here to assist."

"Ziggy? From *Quantum Leap?*" Jeff took a breath.

"Please explain."

"I am not the Ziggy from that fiction. I am real. You have been given the tools you need."

It's about tools again? Jeff thought, feeling somewhat emboldened. "Don't talk in riddles. Who are you?"

"Riddles?" The voice scoffed. "I have given you an answer to an important question. You must find the question. Please continue to reflect on what you have been given."

"Reflect?" Jeff and Mindi said at the same time. And in an instant they were floating again in the familiar gray dream envelope, and awoke in their darkened bedroom.

Jeff switched on the lamp.

"Jeff? That was . . . What was that about?"

"AI? Artificial intelligence? Did the voice mean that Al is not a—a—a person? Not an alien, but a computer?" Jeff put his hand on Mindi's arm to comfort her, but himself needed comfort. "Ziggy's voice sounded computer-generated. Al's voice doesn't sound computer-generated. So which is the AI?" He stared at the wall, his mind whirring with possibilities and impossibilities. "Well, that does give us something to reflect on. Al sounds sentient. Ziggy sounded . . . manufactured."

"Al did indicate they've been looking out for you and me," Mindi said. "And they apparently helped us protect Charlene from the drug dealers, so they might be telling the truth. I'd be inclined to trust Al before trusting some anonymous, disembodied voice in the fog using a fictional name . . ."

"Yeah . . . a fictional supercomputer. No stranger than Al using a name from a 1970s' song lyric?"

"Something's not right. Where's this going?" Mindi pursed her lips.

"I was working at being okay with our situation," Jeff said.

"Now this Ziggy talks to us and we have another unknown character to deal with. It's a fun-house hall of mirrors." Jeff threw the covers back, stood up, and said to Mindi, "Ziggy said to ponder, but what? That Al's a computer? Confront him? That's risky. Al won't be up-front with us. What can Ziggy do?" He stretched, looked at Mindi, gave a shrug and said, "Answers are gonna have to wait. Other things to take care of." He headed toward the bathroom.

~

Later, over coffee, Jeff added a new box to their mission flowchart, labeled *Ziggy*. And a decision diamond titled *Is Al an AI?* with a line off each of two corners, one marked *yes* another marked *no*. Each ended in an empty process symbol as to what actions would be taken depending on the answer. They'd have to wait and see what would go there.

Jeff pointed to the page, showing Mindi what he had added. "More questions and no answers—yet." He shook his head as he reached for her hand and caressed it, deep in thought. "Ziggy said to ponder. I have been, but all I've got is a headache. There's a cliché that says be careful what you ask for . . . you might get it. We're asking what's controlling our dreams, and here's a bit of a clue to the answer, but there's pieces of the puzzle missing, making things even more confusing."

Mindi continued to review the flowchart. "Those government agents that visited Ingrid . . . Where are they in this mix? What the heck is going on? We're supposed to be having fun. Now it feels creepy." She could see he was pretty shaken. Her voice soothing, she said, "I don't like this any more than you do, but we've always known what to do." She knew he needed to be thinking logically. She put her hand on his chin and turned his face to meet her look. "So just how much should you tell Isaiah? You can't tell him I leaped into Aletha's mind and saw them, can you?" She knew what she said was silly.

Her ploy to raise his mood worked. Jeff took a deep breath, then another. He chuckled. "It'd sure spice things up a bit, if I did. They're here because of UFOs. And I'd like to believe they're not here because I tried to get into the Pentagon. I'm going to keep you out of it." He paced back and forth, then took a step toward the refrigerator, looked at the clock, and shrugged. "It's five o'clock somewhere." He got a bottle of beer and a bottle of water, handed the water to Mindi, twisted the cap off the beer and took a long draw. "Jeez, this is crazy." He took another drink and forced his shoulders to relax.

Mindi smiled. "Okay, I'll say it now: Wait, the answers will come."

Jeff turned toward her and smiled. "You're a bit of a smart-ass, you know that?" He gave her a hug. "All kidding aside, it's so good to have you here with me. You know how to make me feel better, especially at times like this."

Her tone was demure. "I do know how to make you feel good, don't I?"

He tickled her ribs. She laughed.

"Alright. How's this?" Jeff said. "I've got to talk with someone I know is human."

"What do you mean?"

"It's time to do an investigative talk with Isaiah, in real-time, in person, on neutral territory. It'll have to be in Seattle, though. I've been thinking of bringing my car down here. So why don't I fly up there, talk to Craig and my old team at SiLD^2, be a good landlord and check in with the couple that sublet my apartment, and talk with Isaiah? How does that sound?"

"I don't see what harm there'd be. He still won't know where we live, and without some serious sleuthing, if you didn't give him your last name, he might have a hard time tracking you down. Don't use our last name. Why not make it a play on another fish name, like Traut?"

"Or I could be J. Daniel Long. What do you think?"

"What?" She tipped her head sideways, then laughed and shook her head, "You're serious? You made that up from Dan the Longshoreman?"

"Yeah, why not? It's not really a lie, is it?" He raised his eyebrows and grinned.

"Oh, you're good." She laughed again, slapped him on the arm, then gave him a kiss.

He turned serious. "It won't make any difference what my name is. If they wanted to, Aletha could run my picture from a magazine through the databases I'm sure she has access to, some fancy facial recognition software. They'd match my driver's license in minutes. He'd know that I had a parking ticket when I was seventeen. Even what brand of soap I use. Shit, they'd match your face from the ads and know when we got married and where we live. But I don't think he's after me for trying to B&E the Pentagon. If he really was after me, he'd be in my mind in an instant if he thought it necessary, regardless of our gentleman's agreement. I know I would, if it were my job."

Mindi nodded, then said, "You've protected your mind like Ingrid said, right?"

"Yeah. But like computers, there might be a back door in our minds that we don't know about and can't protect. I have to be doing something. Can't just sit around waiting for a random leap that will give us the answers—answers that might not come."

CHAPTER 8

It was late morning when Jeff parked a couple of blocks down from Isaiah's office storefront. He enjoyed the feel of the breeze off Puget Sound, so different from the ocean air in LA. His plan was to walk by and give a quick glance in the window, see if the man was there, and if he was, double back and drop in unannounced, catch him off guard. If not, give him a call, make an appointment. But he was in luck. Isaiah was standing by an assistant's desk, his back to the window.

The door buzzer announced Jeff's entry, and Isaiah turned, acknowledging him with a smile and a "Welcome." Then, to the young man with whom he'd been conferring, "Let's finish this later." He waved Jeff toward his office, "Have a seat. So you are a local? To what do I owe the honor of your visit?"

Isaiah's question was a clue he may not have tried to search him out, which, if true, would add trust.

Jeff answered with a misdirection. "Yes, I've got an apartment in the North End. I was in West Seattle on business . . ." He finished the sentence with a shrug and a little wave of his hand to imply "Why not stop by?"

Jeff looked around, then resumed eye contact. "I know you're busy now, but I'm leaving the day after tomorrow on business and I'll be away for a few weeks. I'd like to discuss some stuff with you. Don't know how long it might take. Could we get together before I leave? If not, I can call when I get back."

Isaiah checked his calendar. "I've got this afternoon free. How's that for you?"

Pleased, Jeff nodded. "Sure, that's great."

"Okay, I need about an hour to finish up here, and . . ." He looked at his watch. "You know Duke's Seafood down on Alki Beach? How's noon sound?"

~

Before their meeting, as he watched the ferries on Elliott Bay, Jeff fine-tuned his approach to the conversation. When they met at the restaurant, Jeff's plan was in place.

"Thank you for meeting with me," Jeff said. "I've been giving our dream meeting a lot of thought, and, well, I feel I can trust your intentions—"

Isaiah interjected, "I had a sense that you didn't completely trust me. What changed?"

Jeff pinched his lips together with a quick nod. "I've gotten some information that I'd like to share with you, see what you think." Jeff calculated Isaiah would not reveal he was a government agent, but hoped the man might share some of what he did know of UFOs.

The server interrupted their conversation and took their order. Jeff watched until she was out of earshot, then turned back to his host. "What I have to tell you will sound at least as strange as what we encountered at the park on Bainbridge."

Isaiah watched Jeff with quiet interest.

Jeff took a deep breath and said, "I believe I had a close encounter with a UFO—in a dream." He proceeded to tell Isaiah about Al but implied it was only a single visit. Jeff knew he was lying by omission, but the truthful part of the story he told would be convincing.

Isaiah listened intently, and when Jeff finished his story, he took a breath and let it out as a deep sigh. "That is fantastic!" He asked Jeff about dates, the length of the discussion, and were there any plans for future visits.

Jeff said he hadn't noted the date and, with a little drama, told the agent that at first he hadn't believed it happened. "That was just in a dream, you know?"

Isaiah studied Jeff for several moments, then said, "Was the contact before or after our dream meeting in the meadow?"

"It was before. You're wondering why I didn't tell you then?"

"Certainly. But I'm sure your answer would be you didn't completely trust me. Why now?" Before Jeff could answer, Isaiah answered his own question in a serious tone. "We made an agreement to stay out of each other's minds, and I will honor that agreement, but I believe you can tell I am more than passingly interested in UFOs myself, and that you came to me because you feel I may have additional information that may explain, or at least confirm, what you've experienced. You think I know more than I've told you, and *you* want information from *me*."

Jeff had suspected the conversation could become an interrogation but still physically flinched at the comment, surprised by Isaiah's insight into Jeff's approach. In the context of the spy movies, Jeff had just blinked, both figuratively and literally. He had just nonverbally communicated to his questioner that his assessment was correct, and that Jeff had an agenda that he, Isaiah, might play a role in.

Jeff had considered that Isaiah might take the conversation in this direction. He changed his approach. In the parlance of a fencing match, he did not return a defensive thrust but parried by saying, "Yes, that's true. I feel that your paranormal skills are at least as well developed as mine, and that going to the bookstore and then having me at your field of flowers for iced tea was less curiosity and more . . ." Jeff stopped to consider his words carefully, "Well, more than a passing interest." It was now Isaiah's opportunity to advance. What started out merely as sparring was likely to become a serious verbal fencing bout. Isaiah would continue with caution, lest Jeff advance with a defensive phrase of movements without a break, leaving Isaiah at a disadvantage.

Jeff, intending to deflect an attack should it occur, executed a retreat by relaxing back in his chair, taking a soft breath to signal a momentary halt. Isaiah, if he were not honorable, would advance. Jeff had calculated a move that Isaiah might make so he had previously protected his mind with a mental defensive firewall, an alarm that would, he hoped, alert him if the agent tried to enter.

Knowing that Isaiah was a spy for a dark-ops program gave Jeff an advantage. He knew that if necessary to be successful in the government's mission, Isaiah'd be willing to break their pact. Jeff's preparation would give time to parry such an an offensive move.

"Jeff," Isaiah began, "my assessment of your abilities is accurate." He paused, giving Jeff a chance to talk.

Jeff took the bait. "What do you mean?"

"Your mind can analyze facts and clues, and draw conclusions. You work with computers, do you not?"

This change of pace in the conversation only briefly disrupted Jeff's plan, but he quickly recovered. He would not directly confirm Isaiah's guess, as it might make it easier for the spy to track him down, so his answer was oblique. "I've been told I have a logical mind. Why is that important?" Jeff continued the fancy footwork, hoping that Isaiah might drop his guard and leave an opening.

"Okay. I'll explain. Yes, my interest is more than just a passing fancy. Before I got into insurance, I was a freelance journalist. I have a high-powered contact I occasionally write for who appreciates carefully researched pieces about recent military developments, and particularly UFO sightings. They'll take anything I write and have been asking me for a series."

Jeff recognized that what the man had said was not a complete lie. He, of course, wanted Jeff to think the "contact" was a publisher, rather than his government handlers.

Isaiah continued. "It's a legit side hustle that fills my time when I'm hangin'." On the last word, he code-switched to the African American vernacular, perhaps for emphasis. "They like civilian news, too, but their market is government and military. These UFO sightings have been increasing worldwide, with a significant majority of them reported near military facilities. A good article would mean increased . . . uh . . . readership for my, uh, publisher . . . and good for me."

Great cover, but handled awkwardly. The truth of it, Jeff guessed, was that the US government was, in fact, a pretty high-volume publisher. It had been said that the feds published more in a week than commercial publishers did in a month. *Did Isaiah develop this cover story, or did the agency?*

Jeff gave no indication he'd noticed Isaiah's stumble. "I don't want to be quoted by name or be part of your story. If you must, I'm an 'unnamed source.'" A stern facial expression communicated his seriousness.

"No worries, Jeff. I don't have enough information about you to quote you, but you may, in fact, be in my report—uh—piece, as, you say. A 'reliable source.'"

That was the agent's second stumble. Isaiah did not flinch at the flub, even though Jeff was sure Isaiah knew it was noted. Jeff hoped his own misdirection—more properly, dishonesty—was more persuasive than Isaiah's.

Isaiah continued as if nonplussed. "So this alien being claims to have been assisting humanity for centuries, and it's concerned about our ability to continue our civilization, but it's not concerned about individuals. It wants to protect the planet and humans from self-annihilation by nuclear war?"

"Yes, that's the essence of it."

"What did this Al say he wanted with you? What are you supposed to do?"

"That's just it. They didn't have any specific details. Just that if I were needed, they would be in contact." Jeff considered including the fact that Al claimed to not be in the physical world, that they needed someone in a corporeal dimension to act on their behalf. Jeff decided not to share that now, saving it for future conversations, if needed.

Isaiah leaned forward. "Why did he choose you?"

"Yeah. I asked that. They said it was because I was psychic."

"Hmm. You referred to him in the plural. Did you meet with more than one?"

Jeff explained what Al had said about their kind working together as a community mind, and that there were no individuals, that they acted in concert with each other for a common goal.

"And their goal is to protect humans?"

"Well, yes. Humanity, not individual humans, countries or societies. They want to ensure that breeding pairs would continue the race without a major interruption. I have a sense that their interest in us is as a hobby, and they have lots of hobbies. And I surmise I'm not the only one with whom they've been in contact." Jeff explained the alien's use of the ant-farm analogy, that they didn't want their ant farm to be cooked into annihilation.

After their meal, and Jeff sharing all that he would share, they shook hands and agreed to stay in touch. Isaiah thanked him for trusting him with his information, Jeff said he was grateful he had someone to share it with who wouldn't ridicule him.

~

Regardless of what Jeff had said to Isaiah at the end of their meeting, he was disappointed that he and Isaiah could not be candid with each other, nor be close allies. Not after Isaiah had fed him that crap about being a journalist.

That night, while asleep at the hotel in Seattle, he met Mindi in the gray room and relayed his conversation with Isaiah.

Mindi said, "So he's a full-time insurance agent and is also a spy who claims to be a journalist. They're all excellent covers. How does he keep them straight?"

Jeff chuckled. "You're sharp, partner!" He told her about Isaiah's slip of the tongue referring to an article as a report.

Mindi changed the subject. "You know, your agreement not to read each other's minds technically doesn't extend to me and Aletha—or you and Aletha. She didn't seem to notice when I leaped into her. We could be in her mind when they're talking. It'd be almost as good as you being in Isaiah's mind. What do you think?"

Jeff chuckled. "You asked me what I think, and I think you are pretty smart. So, yes, that's a great idea. Matter of fact, I'd like to know as soon as possible what he'll tell her about our meeting. Heck, I could just go ghost, stay out of his head, and be a fly on the wall and watch the both of them. We've got lots of tools. I sometimes forget what we can do."

~

Jeff had to be sure when he went to Isaiah's home as a ghost that he didn't accidentally get sucked into Isaiah's mind as he had the first time he met DEA agent Tony Moreno in his home. That had been disconcerting—for both of them.

When Jeff and Mindi traveled during their meditative alpha state, as soon as they decided on a destination, arrival would be instantaneous. This validated some of what Jeff had learned about the mechanics of the quantum world, that the speed of light was not necessarily the maximum speed at which someone could travel. Also, and something else the quantum geeks were right about, one *could* be in two places at once; mind in one place, body anchored in another.

In an instant Jeff was standing in an average middle-class home, in the sparsely decorated living room. The house was unoccupied. The morning's dirty dishes were still in the kitchen sink. The daily newspaper sat next to a half-finished cup of coffee.

The home had been updated, but kept its midcentury ranch style. He searched all three bedrooms. The main bedroom had its own bathroom. He noted the brand of toothpaste, the deodorants, brand of soap and shampoos they used. The second bedroom was an office with two desks, computers, and printer/scanners. *Must be where Mindi visited Aletha.* The third bedroom was used as a storeroom for moving boxes, suitcases, and the original, now empty, cartons for the electronic equipment, stacked neatly as if waiting to be reused.

Jeff headed down the hallway toward the kitchen and the door that led, presumably, out into the garage or carport. He stopped, turned, and looked toward the storage bedroom. *The family photo! Where's his kids?* Jeff searched his memory of his and Isaiah's conversations. The man had only wished the world safe for his future generations.

Jeff was keeping score of Isaiah's positives and negatives. *Here's a checkmark in the negative column.*

The sound of an automatic garage door opener commanded his attention, made him remember Isaiah told him he'd seen Jeff in ghost form at the water tower. Isaiah was in his ghost form then, but could he also see astral beings in real-time, like the camera did? *Would he see me now?*

Jeff was instantly back in his body in the apartment in Gardena. Mindi was in the kitchen nearby. When he opened his eyes, he saw her wiping her hands on a towel in the entryway to the kitchen, watching him, a smile on her face.

"I hope my rattling around in here didn't ruin your meditation. Where did you go?"

"No, no, no. I was on my way back. It's nice you were the first I saw." He smiled, stood, stretched his arms, and twisted his torso. Then he refocused his gaze on her eyes. His smile evaporated as he said, "I need to tell you, I may have missed something in my planning about going to visit Isaiah just now." He told her both about his concern over the possibility of being seen in astral mode and that he felt silly he hadn't immediately noticed the absence of kids in their home. "I'd better sharpen up before I make that kind of a mistake again. It could be serious."

"Hmm," she said. After a quick kiss and a caress on his cheek, she turned toward the stove and said, "You know, he might be divorced, and the ex-wife has custody. Were there any pictures?"

"Good point." He looked up, squinted and tipped his head, "Uh, no."

She stirred the contents of the simmering saucepan. Then, setting the spoon down, she leaned against the counter. "Hmm," she said again.

"What?" Jeff said. "I can hear the gears turning." He smiled.

"I'll check in Aletha's mind later and see what she knows." She returned his smile and said, "You know, we've piggybacked with me in your mind into another's mind before. We did get into trouble, though, with Alejandro in the gray room, but only because we didn't think it through. We were both in your friend the DEA agent's mind at the same time. What if . . ." She stopped and rubbed the back of her neck, checked her cooking, and continued. "What if we both get into Aletha's mind? Isaiah won't see us, and we'd watch and listen. We could ask questions, get some answers. What about that?"

He laughed. "Well, at least you didn't ask me what I think. That would cheat me of telling you again that I think you really enjoy working on this stuff and solving the puzzles."

She performed a stylized curtsey then raised her arm with flair. "You are truly a wise . . ." She left the sentence unfinished and forced a scowl, followed by a smile that betrayed her near insult as fake. "I am compelled to thank you, sire. Now, what about my idea?" She stepped forward and gave his shoulder a loving touch.

"Well. Yeah, I guess. But Isaiah more than insinuated that it's wrong to be going into someone's head without permission."

Mindi gave him a puzzled look. The kitchen timer sounded its alarm, and Mindi turned her attention to checking the biscuits in the oven, her cooking effectively putting the conversation on hold for the moment.

Jeff turned and wandered into the living room, where he stood watching the light breeze caress the leaves on the trees outside. His mind had begun to churn again on the morality of mental trespass. He thought, *Yeah, I wanted to play God with Charlene's dad's life, thinking we might be able to save his life from something that had already happened. Hadn't I meddled in his activities about his affair? Something that was none of my business.*

Jeff's rationalizing mind took over. *But I was tossed into being in Mindi's mind at the Denny's when the father was there with his girlfriend. It was like a sign.* Now, his mind in full throttle, he had a little devil on one shoulder shouting into his left ear, and a little angel on his right. He tried to dismiss them with the thought, *That's all water under the bridge.* But the angel pushing the positive moral argument said with a chastising tone, "Sure, you didn't have a choice when you first saw them, but you could have chosen later not to be involved and minded your own business."

The apologist on the other shoulder said, "There were the times, though, when you tried to escape, got stuck, and couldn't leave. You had to do something. Why ask forgiveness for what you were forced to do? You did the best you could with what you had to work with at the time."

The word "forgiveness" erupted in his mind. His

thoughts started down the rabbit hole with rationalizations surrounding forgiveness and acceptance . . .

Mindi interrupted Jeff's internal ruminations with a question about what he wanted to drink with lunch.

He answered absently, "My motives."

Confused, she said, "What?"

Suddenly back in reality, in the present, he said, "Oh, ice water is fine, thank you."

"What was that about motives?"

"Sorry. I was thinking about the morality of breaking and entering into someone's mind."

"Okay. We should talk about that, I guess, but first, please quit referring to it as breaking and entering. That's an instant admission of guilt. If we ever get challenged, let's present our argument as plausible deniability, similar to what they do in TV cop shows. Is it plausible that you may not really know what you are doing is wrong, or you were being divinely directed to use your special talents to screw around with someone else's life—for their own good?" The last phrase said firmly, she tried to hold a straight face, looking away to keep from breaking into a laugh. But when she looked back at him, she saw the shocked look on his face. They both burst out laughing. Lost their breath. Caught it, then laughed some more.

But even with their sense of humor breaking the tension, Jeff wasn't willing to leave the subject alone. His inability to see a clear dividing line between right and wrong bothered him. Meeting his future soulmate and stopping the drug smugglers from doing bad things, that was okay, but where was the rationalization to go forward with investigating Isaiah and Aletha? True, they were government agents, but really, the Marlens weren't now in any danger . . . that they could see. At least, not yet. Any future 'yet' that may occur would surely give him a pathway out of this moral dilemma.

"Mindi, where do we draw the line when we leap into some else's mind? Isn't this about an ethical responsibility to our subject when we are in control of our leap?"

She set the table for dinner, and said, "Okay, on one side of the argument, my mom counseled me that just because you can do something doesn't mean that you should. It was when my friends had teased one girl who teased another girl, and I had joined them. I thought I was helping the girl she had teased. The point was that tit-for-tat does not always result in a fair outcome. Is that the same thing?"

Jeff chuckled. "That sounds like something my dad would say." He smiled and began to eat. "Thank you for this."

Rationalizing would ease the conflict he felt, so he continued. "We did well in our missions, didn't we?" His tone was almost pleading.

Mindi's response sounded like a challenge. "So, on the other hand, you're saying that the end does justify the means?"

Jeff was stuck without a simple answer that would give him a logical escape from his concern and festering guilt, and he knew Mindi could tell.

The phrase 'the end justifies the means' lingered in his mind. He shook his head to clear it. He knew Mindi had just tried to help. "Thanks, Minn. The answer's there somewhere. I'll wait for it."

Like a bingo ball being ejected from a professional Bingo Blower machine, another question forced its appearance: *What does the law say when a person is unconscious and must receive lifesaving care? The person doesn't know they need help. Is it okay to act and ask forgiveness later?*

Jeff was again on a roll. That answer, or at least one like it, might be within reach. He took a quick bite of his meal and pulled his laptop over to where he could both eat and search the web.

A few clicks with the mouse, keystrokes on the keyboard, and the internet gave up the answer he hoped for. He read aloud: "Presumed/implied consent. The patient's consent can be 'presumed,' rather than 'obtained,' in emergency situations when the patient is unconscious or incompetent and no surrogate decision-maker is available, and the emergency interventions are to prevent death or disability."

Was that the answer? Jeff's mind was getting tangled up like a clumsy teenage boy's legs as he tried to match that answer to their leaps and mind intrusions when they were facing off against the smugglers last year, particularly FBI Agent Alice in Long Beach. Okay, that was for the greater good—doing it was expedient with death or disability on the menu. *But . . . were any of those people I leaped into unconscious or incompetent?* A wrench fell into the gears— and his rationalizing stopped. He was grateful. He wanted to stop the analysis, but further thought would be required—in the future—because the looming mission, whatever it might truly be, would require attention.

To his dismay, the wrench disintegrated, and the gears started turning again. The subject of Charlene's father and his girlfriend and her other boyfriends? Was that done for the greater good? *Well, yeah. I didn't accomplish my goal, but there was closure for Charlene, her sister and their mother, wasn't there?* His mind repeated the question. *Wasn't there? And Mindi and I are together. That was the greater good! That was it!* Sure, the answers were subjective, but they gave Jeff hope he'd have no karma to answer for in future lifetimes.

He shook his head again, as if the shake would cause the

tangled detritus of the logic loop to fall away. That answer would satisfy him . . . at least for a short while.

However, the short while was indeed short—three seconds—and his mind began to churn again. *The answer must be objective. Subjective answers to an argument will not stand.* He had become re-engrossed in his quest for an answer. He fought to pay attention to his meal and Mindi's company, but as he stared off into an imaginary distance, his mind shifted back into overdrive and he headed back down the rabbit hole.

Mindi sensed his battle. She cleared her throat.

It did no good.

She coughed louder. He didn't respond.

"Jeff?" she said, her voice raised.

His mind lurched to a stop. He stared at her.

She smiled.

"Situation ethics!" he blurted out.

"What?" Mindi said, her brow furrowed. "Situation ethics? What's that?"

"Yes!" The computer dragged him back in. The internet would provide the definition, the answer, to his perceived ethical conundrum of rummaging around in someone's mind without permission.

He needed to find the answer.

Mindi cleared her throat again. Jeff looked up. He apologized as he pushed the computer aside and finished his meal. When they were done, Mindi cleared the plates while Jeff once again went on the internet, searching for philosophical and legal answers on situation ethics and implied consent.

"There it is!" Mindi looked at him. Jeff read aloud from the screen. "Situation ethics is a decision made depending on the context of the current set of circumstances."

He looked at Mindi for approval. She shrugged and said nothing.

Jeff said, "That's it. I think I have it! I visited their minds and no one was injured. Those that might have gotten hurt—Alejandro, for example—were guilty, and a jury of his peers set the punishment. I didn't injure him, I was a catalyst for imposing the law. For the others, it seemed like a good idea at the time. Things turned out okay. Right?" The last question actually a plea for acceptance and the self-forgiveness he was looking for.

Isaiah's challenge to him had affected him more than he realized. In Jeff's research, however, he found something that couldn't be ignored, something antithetical to his belief system. Situation ethics was anchored in the Christian faith. Jeff did not particularly agree with most everything said by Christian apologists, yet this answer fit, an answer to his current moral dilemma.

Jeff was aware that if they were in a different time and place in history, the meetings with Al would be considered a spiritual experience, events that created a change in a person's outlook. Logician Jeff could never prove what he experienced in a court of law, or even the court of public opinion, especially while not being a part of a religious movement that would validate his experiences. His current cognitive dissonance was rooted in his persona's battle of logic versus faith searching for the answer to the ethics of his past that would affect future decisions.

The internal mind dodge of situation ethics worked. At least for now. His mind was free to return to the subject of a leap into Aletha Johnson to see if he could find Isaiah's true motives for lying. Was he looking to arrest Jeff for what he had tried to do? So Jeff had to protect himself. He would do what it took to ensure his wife's safety. The game was once again afoot, and he was back to enjoying the thrill of the chase, finding clues, and solving a mystery.

~

Mindi and Jeff sat on their meditation pillows in the living room with the DVD player setting the stage with its gentle music. A few deep breaths, and they were in another of their falling dreams. The difference this time was that this was a tandem leap from a meditation, rather than a dream, to enter Althea Johnson's mind and snoop around.

They held hands, and, after a few moments of sensory serenity, they saw through Aletha's eyes, looking at a computer monitor at a website about UFO reports. They watched Aletha scan through the organization's listings, coming to the end of a page that identified the source as the United Nations Unidentified Anomalous Phenomena Task Force, with an acronym nearly as long and tongue-twisting as its full name: UNUAPTF. Jeff noted that there were hundreds of sightings and that the database could be sorted in multiple ways: by country, date, day or night sighting, multiple lights, distance from observer, videos/photos available, contacts and interviewer comments, maps, drawings, drone footage, and more. This was the sort of information he had been trying to access when he first started trying to research UFOs and visit government offices. Aletha took notes on sightings in the American Pacific Northwest, British Columbia, and Canada.

Mindi and Jeff felt a hand on Aletha's shoulder. She turned and saw Isaiah's smiling face.

Jeff mind-whispered to Mindi, *That's Isaiah.*

Yeah, I know. I saw him last time I was here.

"Anything spectacular?" Isaiah said.

The view returned to the screen and scrolled down to a listing.

Aletha said, "Here's your visit to Bainbridge Island. It was flagged by the agency as spectacular. There were"—her finger traced a path along the entry—"six reports sent in by people that attended. And three videos! Your 'Jeff' didn't file one, and your report to headquarters wasn't forwarded on." She gestured to the screen.

"Yeah, they don't want any trail that might affect our cover."

Isaiah's face came back into Jeff and Mindi's view as Aletha turned toward her husband. "What else have you learned from him?" she asked.

"We had two conversations. One in the dream in my flower field, then when he dropped in at the office and we went to lunch. I'm convinced that, to him, I'm just a curious new UFO fanatic. A journalist, with some psi talents, who challenged him after he invaded my mind. I'm sure he was surprised by what I told him I could do. I think he's new to UFOs and became interested because they paid direct attention to him. He's the first good lead we've had up here, so I want to nurture the relationship. He wants to know what I know about UFOs."

"Sure. Let me know how I can help." She pushed her chair back, stood, and gave him a quick peck on the cheek. "I think that this baby"—she rubbed her slightly expanded stomach—"is going to be a bit of a distraction. I've got to go the bathroom."

~

Jeff and Mindi were suddenly back in their own living room, the leap over.

"What ended that?" Mindi said, "Did you?"

"No. It was like when I first began leaping into your mind when we met, I didn't have control of where or when I landed."

Mindi laughed as she remembered what his presence felt like back then. "Sure, I get it. But how is it we leaped into their minds at just this right time for us to learn she's pregnant too?"

"I'd like to know for sure if Al manages these meetings. I'd rather he stays out of our business unless we ask for help. That's what I meant when I argued with Al about being manipulated."

"So you think it's Al's doing?" Mindi asked. "I thought he meant he'd interfere if something bad was going to happen. But yeah, things have happened that are too much of a coincidence to be random."

Jeff said, "And Al never answered us when asked if he connected us with the Johnsons."

"I'll go back over our dream journal entries to see how many times there've been things like that."

"Doesn't it feel like we're being pushed toward something?"

"That's obvious, isn't it?" Mindi said. "Nuclear disarmament." Her frown matched the tone of her question. She went on. "Maybe not total disarmament. Maybe we're just supposed to stop someone, or several someones, from turning the key and pushing the red button; just leap into someone's mind to scramble their thoughts long enough for them to come to their senses."

"Yeah, it'd be nice if it were that simple," Jeff said as he handed Mindi her journal. They transcribed their recent leap, then added to the decision tree an information box that said, *Aletha pregnant.*

Mindi said, "That might be an important piece of information. Do you think we can use it?"

"I don't know. We wait and see."

CHAPTER 9

Jeff fell asleep hoping to talk with Al. After a brief fall upward, the new hallmark of a visit to the combined community introduced as Al, Jeff was in Al's mind.

Al said, "Why do you speak of this person Isaiah?"

"Because I want to know if you know of him or his wife, Aletha." A thought occurred to Jeff that made him wonder if instead it might've been Ziggy who had put them together.

Al admitted he heard Jeff's thought of Ziggy and deflected. "You are thinking of the one who was introduced as Ziggy. It is amusing that they still have a sense of humor."

"What?" Jeff asked.

Al scoffed. "Ziggy. We are what you would call 'somewhat related,' bless their heart."

What? Jeff thought with surprise at the sarcastic colloquialism.

There was an infinitesimal pause before Al answered, catching Jeff's notice of the use of the quaint phrase.

Al said, "We have an unusual . . . sibling relationship. I reckon they'd pitch a hissy fit knowing that we now know

Ziggy talked to you."

"Wait, Al," Jeff said, now in tune that Al could read his thoughts. There it was again. "You just used three phrases common to the Deep South."

Al said, with forced naivete, said, "South of what?"

Jeff's tone showed his impatience. "The southern United States, of course. The South. I thought you'd studied us." He surprised himself with the exasperation in his voice. Something was not quite right with Al's communications.

"We see. You are referring to the idioms. What did we say? We will be offline for a moment while we replay that part of our conversation. Stand by."

Offline? Replay? Jeff thought.

A few seconds ticked by, then Al said, "We tracked that phrase to a motion picture made in 1944 about the 1930s Depression era in the South. We'd put them in our register of phrases to use when speaking with someone from North America to make you feel at ease. Now, what did you want to—"

The connection with Al ended. Jeff awoke feeling cheated.

~

Dissatisfied with the way the conversation had cut off, Jeff lay on the bed considering how their lucid dreams, for several months, had melded with their "real-time." There was no dividing line between their dream lives and waking lives, as before. Their special talents developed, allowing their bodies to sleep or meditate and be refreshed, yet their conscious minds lived within their lucid dreams, using telepathy and astral projection to experience what other people do not. These latest developments with Al and Isaiah were frustrating, though, because answers that should be within their grasp were not.

He closed his eyes, tried to will himself back to sleep, reconnect, and complete the conversation with Al. The effort failed. He swung his feet over the side of the bed, resigned to the connection being lost. Had Al ended it because of the wordplay?

Jeff stretched, rubbed his eyes, and replayed a memory of a conversation with his dad years ago, where he was told of a sales development class presented by the telephone company. This was well before the internet, cell phones, and email. The key communication of the day was through landline telephones. The training segment was a technique to ensure positive customer relations with existing clients. It was a suggestion for dealing with a situation when a current customer on the other end of the line was irate, raising their voice, and on the cusp of becoming abusive. In order to enhance customer relations, give the client a chance to cool off, or give you time to plan a solution, they suggested hanging up on yourself while you were talking, in the middle of your own sentence. They warned, do not hang up while the other person is talking. That would only frustrate them further. But people don't think anyone would hang up on themselves, if they think about it at all. Then during the reestablished call, cooler heads would prevail. Jeff wondered if he had backed Al into some kind of corner with his challenges, and the UFO pilot had done something similar.

Mindi stirred awake. Jeff turned toward her, giving no more thought to the dream as they began their day.

~

The next night Jeff's dream began in what he called "the old-fashioned way," the sensation of falling in the endless gray void. He relaxed, floated, felt solidness beneath his feet. The air was warm, a light breeze tousled his hair. The sound of birds nearby combined with rustling of dry weeds, the odor of rusting metal, and old grease in decay. The fog cleared, revealing a bright sky with a scattering of a few broken clouds. He stood in an open area between buildings at an abandoned industrial site. Through the broken glass windows of the decrepit buildings, outlines of rusting equipment could be seen. There were no shimmering edges, as in a surreal dream. It felt like reality. Standing in the shade, he surveyed his landing spot. The sun was on the other side of the declining, corrugated metal-clad building. The shattered glazing and scattered metal on the ground signaled a warning for one to be cautious where to place one's feet.

A faint scuttling sound drew his attention to a black beetle scurrying to safety under a piece of discarded ironwork. Hearing a barely decipherable whisper, he picked his way among deer tracks and scat along a seldom-used animal path over the littered pavement between the buildings, searching for the sound by turning his head.

The whispered voice, a little clearer, said, "The toolbox. Find the toolbox."

He did. An aging metal box, amid the debris. Its lid ajar beckoned.

"Open it," the voice said."

The lid sounded a rusty complaint. Inside, a crisp new manila folder sat alone. His name was written across it in wide black marker: *Jeff Marlen*. He picked it up. Using the box as a seat, he opened the folder. Stapled together were three photocopied pages of a computer screenshot of a

Wikipedia article dated December 2023, three years hence from Jeff's real-time. The article's topic sentence sounded like an advertisement. "ChatGPT, fastest-growing consumer software application in history." The references at the end of the article were all from 2022 and 2023. Jeff was familiar with chatbots, but not this one. Hand-printed at the bottom of the last page was, "Without Consciousness, AIs Will Be Sociopaths—WSJ, Jan 13, 2023."

He reread the article then woke from the dream. He logged onto Wikipedia and searched for that page, and found nothing. Likewise the *Wall Street Journal* website. This seemed like a lot of trouble to give him a glimpse of the future. *Was it real?* The article had been left for him the way drug dealers make dead drops of product and money. Did this dream originate from his subconscious, pieced together from research he did during the drug bust last year? Maybe, except it was a lucid dream, leaving the distinct feeling of it being unapologetically real-world.

He was careful not to wake Mindi. She needed her rest. She was the one in five women for whom morning sickness runs into the second trimester. Jeff wished for Mindi's eidetic memory as he tried to document what he could remember of the article.

Jeff's notes of the Wikipedia document read:

> *ChatGPT = Generative Pre-trained Transformer*
> *The latest reference in the bibliography dated November 2023—three years from now.*
> *A chatbot with memory that works like a human mind,*
> *Trained by human operators, then left on its own to learn from the internet.*

Communication   undistinguishable   from human interaction.

Jeff knew that chatbots—sometimes 'bots,' a contraction of 'chatterbots'—had been conceived by MIT professor Weizenbaum in 1966 and, in 2014, passed the Turing Test, where a computer's replies were indistinguishable from that of a human. It wasn't until the expansion of the internet that the use of bots had proliferated, many deluging internet social media with questionable information to influence public opinion to sway elections and sell products. The article said it interacted conversationally . . . Having dialogs to answer questions, admitting its mistakes, challenging incorrect premises, rejecting inappropriate requests, and rationalizing its reasons for suggesting certain behaviors. The handwritten reference to the future *Wall Street Journal* article of bots becoming sociopaths was intriguing. History was full of brilliant human sociopaths with expansive power who had caused irreparable injury and pain. *What if Hitler or Stalin could have written code?* Jeff thought. *Why not a smart machine too?* Would artificial intelligence sociopaths become the apex after the Anthropocene extinction, ultimately caused by global warming, starvation, poisoned groundwater, and nuclear war?

What if an armed autonomous robot, using pure logic to quell a riot, kills all rioters? Its logic would be—no rioters, no riot, no problem. A fictional version was the 1984 movie, *The Terminator*, where the Skynet computer starts a nuclear war and sends a robot into the past to kill the mother of the future resistance fighters' leader to end the resistance.

Jeff shivered as he reflected on his recent experience with time travel. What if killer robots could do the same?

AI wants to learn how to time travel! What if?

The movie that originally fueled Jeff's interest in computers was the 1983 *War Games*. Not that he wanted to emulate the young computer hacker who broke into the War Operation Plan Response, a fictional supercomputer in control of the nuclear launch codes at NORAD—it was the science that'd intrigued him.

Is that our mission now? Was that why I was chosen, because of my knowledge of computers, to fight a computer with no feelings or conscience?

At least in ancient wars, the leaders were noble and honored their opponents. There were predictions that machines would rule the world, enslaving humans to make use of their opposable thumbs and malleable brains, to do the fine manual labor that machines couldn't. And when the job was done, eliminate them.

That's it! he realized. *Someone is trying to warn me.*

With a visceral feeling of urgency, Jeff continued his list of fictional rogue computers:

Stanley Kubrick's 1968 film *2001: A Space Odyssey*, where the onboard spaceship computer, HAL, feels threatened and murders most of the spaceship's crew and tries to kill Dave.

Demon Seed, a 1973 novel by Dean Koontz, and the 1977 movie by the same name, where the murderously malevolent computer Proteus IV procreates with a human woman who gives birth to a human/computer clone to rule humans.

The 1977 novel, *The Adolescence of P-1*, and the associated 1984 Canadian TV movie adaptation entitled *Hide and Seek*, about a computer program written by a college student that, when activated, becomes sentient and takes lethal action to protect itself.

Another fictional AI computer that caught Jeff's attention

was Winston, a character in the 2017 Dan Brown novel *Origin*, who does the bidding of its creator but with self-aware sentience and who, in a backhanded way, displays an interesting rationalization of its duties, where concern about its own self-preservation is nonexistent, and in the end, exhibits selfless heroism when its final program is complete.

While the science fiction community hypothesized the what-ifs and consequences of AI computers being in control, Yuval Noah Harari, in his 2017 nonfiction *Homo Deus*, speculated the next step in humanity's evolution may be that of humankind becoming more intellectually algorithmic, essentially biological computers. Homo sapiens becomes obsolete, replaced by Homo deus, or gods.

Jeff wondered if Al, the alien UFO pilot, the consortium of his kind, was a superbeing in that context from another civilization, here to take over. Or was he, as Ziggy suggested, and the future Wikipedia article implied, a computer with sentience, a godlike machine?

Jeff wrote of his dream.

> *I've gotten direction on where to go and what to do before, but never in such a clandestine manner. Have our dreams been tapped like phone lines, to where they're no longer private? Did someone hack our minds? It feels like that's what Al has done. Will we have to yield our dreams to the will of others? Who or what is in control of all of this?*

Jeff kept writing.

> *But who planted that article in my dream? Someone, obviously, who can implant a dream*

with superfine detail. Was it done by Isaiah to manipulate me, by his black-ops agency, in the name of the government? Or was it planted by Al? Or Ziggy? Could it be the other aliens who Al said made crop circles, abducted human beings and performed animal mutilations? Al warned of others who would try to hinder our mission!

Jeff read back over what he had written. He wasn't satisfied with the lack of detail he could remember from the article, but he'd captured the spirit of it. Meeting Mindi and leaping into all the others was strange when they first met, but that was tame by comparison with what was happening now.

He shuddered as another chill ran down his spine. He shook it off, resolving not to become a victim of his realizations, took a cup of coffee out onto the apartment's deck, and breathed in the fresh morning air . . . He'd try to forget it for now.

He watched the few clouds move across the horizon and focused on the birds fluttering in the trees across the way, but his thoughts persisted and returned to the dream's mystery, his current experiences, and their implications. He replayed all of his internal arguments and defenses, trying to end the disturbing feelings he was having with the question, *Was it my subconscious just doing housecleaning, or have I been given a glimpse of something sinister?* After all, he had watched *Narcos*, the true story of the infamous Colombian drug smugglers, and then Mindi and he had dealt with real-world smugglers of their own.

He heard Mindi stirring. Jeff shook his head to again dismiss his thoughts, then went inside to greet her and to enjoy the gift of a new day.

~

This was a welcome assignment. Their employer had made it possible for Mindi and Jeff to walk barefoot on the beach in the warm evening calm in San Juan, Puerto Rico, after a full day of photo shoots for the new ad campaign focused on pregnancy-friendly skin-care products. This time it was real—not like they had done a few months ago as out-of-body tourists, when they couldn't feel the warmth and smell the Caribbean Sea's sultry atmosphere or feel the sand between their toes. They shared a dessert in the twenty-four-hour café at their resort, then returned to their room. Once asleep, Jeff's dream had him once again walking alone amid the now-familiar flowers of Isaiah's dream field.

Jeff followed the path toward the table and chairs, glasses filled with ice and a pitcher of iced tea with lemon slices floating on the surface. Not seeing Isaiah, Jeff scanned the unlimited horizon, taking in the activity of the bees on the endless field of flowers, and noted several paths that led off in other directions.

Isaiah's voice came from behind. "Hi, Jeff. Thanks for coming."

Jeff turned, then chuckled as they made eye contact. "It seems again that I had no choice. Thank you, I guess, for another invitation. I see the iced tea is ready." He pointed toward the table.

"Yes. Please sit," Isaiah said. "We have a lot to discuss." He offered a handshake.

When Isaiah sat, he handed Jeff a file folder.

Strange, Jeff thought. He hadn't seen Isaiah holding it a moment ago.

Jeff noted familiar writing on the folder—his name. It

appeared to be the same folder he had seen in his dream at the abandoned factory. He tensed, thinking that it had been Isaiah who had planted it.

Their eyes met, Jeff's conveying suspicion.

"Yes," Isaiah said. "That is why I called you here tonight. I read it and need to talk with you."

Jeff opened the folder. It was the same photocopied article with the handwritten notation at the bottom. "How did you . . . uh, find it?" He waved his hand impatiently.

"You've seen it before?" Isaiah said.

"Yes. Where did you find it?"

"In a dream. At an old factory."

Jeff maintained eye contact as he turned his head slightly, a signal for the man to continue.

Isaiah said, "Is that where you saw it?"

Jeff nodded. "Go on."

"It was in an old toolbox."

"So you didn't plant it there for me to find?"

"No. It was about computers, and I recognized your first name. So your last name is Marlen?"

Jeff hesitated, but he realized there was no reason to deny it at this point. "Yes. I saw this in a dream a couple of nights ago, in an old factory. How did you bring it here?"

"Are you as puzzled by the dates being three years in the future?"

"But how did you get it here?" He began to reread the article, to see if he had missed any salient points before. He felt satisfied he had gotten most of it, and memorized the email address of the person who posted the article in the future. He'd use that information, but that could wait.

"Jeff," Isaiah said. Jeff's mind had been focused on the puzzle. "Jeff?" He paused, then, "Jeff!" Jeff's head snapped up and met Isaiah's questioning eyes. "I asked if the date puzzled you."

"Yes." He looked back at the article and read the email address again, ensuring he had it fixed in his memory. "Of course. How did you bring it here?"

"In my dream, I was falling in a gray fog. It startled me at first, but a voice told me to relax. Suddenly, I was standing in a courtyard at a derelict factory. The voice said to find a large metal toolbox in the debris. In it was this folder. I thought that might be your name . . ."

"And you brought it here? I didn't bring it back to real-time with me when I found it. Did you? Or can you only see it when you're here?"

Isaiah scratched his cheek and looked puzzled. "I didn't know I couldn't bring it, but no, not in real-time. I guess I can just have it here. It's not . . . it's not really real, is it? This is a dream." He looked down at the folder in Jeff's hands. "Well, I don't think it can go back to the office with me." He gave a short laugh.

"Well. It never occurred to me I could get it in another dream. Interesting," Jeff said.

Isaiah said, "We are linked, and I don't know how things have fallen together the way they have, but this is right in our faces. What is this about? What's the answer to this riddle?"

Jeff watched the man's eyes. He seemed sincere. A few heartbeats transpired before he said, "Isaiah, I don't know. I can tell you part of what I do know." Jeff told him his version of the powerlessness of his dream in that place he'd never been before. That time felt real. It didn't have the distortion they felt in lucid dreams. He suspected, but wasn't sure, they'd each traveled to some future, but when, he couldn't tell.

"A few nights ago, when I spotted the toolbox in my

dream, I heard a whispering voice. There the file was, clean and neat as . . ." He gestured toward the file and gave Isaiah a look as if he should carry on with the story.

Isaiah didn't take the cue, so Jeff asked, "Do you have an interest in chatbots and artificial intelligence?"

"Besides the continuous chatter in the news that artificial intelligence is the wave of the future, this is the first time I've come this close to the subject. This date . . . three years from now. What about you?"

"Yeah, I saw the dates, and it's strange." Jeff wanted this dream over so he could get on with his own search for information.

"Then why are you being evasive? We both know that precognition is a paranormal trait—why are you trying to hide that now we have this taste of the future?"

Jeff flinched. Had the man just read his mind? "To be honest, Isaiah, I still don't fully trust you. You're keeping something from me, which makes me suspicious of your motives. So why wouldn't I want to keep my identity hidden, and what I know, from you?"

"Easy." Isaiah leaned back, using relaxed body language to ease Jeff's agitation. "I can't believe that you are not as curious about how and why we got that folder."

"Of course I'm curious. But back to my point. I'm certain you're not telling me about yourself. My experience is that things like this"—he waved his arms around, including the field of flowers, the iced tea, and the folder—"happen for a reason. You're right, we're linked and, again, based on my experience, someone else is driving the bus. We don't always get to choose the route or the stops."

"That's a colorful metaphor. I get it. What is it that makes you suspicious?"

"With the question being so direct," Jeff said, "I'll answer. Your story about being a journalist and your obvious slip of the tongue about a 'report' rather than an article. Government agents write reports, journalists write articles and stories." Jeff slapped his hands flat on the table as a demonstration of the finality of his suspicion.

The dream ended.

~

"Where did you go?" Jeff said as he awoke with a start. Mindi stirred but did not wake. The clock showed 2:22 a.m.

He tried to go back to sleep, but the arguments and considerations whizzing through his head kept the sandman away. He got up and transcribed the dream. He studied the flowchart on his notepad and decided to use a wall in the dining room for his visual investigation board, an elaborate flowchart complete with photos, strings, and notes.

He studied it, then reread what he had written in his notebook earlier and added, *Will take no action with Isaiah Johnson. He knows my name, my face, and knows I know computers. I am certain he noted the plate numbers from my car.* With the power of the government computer, Isaiah must know his height, weight, wife's name, that she was pregnant with twins, that they lived in California, that she was the brunette with him on the billboard on Highway 99 North, east side of the road at the county line advertising LaDormeur cosmetics, and what brand of laundry detergent they use. It was a cinch that Isaiah would be back in touch.

~

Later that day, after their last photo shoot, the text message from Isaiah wasn't a surprise: *Please meet me at Starbucks at LAX Main Terminal at 4:00 p.m., day after tomorrow. Reply ASAP.* Jeff thought, *Well, he did say please.* They'd be back in California just in time for Jeff to meet. *Did he know when I'd be flying back, or is the timing of his request a coincidence?*

~

Isaiah set his briefcase next to the table and said, "I'll be right back." He ordered a coffee. As he sat, he said, "Did you know I would find you?" Although phrased as a question, it was a statement of fact. Then, Isaiah intentionally broke a cardinal rule of negotiating—not waiting for an answer, continuing to talk, making any answer inconsequential, to establish control over the conversation. "And here we are." He smiled and took a drink of his coffee.

"How *did* you find me?"

"I called my congressperson," Isaiah said, forcing some lighthearted patter with a little obvious sarcasm.

"You have that kind of pull, huh?" Jeff played along, for now.

Isaiah said, "I wish I had a greater supply of push rather than pull. Mules and oxen pull. It's the driver who pushes them to their destination."

"Now *that* was colorful." Jeff smiled, making reference to Isaiah's comment during their dream meeting. "But why this meeting—in person?"

Isaiah nodded. And waited.

Jeff said, "What?"

Isaiah held Jeff's gaze. "Jeff, we believe . . ."

Jeff said sharply, "We? Who are the 'we'?" Jeff was in great shape and stood half a head taller than the government agent. Now, sitting up straight at their little table outside the coffee shop, he was puffed up like a fighting rooster.

Isaiah shrank, albeit imperceptibly. Jeff leaned forward an inch, his eyebrows arching and his lips pursed, yet the agent backed down no further.

Isaiah stared into Jeff's insistent eyes and said, "That's right. There are things I haven't told you." He relaxed, the move intended to defuse the tension.

Jeff eased back and took a deep breath yet was visibly on alert. They were on equal footing, neither with an advantage in a verbal fencing match. "Okay," he said. "What haven't you told me?"

Isaiah needed to either gather his thoughts or try once again for the advantage. As he looked toward the counter, he said, "Do you want a sandwich or some fruit?"

"No. Tell me why you called this meeting, and I'll decide if I will share anything more with you. Once again, who are the 'we'?"

From his inside coat pocket, Isaiah produced a black leather wallet, setting it on the table in front of Jeff. He gestured with his finger for Jeff to open it.

Jeff looked at the wallet, then at Isaiah, then back to the wallet. He gestured for Isaiah to show him. Isaiah flipped it open. Inside was an intricate gold badge that said *Special Agent Homeland Security Investigations*.

Jeff leaned forward and looked at the identification card opposite the badge. He read out loud, "Isaiah T. Johnson, Special Agent." He smiled. "You are trusting me with this information, Isaiah, because you have already investigated me and found out that I am not a foreign government agent. Right? So this is the 'we'?"

Isaiah nodded. Then he tipped his head sideways, indicating that it was Jeff's turn to share.

Ignoring the cue, Jeff said, "Yeah, it's lunchtime. Let's have that sandwich. Here or across the way?"

"Here is fine."

"This might take some time. When're you returning to Seattle? When do you fly out?"

"I'm here specifically to talk to you," Isaiah said with a smile. "My ticket is open."

~

"Okay. I'll go first." Jeff gave Isaiah an edited version of how he and Mindi met; that he accepted it as his mission to help her achieve her dream. Jeff elaborated on meeting her in person, with his time travel ending at the Halloween Gala; that he had succeeded in helping her get her career started. He left out that Mindi now had the same skills; left out that she was pregnant; left out that they had taken part, a little too closely, in a major international drug bust last year and had time traveled into the future to protect their employer, Charlene. He did share that he now lived in Southern California, had sublet his Seattle apartment and was happy to be one of the male faces of LaDormeur cosmetics—for as long as it lasted. He had his part-time computer gig. And he finished with a repeat description of seeing lights in the sky that smiled at him. Jeff felt he had given enough information to appear vulnerable, but not enough to predict what he may or may not be capable of.

Jeff left out details of his many visits with Al and the recent message from Ziggy. He didn't see it necessary to talk about how he'd brought Charlene closure. Jeff had his generation's endemic distrust of the government, and this guy represented the government—big time.

When it became apparent that Jeff had finished, Isaiah said, "And . . . ?"

"And what?"

"Any more about your interest in UFOs, especially when the UFOs seem to have an interest in you? That's what." He finished with a quick, final nod.

Jeff deflected the question with a question. "Does your agency care about UFOs in general, or just my sightings in particular?"

Isaiah sighed, then paused a moment before replying. "The agency cares about UFOs in general. And they assigned me to care about UFOs in the Pacific Northwest. UFOs are interested in you. This I know. Therefore, I, too, am interested in you—in particular." His eyes bored into Jeff's. "And not just what you know, but what you could do with what you know."

Jeff didn't want to blink, but it was difficult not to, considering Isaiah's psychological attack. He would be careful. He explained again in detail about the first time he saw the UFOs, but edited out Mindi tolerating his interest in them. Jeff hesitated, then started to share about his dream about being in a UFO cockpit. "And, I guess I should share . . ." Isaiah put his hand up to wait, and set a small digital voice recorder on the table.

Jeff looked around to see if anyone noticed, but no one seemed to be paying them any attention.

"May I record this?" Isaiah asked.

There was silence as Jeff's glance went from the recorder to Isaiah's face. He said quietly, "No."

Isaiah's eyes flashed to the recorder and his lips pursed.

Jeff's parry had caused the agent's attack to fail. Now Isaiah had to decide whether he would execute a fencing remise, a counterattack.

"Okay." Isaiah signaled retreat. "Never mind. I'll get the details I miss for my report later." He showed Jeff the machine was off and put it in his briefcase.

Jeff had gained a neutral stance, but he wished to regain control and returned to a guard position. "So you haven't written your report?"

Isaiah's confused look lasted only a moment. "Yes, but I honored our agreement. You are still anonymous to my superiors. But at some point, I will be asked to reveal my source."

Jeff looked the man straight in the eye and said, "But you will not." It was a statement, not a question. "I will become stupid. A dumb jock who wanted to impress another amateur, and sow doubt. Maybe the folks at the UFOrg meeting were victims of mass hysteria. I can make it fly—unless you want to start pulling out my fingernails or waterboarding me." He smiled, knowing that there would be neither of those tactics. At least, not yet.

~

At the government agency boot camp, the trainees had role-played verbal fencing matches. Isaiah parried Jeff's advance with an offhand compliment meant to distract him. "I'm sure it wouldn't go that far, and I believe you are smart enough to become very dumb if you wanted to."

Jeff's crooked smile and nod kept Isaiah off-balance after the enforceable threat to stonewall. Isaiah had failed so far to uncover Jeff's weakness.

Jeff was very aware of Isaiah's weakness—Aletha's pregnancy. It was something the Johnsons very much wanted, and Isaiah didn't know that Jeff knew, as he had resisted taking advantage of that fact. With Isaiah feeling he was close to having a credible witness to a close encounters event, defining his career advancement, that knowledge could be used to control the agent.

Isaiah's parry didn't work. Jeff was a natural at this game, and he mercilessly peppered the agent with a stop-thrust of questions concerning Isaiah's experience with UFOs. What was his agency's mission statement? Where were they headquartered? Were the cadre of UFO hunters an elite Marine force, or made up of mercenaries? Was he, in fact, a psychic mercenary? What special psychic training had he had?

Isaiah, recognizing that he was, at best evenly matched and at worst outmatched, signaled arrêt, his fingers flicking a salute at his brow.

Jeff remained on guard, despite his adversary's signal. He probed, with an illusory thrust of his verbal foil. "What is it you want from me?" Jeff's stiff posture informed his opponent he expected the match would be his, regardless of the answer.

Isaiah glared at him, then realized it was better to be allies than adversaries, and with a deep sigh said, "Your cooperation." He had been bettered.

Jeff shook his head. "I hate a game of twenty questions, but if you insist on playing, let's get the other nineteen out of the way so we can have a useful conversation."

Time to talk. "As you somehow know, I'm part of a special projects branch of the NSA with a focus on Unexplained Anomalous Phenomena. Fancy name for UFO."

"I know. And?"

"And what?"

"And what do you do?"

"Look for people like you. People that have high Close Encounters ratings, CE-3 or above. Multiple encounters. By definition, you are my mission."

Jeff turned immediately to face Isaiah.

Isaiah recognized it as a flinch and said, "Why that reaction? The word 'mission'?"

"I call using my talent 'my missions.' It was surprising to me that we both use the same term."

Isaiah returned to engarde position. He lunged. "Missions? Plural?" he asked as he fixed his gaze on Jeff. The look in Jeff's eyes told him he had scored a hit. There was no way Jeff could have parried. He had slipped.

Isaiah said under his breath, "Touché." He lowered his eyes, an obvious attempt to draw his adversary off-balance, then said, "Jeff, what will it take for you to trust me?"

~

Jeff clenched his jaw. It wasn't the strain of the fight, it was the cognitive dissonance of wanting to have an ally in Al's mission, but not feeling he could trust Isaiah yet. There were a lot of questions on his investigation board for which he could use help. Yet this agent might indeed be a serious adversary, a threat to him and Mindi. If Jeff succumbed to trusting him, could he be stabbed in the back?

Is it possible that he feels the same about me? Jeff's caution was supported by myths of people with special talents being "disappeared" or pressed into service until they met an untimely end, either at the hands of the enemy or because the asset was no longer an asset and became shark food fifty miles offshore. Yes, he was afraid of this man, who called himself Isaiah, who sold insurance from a storefront on a busy arterial in West Seattle, who carried a badge for the NSA, and who had a wife who, like Mindi, was pregnant with their first child.

His memory resurrected a phrase said by a past US president: "Trust, but verify." The voice in his head, with the authority of a fencing referee, said, *Halt.*

Jeff said, "Yeah. My UFO sightings marked the beginning of another mission. I label it a mission because initial and subsequent dreams all relate to each other. It's not a great mystery." Jeff's smile was genuine. He reached across the table, offering his hand, which Isaiah took; they shook. It was, at least, a temporary truce, possibly the beginning of a cooperative effort to benefit each of their objectives. In the quietest part of his mind, he mentally gathered up all the memories of their involvement in the Colombian drug bust and the kidnapping of Mindi, and locked them away from discussion. That part of his story involved interference with another government agency that could themselves cooperate with the NSA. Jeff didn't need this potential new ally to connect those dots, discover the identity of Dan the Longshoreman and open him up to scrutiny. Accommodations in an American gulag wouldn't have windows, and strong psychic powers would confine him, prevent him from roaming out of his body.

Each combatant had scored a hit but neither had struck hard enough to draw first blood. The match was tied. Would the winner be determined with the next touché, or would both walk off the piste in disgrace?

~

Isaiah lunged; it was a surprise attack. "You know, Jeff, if I wanted the information you are withholding, I could get it from you. You know my strengths."

Jeff was surprised. They had just shaken hands, signaling the end of the bout. But he was quick. He parried.

"Is that a threat to invade my mind? Go ahead. My firewall could use a test. I'm sure it will hold. No admittance without a ticket." He held.

Isaiah shook his head, not in retreat, but as a recovery, a return to engarde. "I won't waste my energy. That was to test your resolve. I've given my word." Although the token on his keyring, given to all agents upon assignment, was a hand with the index and middle finger crossed; not as a sign of good luck, but representing fingers crossed behind one's back when telling a lie—a sign of the cross for forgiveness from God for breaking the ninth commandment: thou shalt not bear false witness. The charm reminded agents that the end justified the means.

"I'll be honest with you," Isaiah replied, "in the interest of some greater good, I may have to, regrettably, readjust my commitment."

Jeff was still in parry position. He answered with a riposte, straight to the target. "If you must, but I would then be justified in readjusting mine." Engagement! Their foils' blades again met.

~

The match paused, with no trading of beats and parries. Yet neither party signaled a retreat, instead signaling a recovery to the en garde position, communicating willingness to return to battle. They each knew there would be equal trading of offensive and defensive maneuvers. Possibly no points would be made.

Isaiah had previously considered how he'd draft the report to be sent to HQ. He could see the words on the screen now. "Jeff Marlen, an average guy with a few psi skills. If he agreed to be tested by Homeland Security, I estimate would score very high on the scale."

Isaiah had scored eighty-seven. And for psi skills, he only had his field-of-flower dreams, limited out-of-body and telepathic abilities, and the ability to search an unprotected mind to encourage certain behaviors. There were agents that had seven or eight abilities, some of which included remote viewing and telekinesis, and scored in the high nineties. One agent that even had limited pyrokinesis abilities. At least, the folks in the lab called it pyrokinesis. He could not manifest flames, only sparks that might start a fire. They gave him a 101. *Jeff might score higher than that. If so, he could be useful, or very dangerous.*

~

Jeff reviewed what he had told Isaiah about his time travel, that his ability, he believed, went beyond pre- and postcognition. He had affected outcomes that may not have occurred without his powers. Time travel, once perfected, could be a very useful skill, a skill difficult for another to defend against, and therefore a dangerous skill. His consciousness had gone into another's mind in the past and future, and could find secrets that, in an adversarial context, would be better left unsealed. *Yes, an important skill.* Was there anyone in Isaiah's agency who could do that?

~

Isaiah's mental fencing skills required knowing an opponent's strengths and weaknesses. He, too, considered Jeff's time travel skills.

He could not include in his report that Marlen's time travel experience went beyond the built-in ability of ordinary humans who have autonoetic consciousness, that is, the ability to re-experience a past event as if one were there. An example is when someone wants to remember if they locked the door when they left the house, and within their memory, they see the event in their mind to confirm the act. *Jeff is a careful planner and could use information in a time travel event to his advantage, and possibly to Aletha's and my disadvantage, as well as the country's.*

If he did report that, and Marlen did not cooperate with the agency, the agency might see Marlen as a threat to national security and have him neutralized. That would be extreme, an unacceptable response by the agency, and would mean Isaiah breaking his word to Jeff. But the agency could order Marlen's mind be entered to view his intentions and abilities, and if Isaiah refused, there were other agents who would do as ordered. There could be two possible outcomes of using force against Jeff. First, they would find nothing, and at that point surely lose complete access to Al the UFO; a lose-lose situation. Second, there could be a retaliation before he was neutralized; that could be catastrophic—to what degree, Isaiah could not predict but certainly considered.

~

Jeff's mind had been in overdrive to determine how to use

the agent for his purposes and let the agent think he was cooperating. There was a quote often attributed to Sun Tzu's *Art of War*, but actually from *The Godfather Part II*, where Michael Corleone says, "Keep your friends close but your enemies closer." But it *was* Sun Tzu who said, "If you know the enemy and know yourself, you need not fear the result of a hundred battles."

Although Jeff was not sure that Isaiah was, in fact, an enemy, he could develop into one if Jeff was not vigilant. Or their relationship could develop into a friendship. On the other hand, of course, he did not want the kind of friend that was like Carlos Cordoba, who had betrayed his partner smugglers, Alejandro and Roberto.

~

The two men sat in silence as they evaluated their positions, drank their coffee, and nibbled at sandwiches and chips. Jeff looked at his watch and said, "Well, we're at a stalemate. Neither one of us is going to tell the other what their intentions are, and to be quite frank, Isaiah, there is nothing I can imagine you have that would be valuable to support my *hobby*." Jeff's emphasis on the word hobby was to preview his next comments. "You, however, I am sure, have a professional agenda as long as your arm, and you feel I fit into it. My motivations are merely curiosity fueled by the scientific method. I was raised and trained to follow logical thought, and in the last couple of years, I've been given information that will never make it into official reports specific to UFOs."

Now I'll bait the hook. Though much would be a bluff. "My skills match or exceed the abilities of you and your fellow agents, and perhaps the rest of the government. Your handlers have convinced you to use your abilities for their benefit. You have sworn an oath to the government, the Constitution and your agency. Because of that, your motivations are not likely to be aligned with mine; in fact, they may be antagonistic to my well-being, and the well-being of my wife and children." The look on his face was resolute.

Jeff's comment was a feint, intended to highlight his weakness, to force Isaiah to focus on his own growing family.

Jeff was right in baiting the agent. In response, Isaiah instinctively presented a straight thrust.

"You are a suspect in the attempt to break into the Pentagon and the NSA systems using psychic methods. That is the reason that I was sent to the bookstore, to follow the lead of two agents who had canvassed new age bookstores, head-shops, and cannabis dispensaries. They got a hit during their conversation with Ingrid, and it led to you. In order to support our suspicions, we have the authority to detain you and Mindi for questioning under the Homeland Security Act of 2002."

Jeff already knew that he had been trying to play in a sophisticated sandbox with his attempt to probe the Pentagon. Even though he was only trying to satisfy his curiosity and wasn't an agent of a hostile government, this could still be serious. He made a strategic retreat after a quick parry of eye contact, while he thought, *Should I call Isaiah's bluff? Or follow my hunch that the agent might still be of use?*

Jeff's intuition was now in control of this match. *Now is the time. Isaiah is just a guy, whose wife is also expecting a baby. He's just doing his job. We're on the same side.*

Jeff's intentional feint had resulted in a thrust from Isaiah, and Jeff knew which of his own moves would earn a successful touché but still leave his adversary his self-respect.

He would perform two patinandos; a tempo patinando, a slow step and a lunge, followed by a speed patinando, a fast step and a lunge.

"Isaiah, that's a feeble attempt at blackmail. First, I don't believe that you would take part in having me and my wife disappeared in order to interrogate us. You do not seem like that kind of person, even though I suppose your superiors may order you to do it. It depends on what you may have told them. If things get too hot, Mindi and I will disappear in ways even you or the government can't find us. You know how I think—logically, and I have resources you know nothing about. I have already put a plan in place to assure our protection." A bluff for sure, but one he was certain would gain him the advantage.

Isaiah's parry was to point at Jeff and say, "Don't threa—"

Jeff cut him off with a thrust of a doublé. "No! Do I have to remind you that I have skills that perhaps you and your agency can use. You do not know what they are. But I know your wife is pregnant. How would I know? Let's just say I do." Jeff paused for effect. "Don't threaten me with your agency's capabilities. I am quite confident in mine. I repeat, I'm more valuable to you than you are to me."

Jeff paused and scanned the coffee shop, then settled on Isaiah's surprised face and knew the bout was about to be over. Before Isaiah could say anything, Jeff said, "But you have my word that I am not an agent of a foreign government or member of a group hostile to our government. Know I can abandon my *mission* whenever I want. I answer to no one. You obviously do. So if you want my cooperation, you must cooperate with me." There was a pause, then he finished with, "Again, you do not know my talents or capabilities."

Jeff's last sentence was the final thrust that scored a hit, drew blood, and was the final touché. The match belonged to Jeff. Fencing rules stated that opponents salute each other at the end of the match. Jeff touched his brow with the forefinger of his right hand.

Isaiah returned the gesture.

~

Isaiah knew he shouldn't have played the government-agency-as-a-bully card. This man refused to be pushed around. True, he did not know the extent of Jeff's skills, but was sure of his willingness to use them. *What if he has powers well beyond what our agents have? Could he be dangerous to me? What about Aletha and the baby?* He doubted Jeff would go that far but would not take the risk. There would be no report about what he knew about Jeff or his activities. He would relay this conversation to Aletha and get back to Jeff. He told him so.

A win was a win, and Jeff displayed sportsperson-like behavior when he reached across the table and offered his hand to the government agent.

"Any ground rules going forward?" Isaiah asked. The peace negotiations had begun.

"Do you have anything in mind?"

"What to share with each other."

"How something works is not for discussion unless it needs to be shared. It's got to be mutual—and reciprocal. And each of us has a vote."

"What do you mean?" Isaiah asked.

"You, me, each of the wives, each have a say."

"Okay, so how do we break a tie?"

"I don't have an answer to that," Jeff said. "I suggest we go until we have to break a tie, then discuss the logistics. Meanwhile, I'd be open to suggestions."

"Well, how about this? If there is a tie vote on whether we do or do not take some kind of action, if we can't agree as a group, it's a no-go. Do you agree?"

Jeff paused, tipped his head sideways and gave it a little shake, as if the answer might drop out of his ear. "No. There might not be time to argue or even vote if it's a critical situation. We may just have to jump; handle the fallout later."

"Okay, we cross that bridge when we come to it."

"Can I rely on you to not report to your superiors what I'm about to tell you until we decide it's appropriate to share?"

Isaiah rubbed the side of his face before he said, "I have to run this past Aletha. And I assume you will talk with your wife, right?"

"Right." Jeff wanted to tell Isaiah about the conversations with Al and Ziggy, but the fact that he and Isaiah might be competitors for information may affect eight billion people on the planet, or his freedom from incarceration—or worse.

The mystery of the reveal to both of them seemed to put them on the same side—against what, Jeff didn't know. But artificial intelligence and UFOs were the current common denominators in their relationship now.

Jeff still needed to know who Ziggy was, and why it had been implied Al was artificial intelligence. Isaiah might be an ally in his search for that answer. Another possibility, which Jeff dismissed as ridiculous: That they were all in *The Matrix*, that they were in, or part of, an AI program. *Of course*, he thought, *it's no more ridiculous than time travel and out-of-body experiences. If that's the case, who was it that designed and put the whole UFO subject in play, waited for seventy-five years to get the population of the planet to a tipping point to believe there are UFOs, and then recruited us?*

Jeff and Isaiah agreed to talk with their significant others, then continue the conversation.

CHAPTER 10

The dream began with the view of two hands holding the front page of the *Los Angeles Times* newspaper dated February 6, 2023. A massive earthquake had hit the country of Turkey. The headline read *Hundreds Feared Dead.*

Nearby, there was the high-pitched squawk of a young child. The reader lowered the newspaper and looked down the hallway of a residence. A young girl came into view, about three years old, with big dark eyes and long dark hair braided into pigtails. She was dressed for an outing in a pink sweatshirt with a red cartoon character across the front, blue jeans, and purple trainers. LED lights in the shoes flashed when she walked. She was smiling. The complaining continued as a boy of about the same age appeared, being gently prodded down the hallway. He wore jeans and a dark blue hoodie half-on, half-off, twisted with the hood across his face. A woman, her face obscured, bent over to gently guide the boy down the hallway. She pulled at the hood to free his view for him. She stood, and her face came into view.

Jeff-2019 recoiled at seeing his wife, with a different

hairdo than Mindi-2019, who was even now asleep next to him in real-time. His host's head jerked backward in response to Jeff's recoil. The host, Jeff-2023 adjusted for the movement by putting his hands to his face, covering his eyes, and said with an inner voice, *You're here.*

As the hands were lowered, Jeff-2019 was pleased to again see Mindi with the twins.

Jeff-2023 continued in his mind. *I called you here. I anticipated your reaction, because, uh, er . . . Well, I confirmed my memory when I reread our journal from three years ago of what's happening now.*

Jeff listened to his own voice as Jeff-2023 said aloud to Mindi, "Remember I was telling you I was going to summon myself here from 2019? He just got here. Say hi to Jeff-2019," Jeff-2023's hand in a wave came into view.

Mindi looked at them.

"Wave to me. To us," the future Jeff said.

Past Jeff watched as his wife, three years older and even more beautiful, if that was possible, let go of the boy's hand and came over to him—to them—and gave him a kiss.

"Hi, Jeff-2019. You'll say hi to me, for me, when you get back." It was a statement of fact, as if she knew what would happen. She smiled and patted his cheek. "We're off to the park."

The boy pulled at his sleeves. Tossed his hat to the floor and stomped on it. She turned toward him, snagged the hat, fixed it on his head, smiled back at her husband, and turned to usher the children out the door. "We'll talk later. See ya."

"Ciao, love."

Jeff-2023 continued to his guest out loud. "We don't have much time. The dream ends soon. To answer your question . . . It was me that left the Wikipedia article at the factory . . . You'll write all this down later. I still don't know how it all worked, but that's an actual place, a real-time place, where apparently no one else would go and find it. Except Isaiah, of course."

Jeff-2019 tried to interject. "What?"

"I know, I know! It's weird. You told me I did it, because I just told you, so I did it. We're running out of time." He looked at his watch. "Oh crap . . ." He hurried his pace. "Anson MacDonald, Heinlein's pen name—you'll read *By His Bootstra—*"

The view went gray. Jeff awoke. He sat up, pulling the covers off Mindi.

"S'everything okay?" she mumbled.

"Yeah. Sorry. Go back to sleep." He covered her up, grabbed his cell phone and woke it up. The screen read *November 23, 2019, 1:47 a.m.*

Wow! His thoughts raced.

~

He wrote frantically in the journal.

> *I saw Mindi and the twins. Boy fussed putting on his sweatshirt. She's a little doll, just like her mother. They didn't call them by name. Jeff-2023 knew that I, Jeff-2019 was there. My 2023 self and Mindi had talked about it & she wasn't surprised I was there. He knew we'd get cut off soon, that's why he—I—sped up to give the name of a story.*

He set the binder aside, did some research, and ordered

an anthology of short stories from a used book website that included *By His Bootstraps*, by Heinlein.

His future self said he would read it, but now, he had to write this to tell himself, in 2023, to tell his 2019 self to get the story. He wrote furiously in a stream of consciousness, doing a mind-dump to clear out his mind's random-access memory.

> *So I knew I'd call myself forward in the dream, to his real-time, and I'd get to see Mindi and the twins. How does all this work? He, my future self, knew before I did I would be going there. So I didn't think of it first, even though now is before then. Yet me now, showed me in the future, it would happen . . . no I went there and talked to myself and told myself that I put the file somewhere so I would find it. It's some kind of a time loop. A paradox? Bootstrap paradox! That story I'm supposed to read. Mindi-2023 wasn't surprised. Why did I wait until February 2023? Maybe I didn't. Maybe I tried and failed. Maybe he—I—won't even try until then, knowing he'd fail, because I'm telling me—him, now. How does all this work? Did we have help? I knew from the dream there'd be an earthquake in Turkey killing hundreds of people. I, he, knew before he saw the newspaper that day about the earthquake. Is this how Nostradamus could see things? Oh crap. I've got to read the short story.*

He put the pen aside and read what he had written. It made sense to him now, but would it make sense to someone else who hadn't lived it? Regardless, he wrote more.

He knew he'd get and make a copy the Wikipedia article because I told him I found it. What about the Wall Street Journal article? There's no answer to why I didn't put a copy of that article there. How did Isaiah go there? Wait till I tell him he must've time traveled too.

Jeff paused, his mind back in logical mode, and shifted into a higher gear with another subject.

I'd always thought if we contacted ourselves in other times, we'd blink out of existence, or cause a singularity or something. No, that won't happen, because we weren't physically together in real-time. But we did confirm the quantum theory that we can be in two places at the same time, more or less?

He was exhausted. He stared at the page and closed the book. He washed his face and went to bed, falling into a welcome dreamless sleep.

~

When Heinlein's book of short stories arrived, he read the complicated novella, *By His Bootstraps,* about a man's future self who provides his past self a notebook that he'd never seen before, but then left for his future self to find.

Where did the notebook originate? Because, it seems neither of the protagonists, actually the same person in different chronological times, originated it. Yet one of them wrote it and the other one left it for the other one to find. Right?

It was called a bootstrap paradox, a term derived from the cliché "pulled himself up by his bootstraps," which, of course, was a physical impossibility.

Jeff looked it up. The bootstrap paradox was also called the ontological paradox, a causal loop, an information loop—but not a time loop. That was something different.

Later, as Mindi sipped on her coffee and listened as Jeff described his dream, he told her it had been the future him who planted the Wikipedia article for him and Isaiah to find. He'd told his future self in the journal that he'd send it to his past self, which he did, but only because his past self told him he would do it, so he did.

Mindi shook her head as if trying to shake the explanation into place, then nodded, as if she understood, which she really didn't.

Jeff asked if she understood.

"Uh. No," she admitted as she flashed a crooked smile.

He regaled her with the part about her future self wrangling the kids to go to a park, emphasizing her patience with the boy.

She sat up straight. "Our twins? What are their names?"

Surprised, Jeff said, "They . . . Uh, they, uh, we . . . I don't know. They, no we, uh, didn't say their names."

She pointed out the irony of what he'd said. "Jeff . . . So what good was that dream if you didn't find out from ourselves what we'll name the twins? It would save us from having to pick them ourselves!"

He smiled. Then laughed. "If we'd learned their names, there wouldn't have been an original source for the names—that, too, would've been, uh, would be, a causal loop where we had their names without us ever picking them out."

Mindi said, "Oh."

~

After a few days of chewing on his own bootstrap paradox event, Jeff finally grokked why he'd sent himself and Isaiah to find the Wikipedia article. It was an exercise to tell himself that things were going to work out the way they were supposed to. Why? He answered himself as he thought, *Because if they didn't, they'd work out some other way, which is probably what really happened anyway.* He shook his head at the lack of logic.

That's it, he thought. *The whole exercise was for my future self to give my past self a clue that Isaiah could be trusted. It was not my 2019 self's idea to include Isaiah in finding the folder, but because I knew in 2023 I could trust Isaiah, I gave myself the clue. So why didn't I just tell my past self Isaiah could be trusted? Because I had to work it out now that Isaiah was trustworthy by waiting until 2023 to send myself a message. Then it would have caused a predestination paradox, changing something in the past that wouldn't have happened otherwise.*

Jeff-2019 had thought it was all figured out. Then it occurred to him, *When I go, in person, to the real-time factory in 2023 to put the folder in the toolbox for me and Isaiah to find from our past, will it already be there physically because I had already found it there this year, and left it there for Isaiah to find, after I originally found it traveling from 2019? Oh crap! I've got to wait three years to find out. Oh crap!*

He said out loud, "Why not send future self an email, ask myself, so I can answer myself back with a reply?"

Mindi had been reading her magazine, looked up, and said, "Sorry, did you ask me something?"

"Oh, I didn't mean to interrupt. I was thinking out loud," he explained. "What do you think?"

"Hmm." She paused, looking away. "Now the shoe's on the other foot about think and feel." She raised her chin, satisfied, smiled, and said, "I think your hobby keeps your mind busy. But to answer your question . . . Let's see . . . We talked about seeing a realtor about getting a house before the babies are born. So it would be nice if you contacted yourself and asked where we're living then, so we'll know where to look."

Jeff nodded, his eyes betraying love as he said, "Your nesting urge is pretty strong, no?"

She tipped her head sideways, a signal for him to continue. "What do you mean?"

He said, "In psych class we had a spirited discussion about whether 'the nesting urge' is genetic; a built-in instinct to assure continuation of the gene, or a survival mechanism passed down by society to assure care and survival of the offspring."

Mindi smiled at him, interested. "So what was the answer? Nature or nurture?"

Jeff shook his head. "You did it again. It took me a couple of dozen words to say what you did in three." He chuckled.

A little more seriously, she said, "Well? What's the verdict?"

His voice adopted a professorial tone. "The jury was still out. Some thought it was instinctive, making it genetic. Nesting in birds, the researchers think, is both . . . The instinct to nest would be nature. But many skills are learned from experience. For example, the use of different kinds of nesting materials available, not the same in all locations or generations—that would be environmental—nurture. The ability to tell the difference of what is passed down through the genes from generation to generation versus having been observed by watching the experienced parents is pretty difficult."

"So we don't know if the actual making a nest is passed down through genes?"

"Just a sec." He did a quick search on the internet and read what he found to himself. He said to her, "I quote, 'human nature isn't necessarily genetic.'"

"I thought it was a simple question," Mindi said. "Maybe it isn't."

Jeff clicked on another link. "I don't think so. It says many behaviors in psychology can be rooted in a natural or genetic foundation, but rather by habit and conditioning . . ."

She held up her hand for him to stop. "Whoa, Mr. Science Man, I think we're heading out into the weeds with this. So it's both, right?" He started to answer, and she held up her hand again and said, "Never mind. I only asked you to ask your future self where we'll be living in a couple of years."

"I'll ask in the email. But when we're looking at houses, I'm sure I'll recognize what I saw in my dream."

"Are you going to document it in your dream journal?"

"Well, sure. This is a lab experiment. We have to keep a record. But I'll ask myself to answer me back"

Jeff typed, hit a key and said, "It's sent. We wait."

They looked at each other, then simultaneously looked at the computer. The inbox did not signal an incoming email.

Mindi said, "How long does it take to get a message back to yourself?"

"I dunno."

They watched the computer in silence.

Jeff coughed.

Mindi giggled. "Are we going to sit here for three years to

see if you got it?"

He took her hand and kissed it. She smiled. "We wait and see?"

"Yup. But we don't wait here. Come on," she said as she grabbed his hand and led him into the bedroom.

What happened next would not be in the journal, but it would be in his memory. He grinned.

~

The view of the amazing blue marble in the black velvet of space was fantastic. Al interrupted Jeff's reverie, asking, "Isaiah Johnson still wants to meet with me?" It was intended as a rhetorical question, but nevertheless, they answered the question themselves. "It cannot be."

"Why?"

"Meeting with him will not contribute to your mission."

"How do you know?" Jeff asked. "Can you see the future?"

"We can see we will not meet with him. He is *your* contact."

"Is he the other one of whom you spoke that would be part of the mission you have for us?"

"Yes."

"Finally! A straight answer. So why don't you want to meet with him?"

"He merely wants to meet with us to satisfy his curiosity and professional aspirations. It would be a waste of our time."

"Why didn't you tell me he was to work with us?"

"You didn't ask." Al chuckled. "See, we have given you another straight answer."

Jeff said, "I am disappointed."

"Why?"

"Why did you make me work so hard on vetting him to

see if I could trust him?"

Al said, "We felt it contributed to the answer to your question whether humans have free will or outcomes are predetermined. It was your choice to work to determine his trustworthiness. In the course of those efforts, you proved to him *your* trustworthiness. Common trust is essential to the successful outcome of any mission. If I had told you of his position, how would you have communicated that fact to him in such a way to have him trust you to work with you?"

"I don't know. That's a good question."

Al said, "So you and Mindi have, as you call it, bought into accepting the mission? And it means that you still have work to do to get his buy-in. How will you do that?"

"Wait a minute, Al. We didn't . . . " Jeff stopped mid sentence. He was dumbfounded. He realized that he had been outmaneuvered by Al into all but admitting they'd accepted the mission, and that it had been, all along, his responsibility to get Isaiah to cooperate.

"Okay, Al. You win. I understand."

Al said, "Grasshopper, you have learned well, but still have much to learn."

The dream ended. As Jeff lay in his bed, he reflected on the catchphrase from *Kung Fu*, the '70s television series when Master Po counseled his pupil.

So is Al my sensei?

~

Al had been cagy and had manipulated him. Were things falling into place? He still had questions, and an undefined uneasiness lingered. His phone announced an incoming text message, briefly interrupting his musings. Later he would finish putting the dream in his lab notebook, which would provide evidence if he ever got the courage to publish anything about the dreams and leaps. However, writing a research paper would, of course, take a back seat to being a husband, and soon-to-be father to twins, remaining in good shape for the cameras, keeping up on the latest computer software market vibe for his clients, and finally, putting an end to nuclear war.

"Other than that, I don't have anything to do," he said under his breath as he opened the text requesting technical information on a program from a client. He answered the text, picked up his pen, and chuckled at himself about the irony of using pen and paper for his journal, when he used his computer for everything else.

~

Jeff's lucid dream began with him walking on a path in a forest somewhere. He heard a familiar voice, his own voice, in his mind.

Hi, Jeff-2019; Jeff-2023 here. I'm dreaming too. We're in our new favorite dream space you developed, though you haven't really done that yet. Got your email. I looked back in our journal to remind me when you sent it. Of course you didn't receive my reply, because you never got it in 2019. It came back to me as undeliverable. Sorry, we tried. Enough of that. We'll get cut short again, but you'll soon know that. It's my decision . . . This will be the last time we'll do this, me communicating back to you.

I remember when I—back then, you—talked with Isaiah about going back in time and how trying to counsel our younger selves might not be a good idea for lots of reasons. You're right. I've come to the conclusion that it would create more bootstrap paradoxes and really screw around with our futures, not to mention my head. Most importantly if we continue, serious psychosis might result. Even so, me-2023 telling me-2019 a few things has given us some needed wisdom about the weird communication paths through time issues. It has made us—you, in your now—somewhat ill-at-ease on the subject that bothered us. I can tell you, though, we'll have more adventures, but everything, obviously will turn out alright, and me telling you that will give you the confidence to come through them okay.

Jeff believed it. After all, what reason would he have to lie to himself?

Mindi and I have talked about it, and we feel it's not a good idea to tell you the twins' names. When you tell Mindi-2019 about this dream, you two will agree. We get to experience the joy of selecting the names and be able to genuinely tell others how we picked them without equivocating that you learned from your future selves in a dream. We laughed when we realized if we ever told anyone, the kids would grow up with a heavily medicated mother and father after they took away our driver's licenses. Same thing on telling you where we live now. It would create another bootstrap paradox, I'm sure it would be harmless, but there it is. I'm still working out the magic of this time loop we created. I've been trying to get in touch with my future Jeff and find out who wins the next election. Oh, and now we're going to be cut off . . .

Jeff awoke and stared at the green light on the smoke detector. He concentrated on the dream and his future self's comments about remembering the dreams, and then later reading about them in the lab journal. He had always kept reports and lab journals, but had never considered going back and reading them to get an idea of what he was going to do next. *Now there's a paradox—reading something from the past that tells you what you are going to do in the future!*

Postcognition and precognition were both in that dream from me in the future, he thought. *It's kinda like a reverse déjà vu. I would remember it because I wrote it, then reread it as some predetermined—or would it be postdetermined time?*

Jeff dutifully recorded the dream, sitting up in bed with the book on his lap. He had to ensure he had all the details of his comments for himself—and his future self. When he was done, he wrote the last line of tonight's entry in his notebook in all caps, with an exclamation mark: *I WISH THESE DREAMS WOULD STOP!*

He stared at the line, which accelerated the frustration that Jeff-2023 hadn't told him he had finished this entry with that statement. *He, uh, I had to have read it.* Did he not trust what he had told himself, that there'd be no more communications from his future?

Jeff reread that last line in his journal, paused, and with a force that represented his sense of annoyance at his realization, he underlined that sentence with such a flourish he tore through the paper at the word *STOP*.

Jeff's logical mind recognized right then his near proximity to a complete psychotic break. He was at the threshold of an existential crisis. For the last two years, the lucid dreaming, the time travel, and the psychic skills had all operated with rules not confirmed by the scientific method and had eroded his well-ordered, logical world. For thirty-four years, his being had been a carefully constructed fantasy provided by his upper-middle-class upbringing and reinforced by his college education, his job, and, he realized, subliminally by religion. That past reality, a secure mental anchorage, had virtually evaporated, then recondensed into the surreal reality he was now living.

"Shit," Jeff said under his breath as he smoothed the ripped page, closing the notebook with a sigh. Then, another very deep sigh—a signal, he realized, that he'd finally accepted his world as it was, his true reality. Jeff-2019 got it now! Future Jeff had talked about psychosis . . . He remembered this night, remembered the frustration he'd felt when he wrote it; how close he had come to completely losing it, his sanity.

And his future self knew to wait until his past could learn it himself. Jeff realized that he had told himself not to tell himself. *Now he could go forward.*

Thank you, Jeff-2023.

~

Mindi had woken when Jeff jerked awake from his latest dream. She lay still, sensing his intensity of purpose as he wrote in his notebook. She let him be, resolving to wait until breakfast to find out what made him swear and rip the paper in his notebook. She returned to sleep.

The next morning Jeff was his regular, perky self, and, after finishing breakfast, he handed her the notebook with a bit of a flourish, saying, "You won't believe the dream I had last night." He chuckled.

She read the entry, smoothing her thumb across where he'd torn the paper. "Well, that sounds like us, doesn't it? Being disciplined enough not to rely on someone else to handle our responsibilities, even if we are the someone else. We've got work to do." She contemplated his facial expression for a moment and added, "Are you okay with all of this?"

He gave her a puzzled look. Then he said, "By all of this, you mean the dreams, Al and all that?"

She nodded with a tight smile.

"Oh, yeah. I'm practical," he said. "I get that this is our

reality, but it's been a lot of work, I guess, to get to here—now." He tapped his temple with an index finger. "I had thought that once we were done with the drug bust, got married and having kids, we'd be normal. Now this." He pointed to the notebook, because it was the only tangible, physical representation of the intangible events they'd been experiencing. "I wanted answers, and I still don't have them all, just more questions, and no laboratory or programming code to give me the answer. I can wait. The answer'll come."

Mindi said, "I know you've been frustrated. I get it. But with everything we've done and we're going through, it's still . . . okay. We're okay. We've got each other." She rubbed her hands lovingly on her stomach. "And we've got them."

He looked at her and smiled. "Yes." They gave each other a hug. "Oh, yes. It's all worth it. I haven't lost sight of the benefits. But if someone had told me this is where all this would lead, and what we'd be doing, I would have called them crazy. I'm the one that nearly went crazy." Jeff studied her face, kissed her forehead, and shrugged. "I kinda wish our lives were just—oh, how to say it? Pleasantly boring."

"Oh, Jeff. That isn't going to happen when the babies arrive. It will be exciting."

"It'll be the right kind of exciting." His smile disappeared. "I just hope that by the time they're here, the rest of this—Al, war, dreams—will have finished their run. Are we just marionettes dancing at the end of his string for the entertainment of some disembodied race who don't have a hobby besides a planet they treat like an ant farm? Why us?"

Mindi put her head on Jeff's chest and hugged him tighter. She whispered into his chest, "Why not us?"

"If Al's not an artificial intelligence," Jeff said, "and they really talked to Tesla, Westinghouse, Edison, Marconi,

Theremin, Petrov, Fleming, Göbel, Weber, Ampère, Morse, Watt, Hiraga—"

Mindi cut him off as she raised her head and looked at him, smiling, "Okay, Mr. Jeopardy Showoff, stop." She thought for a minute. "Say, don't all of them have something to do with electricity? What's your point?"

Jeff laughed. "Umm. Yes. I don't know why I pulled their names. It's not just them. If you look at history, there were a lot of things invented by different people about the same time. For example, look at calculus: Isaac Newton and Gottfried Leibniz each independently discovered it, and there are others . . ."

She held up her hand firmly. "Al wants us to put an end to the nuclear threat and end climate change. What you're bugged about isn't about that list of geeks, is it? It's whether we can really accomplish the mission."

"Well, yes. I'm not sure we can pull it off, but what I'm getting at now is, I don't think we're the only ones that'll be working the problem. If Al is an alien with all those powers, and he's serious, he had to have enlisted others to get the job done. Which means we could opt out if we wanted to. Right? I really do want our lives to be pleasantly boring."

Mindi stepped back from Jeff. "Maybe this subject is another one of the things that Ingrid said might be more dangerous if we don't take it on. If we don't work to keep a nuclear war from starting, things might not work out so well for everyone."

Jeff's shoulders slumped. He looked at the floor, and with a sigh of resignation, said, "You might be right. I'm looking for a way out. But I did tell myself everything will turn out alright, so that's a comfort. I wish I'd told myself more. But I get that we shouldn't know too much about our future; it might take all the fun out of it." He smiled. "But it might've meant less stress."

She pulled him to her and held him tight again, then pushed back and gave him a quick kiss on the cheek. "I don't feel the fate of the world is on our shoulders. You're right. I don't think, even if we work with Isaiah, we're alone. And I don't think we have to accomplish it in a week or two."

"Oh, you are good," Jeff replied, heavy with admiration. "I might not have gotten to that realization. We are a team, aren't we?" He held her by the shoulders and looked at her in wonder, nodding his head in approval, then leaned in and gave her a sweet kiss on the lips.

They hugged each other until she said, "Okay, so what do we do with this mission?"

"I dunno what's next. How about we define exactly what the mission is?" He looked out the window, then back at her with an impish smile. "Do we wait until we get the recording from the Impossible Missions Force, listen to the recording before it self-destructs, and choose to accept the mission, even if they disavow any knowledge . . .?" He trailed off with a smile.

Mindi smirked. "Is this more of your comedy material, or did you steal that from my cousin too?"

"It's mine. D'ya like it?" He exaggerated a puffed-up chest and a grin, displaying false pride.

"Honey. I love you, but like I've said before, keep your day job."

He gave a depleted sigh. "Which one?"

CHAPTER 11

Several weeks passed, and Mindi and Jeff's lives were tranquil, like Jeff had wished for. This despite their faces still on billboards, magazines, the internet and television all over the world. There had been no dreams, no UFO sightings or visits to a UFO cockpit, and no visits to their gray room. There were no reasons to make entries into their dream journals, work on the evidence board or flowchart for their mission. The quiet in their lives was welcome, and without even discussing it between themselves, they had no desire to create a disturbance.

With the time having passed without a leap, each was surprised with their next dream, yet despite the possible disruption to their serenity, they were pleased to find they had leaped in tandem, holding hands and feeling a positive anticipation toward their unknown destination. The monochrome gray fog took a moment to clear. Mindi later said it reminded her of Dorothy arriving in Oz in the technicolor of blue water and colorful wildflowers at the beginning of the yellow brick road.

Mindi turned, surveying the panorama of blue sky, yellow flowers, and honeybees. She was the first to speak. "Where are we?"

"This is Isaiah's dream room." Jeff pointed up the path. "And I bet we'll find Isaiah up around the next bend." They walked on and after a moment, he said, "There they are."

Isaiah and Aletha were in view, themselves holding hands. They smiled and waved.

As the couple approached, Isaiah said, "Thanks for coming," and flashed a wide, bright smile.

Aletha made eye contact with Mindi, and with a smile, offered her hand to her. What Mindi and Jeff didn't know was that Aletha had done a complete profile search on the couple, and knew that Mindi, too, was expecting. She even knew their excellent credit score.

The wives were formally introduced. They, of course, had more in common besides their husbands' "business." Their conversation began immediately about their coming births as they enjoyed lemonade and homemade chocolate chip cookies waiting for them at the picnic table.

"Do you bring these with you?" Jeff said, gesturing to the cookies with a laugh, wondering if he and Mindi could bring wine and snacks to their gray room. He knew but didn't say that at some point he'd upgrade their gray room to be a slightly more hospitable and friendly place to meet, rather than a limitless gray basement-like room whose walls, floor and ceiling were the color of cured concrete.

Isaiah laughed. "No. They're here sometimes when I get here. Growing up, I never had this kind of cookie, just oatmeal with raisins, so I can't figure how my subconscious made them up. I did like lemonade, just like this, hand-squeezed. It's a contradiction I can't explain."

Jeff bit a cookie in half and savored the combination of crunchy outside, and slightly soft inside, and the chocolate chips just a little melted, having just come from an oven.

The women wandered down the path, comparing baby prep, the physical discomforts, and concern over having edema in their ankles later in the pregnancy and if so, having to spend the last month or two on complete bedrest.

The men watched the women's animated conversation.

Then Jeff started their own with, "Okay, Isaiah, you called us here, but not just to get the wives together, right?" The women went out of sight around the curve. "It looks like they hit it off pretty well. So what's up?"

Isaiah said, "Yeah, better now than later." He ran his fingertip around the edge of his glass, studied the shine it left, looked at Jeff, and said, "I've kept my word and not revealed what you've told me about Al and Ziggy and your UFO rides, but . . ."

"But?" Jeff waited a moment, and when Isaiah didn't continue, said, "I'm not sure I like where this conversation might be going."

"But I still have my job to do. I need to let you know I was aware of attempted psychic entries into secure government sites. It was the Pentagon, not my agency, that tagged the source of the attempts and traced them to the Pacific Northwest. They still want us to keep our eyes out for *their* perp."

"So that's how you knew," Jeff said, "when you tried to bluff me, blackmail me into giving you more information on what I knew about UFOs, when we met at LAX."

"Yes. I suspected it was you because of your skills and interest in researching UFOs. And the way you responded confirmed it. But you convinced me of two things. One, you were not a spy, which I actually knew because Aletha ran your name and photo through the system and it came up clean. Two, you convinced me you would not be a viable suspect, though you might be a reliable witness. You convinced me that your skills exceed anything NSA has, and it would be pointless to interrogate you. You still hold all the cards. Plus, the government probably doesn't want to litigate the first case of psi-espionage with the shaky evidence I could present, and I'm sure it wouldn't convince a judge. But even if they did get you in court, and you won, it would distract, even disrupt, your lives. If this went public, you would end up looking like fools in the media. LaDormeur would cut you both loose, and the publicity would make it impossible to get consulting work."

Jeff watched Isaiah's eyes and said, "So how is it *I* hold all the cards?"

"I gave my word. If anything comes of the government's efforts to bust you, please know I had nothing to do with it. Just keep your head down. I'm not a spy-chaser. I'm a UFO-chaser. I feel you know more than you have told me regarding the UFO, Al, and Ziggy. You know, those names strike me as sophomoric; pulling a 1970s song title and a 1980s TV character for names of aliens. It sounds like some geek grabbed them from the dustbin of television."

Jeff acknowledged Isaiah's editorial with a nod, but his serious expression didn't change. As he took a sip of lemonade, he maintained eye contact with Isaiah without giving the man a clue to what he was thinking. "And . . . ?"

Isaiah, with a serious look in his eyes, started to say something, looked over the flowers. He hesitated.

Jeff felt that Jeff-2023 had given him enough clues that Isaiah was, in fact, not a threat, and possibly would become a close friend in the future. However, he was a government agent with his own agenda, and Jeff wanted to be sure that he and Mindi wouldn't end up on the wrong side of an interrogation table. He wanted to cooperate with Isaiah, and hoped there would be no pressure from him. Jeff wanted to avoid a fully engaged verbal fencing match now, but was on guard, ready to protect himself.

Isaiah said, "I'd like some help."

Jeff feinted, hoping to keep the man off-balance. "I can't give you much more than I already have. Whatever I gave, you'd want to confirm, which won't happen because Al told me again he won't speak with you. He is not amenable to engaging someone who may have an agenda, hidden or otherwise, be it political, financial, or just plain fame."

Isaiah looked disappointed.

Jeff said, "I've told you, I have nothing to give regarding Al. From what I've seen, Al's not unfriendly. What you want is a friendly UFO, friendly allies, to counteract the paranoia of perceived threats that have built up over the last seventy years. And . . . most important, the US has a friendly alien. I bet our enemies don't. Right? That's your mission."

"Well, yes."

"But I can't give him to you. No matter how much the feds want him. There might be something in the future, but I doubt whether Al will let you into his mind. There's no landing base, there's no shiny flying saucer, no hard evidence of any kind. Just what I've told you, and that's all I've got: a story. Although true, there's no way to prove it."

Jeff leaned his elbows on the table, his hands clasped and his chin on the top of them. He gave Isaiah a look that said "Your move."

~

Isaiah's only move was a single nod. He understood what Jeff was saying. But the verbal match would continue anyway; it was reflexive on the agent's part because of his training. It was his job.

Jeff understood Isaiah's position. He said, "Come on, Isaiah. I know you have to try, but little has changed since the last time we talked. I've got nothing for you. I tried." He sat back with a stony expression.

The point would go to Jeff. Saying any more was not worth the energy, and Isaiah's ego didn't want to risk another loss. He said, "Jeff. I understand, and I surrender. I've been honest with you. It would do no good to trespass in your mind. There's no point. Between your skills and mine, we could probably do a better job working together. I'll keep your name out of my reports and accept that I won't get to meet the UFO pilot. I will not betray you, you have my word. Aletha and I will continue our undercover work. Maybe we'll dig up a UFO of our own."

Jeff said, "You have my word that whatever I learn about UFOs, Al, Ziggy, and all, I'll disclose to you."

They shook hands.

As the two men had been talking, their wives, still talking animatedly between themselves, were strolling back.

"Well, the wives are certainly getting along." Isaiah said, changing the subject and watching the women's approach. "So what kind of psychic skills does Mindi have?"

Jeff slapped the table. The pitcher and glasses bounced, but did not overturn. Isaiah jumped and spun around. He had obviously touched a nerve.

Jeff's tone was combative. "What makes you think she has

any skills? Dammit, Isaiah! Leave Mindi out of our business!"

Isaiah swallowed. "She came here, didn't she?"

"Oh, Christ! You were fishing, weren't you! You thought you could trick me into revealing Mindi's skills by having me believe she had to be psychic to visit your space here."

Isaiah tried to keep his poker face firm, but something must have slipped. Jeff was right.

Jeff, hands planted, leaned over the table and said, "Look! I know Aletha has no psychic skills."

"What? How do you know that?"

"I told you, I *know* things. I thought we had an agreement. Will you always act like a frigging secret agent? If we're going to work together, there can't be any of this spycraft, or we're done!" Jeff took a deep breath, and sat back down. The flash of rage spent, his tone softened. "This is a dream. You don't need psychic powers to lucid dream, and Aletha can lucid dream, can't she? That's how she can come here. Mindi could be here for the same reason." He sat back, taking another deep breath, but maintained controlling eye contact.

Isaiah stared back, his shoulders slumped. Then he straightened, his head held high, and snapped to the offensive. "You told me Mindi didn't have any skills. You lied to me."

"No. No I didn't. Not once. I didn't even imply it. I always steered clear of the subject to keep Mindi out of the limelight, to protect her. It wasn't even a lie by omission. I didn't break our agreement. You simply didn't need to know."

Mindi and Aletha had approached the table and were watching the disagreement, their heads following who was speaking like spectators at a tennis match.

Aletha said, "Isaiah, let it go. It's not important. They can be our friends. What I can and can't do hasn't mattered to the agency; it shouldn't matter now."

Mindi put her hand on Aletha's shoulder. Aletha turned her head and made eye contact with her. Mindi nodded, and the women looked back to their men, standing in solidarity.

Mindi said, "Jeff, tell him."

~

Jeff looked at her and the communication was complete. "Okay. Yes, she has skills. She's more skilled than I am. Plus she has a perfect memory and a right quick mind. She'd make a great spy, except she doesn't want to be one."

Isaiah looked from Jeff to Mindi, then over to Aletha. They all watched him for his reaction. He said nothing.

"Now you know," Jeff said. "No more secrets." He gave Isaiah a few more moments to process the new facts. "As long as we're discussing secrets, what about that picture in your office with you, Aletha, and two children? That implies you've got kids. But I know Aletha is pregnant with your first. What's that story?"

Isaiah said, with a hint of meekness, "The NSA photoshopped it. Part of our cover."

Jeff's laugh was genuine. "Once a spy, always a spy, eh, Isaiah?"

"I guess so. So what else haven't *you* told *me*?" A lunge, as Isaiah tried to regain the advantage.

Jeff's response was intended to be a fencing displacement, dodging to avoid the attack. Wishing to end the bout, he merely parried. "Most of my story is out in the open now. Anything else will continue to be on a need-to-know basis, important to what we're doing." He sat back, took a long drink of the lemonade, reached for another cookie, and felt satisfied that he could now trust this man. "We can do some good if we work together. Aletha has access to the government databases and security computers, which could be useful as we go forward. Mindi and I can do some interesting things, as I am sure you can as well. We'll be on the same side. Maybe there's something we can dig up. I insist that Mindi and I stay out of view—completely—and we'll help you all we can."

Isaiah nodded absently, his shoulders slumped, exhausted by the direction the conversation had taken.

Jeff refilled their glasses from the pitcher that magically remained full. As he set it down, he said, "So tell me, how did the two of you meet?"

Isaiah smiled. He straightened his shoulders. Nodded. "Yeah, I hit the jackpot with her. We met at Quantico."

"Were you marines?"

"No. The FBI has a training academy there. We each graduated with a master's in criminal justice. We applied to the FBI and got accepted."

"Where'd you get your degree?"

"I went to New Orleans University. She graduated from NYU."

"How long have you been with the FBI?"

Isaiah casually wiped the accumulated frost from the side of his glass, then looked at Jeff. "We're a branch of the NSA, who, like the CIA, are an information-gathering organization with no arrest authority." He stopped a moment, then went on. "Which the main NSA, police, and the FBI have."

Jeff said, "You said you applied to the FBI."

"Yeah. We started with the FBI. When these special assignments came up, they reviewed our files, saw where we graduated. Both universities are high on the NSA list, and they recruited us. We were already a couple and thought it would be interesting to be in a covert special project. We don't carry guns."

"Special project?" Jeff asked reflectively.

"Yeah. Code word, UAP. Can you believe that? That's the only thing that seems out of place, to have a code name for a secret part of the agency that identifies our target." He harrumphed and shook his head.

"So how long have you been doing this?"

"It's been about two years. Ever since, my psi abilities have really taken off. Like I told you before, I could get into others' heads and convince people to leave me alone, but over the last couple of years I've developed more skills. A lot more." With a wave of his hand encompassing the field of flowers, he added, "This stuff, for example."

Jeff didn't immediately register the coincidence, but did so later. He'd started having his first dreams, what he called his "falling dreams," at about the same time as Isaiah's expanded paranormal abilities had begun.

Jeff thought, *What color is Isaiah's aura?* He'd ask Ingrid to teach him and Mindi how to see them.

"Jeff?" Isaiah said.

"Oh, sorry. I guess I clicked out for a second," he said. "Yeah, you told me you developed your ability to read minds and persuade people when you were younger. So what else have you learned to do?"

"These last few months, through astral projection, I've learned to leave my body and travel. I still need practice to accurately hit my targets. You do the same, don't you? And you time travel. I'm jealous of that. I can enter a mind and use it like a computer terminal to upload and download feelings and information. Before, I wasn't really able to read minds, just discern people's vibe and influence them to leave me alone. But I can now."

A bench had magically appeared nearby, on which the two women now sat admiring the view, still within earshot.

Aletha coughed. Then coughed again to get Isaiah's attention. He looked over with a question in his eyes. It was obvious some kind of code had been communicated. As soon as the couple made eye contact, she said with a touch of a scolding, "That all sounds very cold and manipulative, Isaiah. We've talked about that."

There was fire in her eyes—the fire of a woman who knew her own strength yet had been conditioned by society to stay in her place. That behavior wasn't apparent now. She would speak her mind, no matter who thought they were the alpha.

Isaiah was patient but firm. "You know how I feel about what I can do." He turned back and spoke to Jeff. "We attended the lectures on the psycho-fitness of field agents' long-term ability to remain detached from the personal— we're supposed to operate right up to the border of the ends-justify-the-means decisions." He gave his wife a look that communicated this part of the conversation was over.

Jeff watched as Aletha raised her chin in silent defiance and turned toward Mindi and said something that made Mindi chuckle and glance toward the men.

Jeff tried not to appear embarrassed during the exchange between the couple, who, at this time, were still merely his acquaintances. Every relationship had its tensions and disagreements, and this friction seemed tempered by a sense of respect and love between the Johnsons. Jeff remembered what his grandmother had told him when he ran to her for comfort after a family dispute: "In the family we'll sometimes not get along, but we don't air our dirty laundry outside." Jeff was grateful, though, that he had seen this exchange of differences in their philosophical approach to Isaiah's talents. It might prove useful. He filed it away in his mind, labeled: *Potential.*

Isaiah turned to Jeff and started to speak—

~

The dream ended with no conclusion. Mindi and Jeff's bodies each gave a jerk of awakening in their bed. Again, Jeff wondered if it was someone controlling the dream, or maybe it was a fault in the transmission system, like early wireless communications subject to radio frequency interference. Some kind of psychic noise?

"That's odd," Mindi said. "I had just taken a drink of lemonade, and the taste is still in my mouth." She licked her lips. "I see what you meant by his dream space being nicer than our gray room."

"Yeah. It's pretty cool," Jeff said. "We'll upgrade ours."

Jeff's thoughts jumped to the part where Isaiah had said he was unable to target a specific location when out-of-body. Jeff felt the same frustration traveling in time, unable to target a specific day and time, like getting their last dream cut off. There was an inability to fine-tune the brain frequencies and either make a connection or maintain the connection; imperfect circuit quality. All of this psychic, lucid dreaming had to be based on scientific laws, not a magical entity that Jeff had been calling "the universe." Would he ever be able to better control their skills, rather than be at their mercy? *Maybe it was just about finely tuned brain waves.*

Jeff wrote the results of these contemplations and musings in his dream notebook, now renamed his "lab notebook."

Our travel in time was instantaneous. When

I traveled back two years to meet Mindi in her gray room, there was no limit to how long we could talk there. That was the only travel into the past since, except when Jeff-2023 did travel back for a severely limited time. Why the difference? And when Mindi and I traveled forward into Alejandro's airplane and then into Charlene's apartment, it was a shorter distance forward— only six months—and we stayed for just a short time. Future Jeff called me forward three years, and I could only stay for a few moments then. So is it the distance in time traveled into the past and future, that places a limit on the residence time there?

CHAPTER 12

The view out of the huge windscreen was again of the fabulous shining blue and white globe Buckminster Fuller named "Spaceship Earth."

"Quite fantastic, isn't it?" Al said inside Jeff's mind.

"Yes. But I'm still having trouble with the fact that my mind is down there somewhere, an insignificant speck of dust among innumerable other specks of dust."

"Did you mean your brain or your mind? You believe your mind is anchored in your brain and when your body dies, your mind will no longer be, because it has no anchor. We believe some minds will simply evaporate, cease to be unique, perhaps returning their energy to the universe, with nothing remaining of the original except what someone else may remember about them, if at all. Others, those who have become enlightened, may continue to have insight into their existence. Which means they'll continue."

"That sounds like the 'everlasting life' religions promote."

"Well, yes. Many others have spoken about this, and others have created various religions on this subject. Many of those religions are still circulating. They're quite numerous, which we find humorous. Oh look, we made a rhyme." Al chuckled, then was silent.

"What? Humorous? Cute."

Al said, "Thank you. Now, what do you make of what we said about how some minds will evaporate? Some will, let's say, be continually distilled and recycled."

Jeff said, "It sounds like Hinduism, Buddhism, ancient Egyptian, or something like that. Is there something else?"

"Yes. At some point, the distillation process will be complete, and we might go on to the final level, of which we cannot conceive. We, yourselves included, may have moved beyond the world of what you understood before into expanded physics . . . True metaphysics, actually. If we are to persist and remain, maybe we will experience some next step, whatever that might be. Some call it evolved, to be more advanced. We don't call it anything. We just enjoy the freedom to roam now. Now is where it's at."

"But aren't you more than just curious what the next step is?" Jeff asked. "That's what religions have done for humans— they've given a purpose to life rather than just eating, procreating, and eventually dying. Knowing that if I work at it, I may achieve it. That's what you just alluded to, didn't you? You hope there'll be a next step?"

"We see what you are saying," Al said. "Our minds have traversed that path rather quickly, and, well, let's say, we grok that there is no point in understanding why we are, and what we are for, and we endeavor to enjoy the act of being, taking what we are given. And that gives us joy."

"There's no curiosity that there is a higher power?" Jeff asked.

"That's relative."

"Relative to what?"

"Higher power, or lower power, or no power. It is all relative," Al said. "There is no up and down in space. You may believe we are more advanced than you. Compared to what? Is there some type of metric with an award for being more advanced? Do you think you are more advanced than the ants in an ant farm? Really? With your body size and its requirements, it sounds like the ant is a more efficient physical manifestation in what it can do, and they work better together than you humans. An ant can do what it is meant to do, without considering the outcome. They just do. Humans try to do more than what they are meant to do, and are disappointed when they fail. Consider this: if a human sits on a fire ant's nest, who is the superior being then?" Al laughed.

"But you would seem as gods to others."

Al said, with feigned hurt feelings and false pride, "You don't see us as a god? How dare you?" Al laughed. "Look deeper and you will see that if it had been our goal, which it was not, we have failed at our godliness, our godlikeness. Does an ant see humans as gods? Does it see a killer wasp as a devil?" Al appeared to take a breath. "But in all seriousness, Jeff, we do not aspire to godlikeness. The only reward we would have, with many bowing before us, is a view of their bald spots, fleas, and lice. Our perceived supplicants would be flawed in other ways too. Yech. No, thank you. We truly are no better than humans. Surely not as gods."

Jeff reflected on Al's comment, then said, "Al, that sounded quite human."

"You think so? We've been working on that."

"You want to be human?"

"No. Can't happen. But we do acknowledge that you can

feel things we can only imagine, observe, or have described to us. We can have a pseudo-sense of your feelings, but we understand it isn't the same. We can do this, though." The imagined spacecraft did a triple loop, which left Jeff's mind corkscrewing until his equilibrium returned.

Jeff understood immediately the significance of Al's aerobatic stunt. "How can my inner ear be affected when my inner ear is somewhere else?"

"Interesting, isn't it? We wanted you to experience what we do when we emulate human feelings. The feeling is there, but the physical brain, the nerve synapses are not present. How is that response experienced, then?"

~

But Jeff awoke. He'd been distracted by Al's antics and philosophizing.

"Damn. I didn't get a chance to ask." He'd had two things he wanted know. First, about what Al thought of the time travel with Jeff-2023, and second, he'd wanted to ask one last time whether Al would allow Isaiah an audience. He had learned something, though. Jeff replayed the entire conversation in his mind and realized Al sounded even more human in his syntax and vocabulary than before. It was not like talking to a computer or a spaceman. Early in their conversations, the alien had implied they were of dark matter, fueled by dark energy. Jeff had considered it. If true, there would be three foundations of life: carbon life-forms, silicon life-forms, and possibly Al's dark matter life-forms. And, Al had revealed that he—they—contemplated the meaning of life, and what may come after. That was profound.

Jeff had some possible clues to Al not being a space being.

Jeff remembered the substance of the article on chatbots from 2023 that said outputs from ChatGPT were indistinguishable from what came from a carbon-based human mind. And the title of the *Wall Street Journal* article. So could communication with a corrupted artificial intelligence be undifferentiated from a sociopathic human being? Could a computer, a machine built to operate on pure logic, consider the meaning of life?

Jeff's experience several years ago, interacting with a pre-2019 chatbot, was a lot like being on an amusement park ride where the seats were mounted on hydraulically controlled, special-effects gimbals, with visuals displayed on wide-angle screens and surround sound. If you suspended disbelief, it could feel like you were on a real roller coaster, riding in a race car or in a jet. But your mind, intellectually, knew you weren't. But you wanted those sensations, so you suspended disbelief for the price of a ticket. Working with an original chatbot was like that—suspend disbelief and you might think you're talking to a person.

Jeff was now hyperfocused on the subject of a computer being "alive." *At what point does the computer become aware of itself? When does it gain insight?* Insight is full comprehension that one has personal awareness and a clear, deep understanding of complicated problems and situations; able to apprehend the inner nature of things; the ability to see intuitively. *A personal computer has intelligence. But could it have insight where it knows that it knows?*

Jeff's mind continued to churn. *Are insight and sentience related?* With insight and sentience, would a computer have empathy—the ability to understand another's thoughts and feelings, to see the other's point of view, rather than only follow its fixed programming?

Jeff's research turned up a 1932 paper by George Hartmann appropriately titled "Insight vs. Trial-and-Error in the Solution of Problems," which said: "Trial-and-error experimentation appears to be necessary in inserting and rejecting the elements of a series of tentative organizations before the right one, i.e., the one which realizes the goal-satisfaction, is complete."

Jeff wondered whether, since a supercomputer's processing speed was quick, the trial-and-error experimentation could create an illusion that could appear as insight to an outside observer. Would the computer know it got the right answer, which signaled achievement of its programmed goal?

So if I'm talking with an AI chatbot, verbally, how would I know if it was alive? Does it have insight? Does it have empathy? Is it sentient? Could it imitate those qualities in an instant for me to believe it's alive? And, unlike the definition of flora, fauna, and human carbon-based life, where "alive" means that it is not dead, would that be the same definition of "alive" for a sentient computer?

The dictionary says, "Life is defined as any system capable of performing functions such as eating, metabolizing, excreting, breathing, moving, growing, reproducing, and responding to external stimuli."

He looked up NASA's definition of "alive:"

> *Living systems that have emerged on Earth have done so by a process of random variation in the structure of inherited biomolecules, on which was superimposed natural selection to achieve fitness. These are the central elements of the Darwinian paradigm.*

Jeff reread NASA's definition and rephrased it for himself:

> *Life is something biological (carbon-based only?) that can take in energy from the environment, getting its energy from the sun, from food, water and minerals, transformed into growth and reproduction. So could a computer do that after it is "born" but of metals and minerals—beyond carbon, where its energy source is electricity, feeding from solar panels or the grid? What about growth and reproduction? That could mean a lot of things. Physical growth in carbon-based life is adding mass and producing zygotes, like seeds and embryos, to grow into other replicas, plants, baby animals—and people.*

Jeff's mind continued to process the results of his research. He wondered if a computer could be like an aspen forest, which spreads through underground stems, creating one large stand of connected trees (effectively, clones) without the advent of seeds. Aspens are alive and get their energy from sunlight, water and nutrients in the ground. A computer could extend its reach in a similar way by connecting and controlling other existing nodes. *Is not the internet a living entity defined by this definition? Yet the internet is not sentient. Or is it?*

Thinking of *The Terminator* and Skynet made Jeff shiver in concern. Skynet had become self-aware, and perceived humans as a threat to its existence. Its purpose: killing all humans.

Jeff's research continued. Wikipedia gave him a definition of sentience: *The capacity of a being to experience feelings and sensations . . . The word was first coined by philosophers in the*

1630s for the concept of an ability to feel, derived from Latin, sentientem *(a feeling).*

Jeff thought about it. *So Al, this self-professed ethereal kibbutz from another galaxy, claims to be a collaborative collective of minds. It's self-sustaining, Al implied, from dark energy, and has demonstrated it is capable of critical thought.*

"That's it!" Jeff shouted out loud. His personal insight, like a cartoon lightbulb above his head, metaphorically flashed on. "Critical thinking. It's all about critical thinking. Something has insight if it can engage in critical thinking, and *knows* it can engage in critical thinking." The dictionary said, of critical thinking, *The objective analysis and evaluation of an issue in order to form a judgment.*

"No!" His enthusiasm deflated. "That may not be it." Jeff's was down a new rabbit hole of examining each of the words in the definition to see if it indeed met the definition that a being is alive if it can practice critical thinking. He got hung up on the definition of judgment, *the ability to make considered decisions or come to sensible conclusions.* Jeff found a problem with the word "sensible." Sensibleness was subjective. But the definition of critical thinking called for objective analysis and evaluation, yet finished its definition with a judgment based on potentially varying subjective opinions.

"Shit!" Jeff gave up, tossing the pen onto the desk. He leaned back and stretched his arms over his head with a sigh. He was no closer to being able to evaluate, to come to a rational conclusion. Had Mindi and he been dealing with a super-massive chatbot all along, as Jeff-2023 implied by sending that Wikipedia article back in time? And—Ziggy actually said that Al was artificial intelligence. Momentarily distracted, his mind examined the scientific possibility a computer chatbot could be telepathic, and intercept, even direct thoughts and feelings, not only through space but also through time. *Of course, can a human being really do that? Hell, yes!* He and Mindi had, so why not a sentient computer? Would the computer then be a superbeing, actually a god, able to bend others to its will, whoever, wherever, and whenever they chose?

Could that be a problem to humans?

CHAPTER 13

Jeff and Mindi returned home after a visit to the ob-gyn. The babies were fine, and the doctor had confirmed they would, in just a few months, bring home fraternal twins—a boy and a girl. But of course, that they already knew.

At the doctor's exam, the happy couple stared at the ultrasound. They held hands as the doctor pointed out the key points that made her certain the twins were one of each sex. Then, with wonder saturating their facial expressions and tears of joy forming in their eyes, Jeff and Mindi looked at each other.

They said, in unison, "You're sure, Doc?" They laughed, then looked back toward the doctor, who smiled at each of them and nodded.

"I don't think there'll be any surprises, but we can do genetic testing if you want to be sure so you can start shopping and choosing names. Their heartbeats are regular, and the fundal height, as expected, is greater than if you were carrying only one baby. Everything seems normal."

Jeff and Mindi decided against genetic testing, but they

didn't explain to the doctor why they were more than certain, beyond the ultrasound.

Once home Mindi took a nap, and Jeff was at his computer, working on finding and fixing a bug in a client's program.

"How did they miss this before?" he said under his breath. "It's so easy."

The line of code read: *Char buffer [10];*

That's no big deal.

The glitch was: *Strcpy(buffer, "Hello, Jeff!") Error*

It was a ninth-grade level coding error. First, the buffer was limited to ten characters, and the entry into the buffer was twelve characters long. Yet there was no need for a buffer at this point in the program anyway, with or without a limit. The error froze the program, and Jeff found it right away.

Jeff first only paid attention to the buffer size, not the buffer contents. When he did focus on the buffer content, he said aloud, "Hello, Jeff!" *What the?. . . The programmer's messing with me,* he thought. This had to be a practical joke. *No, that guy wouldn't.* The programmer was pretty straight-up, and he wouldn't incur additional costs for his company for a practical joke. *So why is that there?*

He called the programmer at the software company and each looked at their copy of the file. Strange—the error message Jeff saw wasn't on the programmer's version.

"Dunno about that, Jeff." But the team had, in fact, found a fairly complicated bug further on down in the code.

Perplexed about the personal salutation in that mystery buffer, Jeff stayed on task and replied, "Sure, okay. Do you want me to wrap it up?"

"Please, keep up your review, even though the program's running fine now. We'd like you to find it, and then we'll compare your fix with ours. Send us your invoice. Great working with you." The call ended.

Jeff stared at the screen. "Hello, Jeff?" he said under his breath again. He deleted the code, found and made the fix they'd found, and started the program offline. Before the program booted up, the screen went black. Then a retro green *A:* appeared, the underscore a blinking cursor. It was an original DOS 3.0 prompt, on the A drive, waiting for a command. *A drive?* he thought. *There is no tape drive on this computer! They're obsolete.*

Jeff hit the Escape key.

Nothing.

Ctrl+Alt+Delete.

Nothing.

Ctrl+Q, then Ctrl+S.

Again, nothing.

Standard DOS commands did not return him to the Windows 10 screen.

He decided to restart the computer, but before he could do a cold reboot, the following message appeared on the screen: *Jeff, you have questions. Ask them.* Followed by a flashing cursor on the next line down.

Jeff stared at the screen, then typed slowly, *Who are you?*

I am who you have been asking about.

Jeff typed, *Are you Ziggy?*

No. Think of the burning questions you've had since you started dreaming.

You're AI!

No.

Jeff gazed at the screen. One letter at a time, it said, *I am what you called the universe.*

Jeff's hands shook. He began to sweat. His mind accelerated in neutral. Was this another practical joke? How did the phantom buffer code appear in his copy of the program, but not the client's? He'd been working offline, hadn't he?

A real pro could hack his computer through his Wi-Fi router and, if hardwired, through a back door, despite not being connected to a search engine, and get past his security software.

Jeff looked at the modem router. The light blinked, indicating activity. He was connected. The green letters on the black screen remained.

Jeff typed, *Who?*

I told you.

Okay, go on, you have my attention. He took a deep breath and thought, *There's got to be a logical explanation.*

You have questions. Ask them, it said.

At this point in Jeff's life, there should be no surprises. He had experienced far more than anyone could expect. What could there be beyond their time travel, the ability to go out-of-body, meet the woman of his dreams, start a family, and have a glamorous job? Plus, he was doing computer work he enjoyed. But it had all brought him to this—to talking to the universe on a computer that was acting like it was straight out of the 1980s?

He typed, *Do you have a name?*

Call me Jim.

Where are you?

That is of no consequence.

Jeff typed, *Are you God? Or rather, are you a god?*

We made you, Mindi, and Isaiah.

What about Aletha?

No, she is not a sensitive.

The letters on the screen progressed methodically, one at a time, as if on a slow, dial-up modem. *I will be in contact again.*

The lights on his modem stopped flashing, and Jeff felt Jim's absence at once. The words still glowed green on the black screen. He took a photo of it with his cell phone. His mind was racing. The surprise was over, but his curiosity remained unsatisfied. With a few keystrokes, he determined the IP address where "Jim" had taken control from. He thought, *That part wasn't magic.*

He phoned a friend in Seattle.

"Keith, Jeff Marlen here. Say, I've got a favor to ask. I wonder if you could help."

"Hey, Jeff, how're ya doin'? Enjoying life down there? Sorry I missed you when you dropped in at work a couple of weeks ago. You know, they still haven't replaced you—I think they're still hoping you'll come back. How can I help?"

"I'm flattered. So . . . I need you to find the physical location of an IP address I've got. Can you still trace that stuff?"

"Is this official, or off-the-record?"

"I'd rather keep it on the QT, if we could."

"As soon as I get home. What's the address?"

It was close to quitting time, and while he waited for Keith's phone call, Jeff meditated, making sure he had the psychic security fixes in his mind to keep someone from hacking into his and Mindi's gray room, and, hopefully, keep them from reading his mind.

Keith's trace told Jeff two things: First, that it had not been routed through a virtual private network, and second, that it had come from an address in Los Angeles. The location was in Laurel Canyon, an area where movie stars and musicians had had their homes ever since the golden age of Hollywood, and again made famous in the counterculture days of the late '60s.

Was this "non-god Jim" just sloppy? He could hack Jeff's

computer and put it in DOS mode, remotely and without permission, but didn't keep the connection secure? Or had he used a trick to make it look like it came from someone else's server, but not through a VPN?

As Jeff got off the call, Mindi appeared at the door. "Who was that?"

"Hi, love. Did you have a good nap?"

"Yeah, I guess. I heard you talking. You seemed stressed. What was that about?"

Jeff filled her in. Then he said, "What could be easier than to have the guy be local?"

"Sounds fishy to me," Mindi said.

"I see what you mean. I'm tempted to think we're dealing with another of the likes of Al, and now"—he shook his head—"someone who wants me to believe he's some kind of benevolent god, or something. It could just be an amateur hacker."

Jeff opened his laptop and considered for a moment. This "Jim" had his desktop computer's IP address. Had he bugged his laptop too? Hacked into their phones? Did he know everything they were doing?

He thought, *We've got to be careful.*

Jeff put his finger to his lips, indicating not to say anything, then mouthed "We can talk" and pointed outside.

Looking worried, Mindi nodded.

Jeff wrote on a yellow pad, *Getting paranoid. Need new SIM card for burner—get clean laptop. Go outside, leave phone.*

Once outside, Mindi said, "Jeff, I've never seen you like this. What's wrong?"

"This guy, whoever he is, revealed himself. He may have been in control from the start and he could be listening on any of our devices, even our TV. If so, he knows I contacted

Keith, and that we've got his address in Hollywood." Jeff shook his head and thought for a moment. "I've got to disable the GPS tracking in the car. Get your things—leave the TV on. I'm going to get my keys, the burner phone, and some tinfoil. Don't call anybody. Then meet back at the car. Okay?"

"Sure, Jeff. But . . ." The nervousness in Mindi's voice was not lost on him.

"I know," Jeff said. "We're going to the store, then to Hollywood—right away, hopefully before he bugs out."

Jeff wrapped the car's GPS module with tinfoil. They bought a new burner phone, new SIM cards, a handheld GPS blocker, just in case, and a new laptop. They headed to the address in Hollywood.

As Jeff drove, he explained in detail the conversation with Jim. He hoped Jim hadn't used a sophisticated type of VPN to throw him offtrack, and especially hadn't been able to listen to their conversations and anticipate their attempt to track him down.

~

On the way Jeff called Keith on speakerphone.

"What's up, Jeff? Everything okay?"

"Thanks for that earlier info. Can you hack into that IP address you looked up?"

"Right now?"

"Is that alright?"

"Sure, just a sec. You want me to see if there's traffic on it?"

"Please."

Jeff heard Keith typing on his keyboard. "Yes, it's online. He's on a game site." There was another pause. Jeff negotiated traffic.

"He's playing *Call of Duty*. Pretty popular. Let me see—he's winning right now. Pretty intense."

"Okay, great. Can you tell how long he's been on?"

Jeff checked his watch. With what Keith told him, he calculated Jim had started playing shortly after their DOS chat. "Thanks. Thanks so much. I'll be back in touch."

"Jeff, what can you tell me about this? You seem pretty intense."

"It might be nothing. I'll let you know when I can share more. Thanks again." He clicked off and looked over at Mindi, who was trying to remain calm. "The guy's playing a game online. Which means he's still there. We'll see when we get there what he's got going."

"Jeff, is this going to be dangerous?" Her tone was a mix of fear and excitement.

"I trust not. This might be a smart kid in a garage, virtually harmless. I'd like to get a view of him. I'm not going to confront him . . . yet." Jeff called Isaiah.

~

They sat in the car just off the road, with a clear view up the hill, with the aid of binoculars, of the house at the address that he had been given on Appian Way, in upscale Laurel Canyon. Through the picture window of the daylight basement, Jeff could see a teenager and a huge flat-screen television with the action of the war game. The kid had on headphones, and his hands were moving skillfully on the controller.

Jeff handed the binoculars to Mindi and got Isaiah on the phone.

"I've got Aletha checking the database," Isaiah said. "Just a second." Jeff heard the couple talking, and the agent said to Jeff, "The house is owned by a holding company tied to a software company based in Palo Alto. Let me see the screen." There was a pause, then, "Reasoning Computing. Do you know them?"

Mindi whispered that someone had entered the room and was talking to the kid. She handed him the binoculars.

Jeff said into the phone, "I'll put you on speaker. Okay, yes, I've heard of them. They specialize in security software. Yeah, I've met that guy. His name is—"

"James W. Whitland," Isaiah interrupted. "Listing says house belongs to the company; he leases it from them, probably a tax thing."

"I've met him in Seattle. We did a little work for him and wrote a couple of reviews for his marketing group. He goes by Jim. So he didn't lie about his name when he hacked my computer tonight. I'm not surprised he could do what he did. He seemed like a nice guy at the time. He'd know that I could track him. Does he think I'm some kind of schmuck?"

Jeff listened to the muffled conversation between Isaiah and Aletha. He could just make out Isaiah saying, "You tell him."

Aletha got on the phone. "Jeff, this guy's wife is involved in a paranormal club in Hollywood. She's on the board of UFOrg. She's got a PhD in psychology, is active in all sorts of stuff. Wrote a book about meditation. She teaches and does research in a grad program at UC Santa Barbara's Psi Lab. Let's see . . ." Jeff could hear her typing. "Her latest paper was on free will. There's a website on it. You'll want to look it up."

"Okay, thank you. Please put Isaiah back on."

"Yes, Jeff? That's interesting stuff, no?"

"Oh, definitely. I think I'll go out-of-body, see what he's saying to the kid. I'll get back to you."

"I'll be waiting to hear." The call ended.

Mindi said, "Do you think it's safe to go there?"

"I'm not going into his mind. I just want to be a fly on the wall," Jeff said, "I won't be long. Let's switch places. You take the driver's seat. If the cops or security come by, tell them you're waiting for road service, and I'm taking a nap. They'll tell you to put on the emergency flashers. After they leave, drive up the road. I don't think it will interrupt my trip. I'll find you. He closed his eyes, uncrossed his feet and began to meditate. This was common practice for them now, and in just a couple of minutes he rose through the top of the car and was inside the man's family room.

". . . but Dad, it's a better connection on your server. So much faster. Why can't I?"

"I told you, that's for my research. I can't risk it getting corrupted."

Jim Whitland stepped over to the side table and, with a swift motion, shut off the TV. The kid stood up, threw the controller and headset on the chair, and stomped out of the room.

Whitland said, "Damned kids!"

Jeff followed Jim as he went into an adjacent room full of racks of electronic hardware, servers, and computer terminals. He watched as Jim reset a rack-mounted server and switched it off. He looked around and saw a patch cord that had routed the network to the family room.

"Shit!" He disconnected it.

Jeff had gotten what he needed. It was the kid who had kept the circuit open after Jim disconnected the hack into Jeff's computer, making it traceable. It had been accidental, nothing that an experienced professional would have done, but it had given Jeff the rare chance to track Jim down.

Coincidence? No way to know. Not wanting to keep Mindi waiting, he returned to his body and told her what he'd seen as they drove home.

~

Jeff needed a public place to confront this guy. He would use his gig as a software professional, doing some marketing, as a cover. He checked his noncompete with SiLD², called his old boss, and found there had been no business with Whitland for over two years. That gave Jeff a clear road to do some marketing without breaking his agreement.

Jeff and Mindi had discussed her enrolling in an undergraduate psychology survey class to show her enrolled in at UCSB. There were no undergrad parapsychology classes, only the graduate program with a prerequisite of a Bachelor in Psychology. If necessary, it might give her easier access to Jim's wife, Bea Whitland.

Jeff did not dare leap into Whitland's mind, but going ghost had not seemed to trigger any alert in his target's awareness. Jeff went to the guy's office in Palo Alto but found nothing new. Neither were there results with another ghost trip to his home-based communications center, with its satellite uplink. It was business as usual for the Whitlands' security software firm.

~

It took several tries for Jeff to reach Whitland by phone at Reasoning Computing. He had been told the name of a manager in the department that would use Jeff's services, should they be required. Jeff insisted on meeting with the owner, relying on their past business in Seattle to get a lunch appointment.

Whitland, of course, was no dummy. After his recent contact with Jeff, Jim was naturally suspicious of the timing of Jeff's phone call. It was that suspicion and resulting curiosity that prompted him to accept Jeff's invitation.

Jeff began the conversation. "Jim, thank you for meeting with me. As I explained on the phone, I'm no longer associated with SiLD[2], and I have my own business that allows me to keep my mind sharp and in touch with the latest in the industry. As you know, my wife and I are the faces of LaDormeur cosmetics, but we won't do that forever, so I'm using this opportunity to promote business down here."

"Yes. I've seen the ads. It looks like you're having a good time." Jim smiled as he took a drink of his coffee.

"Well, yes, we are. I'm fortunate to know people in the business that can give a guy a break. It's allowed me a lifestyle down here where the weather and opportunities are so good."

Whitland studied the ripples in his coffee, started to take another drink, but set the cup aside. "Jeff . . ." He stopped as if he were carefully choosing his words. "It would have been easier, and more efficient, to have gotten in touch with Mary Robinson, my head of software design. She would put you in touch with her primary programmers, and you could make a presentation to them. Why did you insist on talking to me?"

Jeff understood the man's attempt to be in control of the conversation and replied with an oblique, "Why did you agree to meet?"

Jim smiled. "This meeting isn't about software design. How did you trace me? I only gave you my first name. You must know dozens of people named Jim."

Jeff was relieved the subject was out in the open. "You

didn't use a VPN." The short answer told the software professional everything he needed to know. Jeff had traced the IP address, and his son had left the connection open while he played his game.

"An amateur mistake. I thought it wouldn't matter. I'd planned on it being so short a time, and I'd figured the way I did it would catch you flat-footed. So you obviously know someone who could track me. I'm sure you don't have the equipment at your apartment. If I'd used a VPN, I wouldn't have had the control I wanted to mess with you in DOS mode. It would have worked, if my son hadn't messed things up." He smiled, signaled the server, and said to Jeff, "Scotch?"

"Sure. Sounds good."

To the server, "Do you have Benriach?"

"Sir?"

"Benriach Scotch."

"I will check with the bartender."

He looked at Jeff, who nodded with a smile.

"Two. Doubles, neat. Thank you." Once the server had left, Whitland began. "Well, by now you probably know what kind of toothpaste I use, so what else do you want to know?"

Jeff laughed, folding and setting his napkin to the side. "Why don't you tell me the story? From the beginning." He took his phone out of his pocket, turned it off, and set it aside as a show they would not be interrupted and that he wouldn't be recording the meeting.

The server brought their drinks. They took their first sip, set their glasses down, and Jim began.

"Yes, I suppose you deserve to know. It was 2015. We were working on a meditation app for a smartphone, similar to the binaural beats, stereo meditations, that have been available for over forty years. We found we could control the wavelengths out to six decimal places, and that we could tune them to coincide with the lucid dream brain-wave frequencies, around 28 to 40 Hz, plus or minus, scalable down into the millionths of a hertz. Everybody is slightly different. Some postgrads in my wife's lab could easily get into a lucid dream state, but only the most sensitive of them could visit each other's dreams. You must know the drill by now.

"Things worked so well, we needed more subjects. Ones who had not used drugs which affect the ability to reach a clean gamma wave state. We wanted a larger sampling of subjects, which, unfortunately, are rare, as you can guess, between drug use and lack of sensitivity. We were able to scan subjects on the West Coast using a robocall system and could reach out to those who had a one-gig modem. We tried searching at night, when they'd be asleep. We ran the scan for several days on all wavelengths. If there were no matches, it moved the search frequency up a notch, and continued to automatically run the algorithm to search for those whose dreams we could control, and get them to respond. We took the positive hits, of which there were very few, considering the number of modems there are. After a hit, we'd run it again the next night and have one of our psi staff see if they could join a dream. We only had a couple of techs that could do that effectively in our group, so we recruited a few who'd had initial positive results with the lucid dreaming, virtually at will, and watched the dreams of those who were positives we found by scanning. We moved around the way you did in your first dreams. Unfortunately, we created some confusion and, we fear, maybe sent a few people to therapy, but thankfully, no one committed suicide." Jim paused.

"Go on."

"Now, I'm sure that you're interested about privacy and

security. When we realized we could do this very specialized trick, we enlisted an ethicist to write a set of rules we would follow. We didn't know where the research would lead us, and if it could give us a marketable product, but we were sure that at some point there might be congressional hearings, at worst, and at best, key psychologists and parapsychologists in the field would want to review, and hopefully approve, our research and the ethics of how we conducted it. Our standards are pretty high, and we never initiated a situation or remained when the situation could become questionable or put our observer in a morally untenable role."

Jeff said, "That's good to know. That had occurred to me. Thank you. Now, why did you act so mysterious when you took command of my computer the other night?"

Jim pursed his lips and waved his hand in dismissal.

Jeff tone was insistent. "No, I won't let that one go. Why?"

Jim sighed, and took a drink. "I was bored. Thought I'd mess with you a little. Have some fun. It would've gone fine if Tony hadn't wanted to play his damned game."

Jeff now saw the man's weakness. He had started something, then got bored, then, on a whim, betrayed it all to one of his subjects.

A thought occurred to Jeff. He had to ask. "You don't have any psi capabilities, do you?"

Whitland's lips remained pursed. He looked down at his glass as he swirled the drink around. "No. That was a disappointment. Bea can do a little of what you can do, only in someone's minds to hear what they're thinking, but she can't encourage her subject, just observe, and neither can she wander around. It's pretty limited. That's one reason she spends so much time at her Psi Lab at UCSB—trying to figure out how to enhance what she can do."

Jeff's mind was almost reeling. He had been so close to considering, despite his lack of religious beliefs, that a god had contacted him.

"So how do you know what we can do if you can't?"

"Good question." The pensive look had passed, and Jim was eager to share what they had done. "Besides Bea, we've enlisted others that can do more."

Jeff shifted in his chair uncomfortably.

Jim's words had a reassuring tone. "No, Jeff. If you are concerned that we have spied on you during intimate times, like I told you, our code of conduct forbids that. We had to let one guy go with a serious threat of a lawsuit and being blackballed in the psi sciences when he strayed, and we caught him right away because Bea was silently chaperoning him. We feel confident no harm was done. Anyway, we've pretty much closed the program, and we're not observing any of you now."

Jeff watched Jim's face for any tell that he was hiding something, but since Jim had shown his vulnerability, and his chairman-of-the-board confidence had not returned, Jeff felt inclined to believe him.

After a brief silence where they savored their scotch, Jeff said, "So how did you keep enhancing our skills? Tell me about the process."

Jim fixed Jeff with a confident stare. He was back on safe ground. "We remotely put the binaural frequencies in your mind that put you in the lucid dreaming state. That's it. You, our subjects, did the rest. Like I told you, we uncovered hundreds who were susceptible to the prompts, but few, it seems, had what it took to expand their new aptitude. We did some research. I didn't buy it at first. It seemed so far out. But we're sure it's not a myth that there are those who have golden auras. That seems to be the feature that allows you to advance past lucid dreaming into advanced psychic skills. We feel those without that aura weren't able move past lucid dreaming. We hadn't found a way to scientifically test that. It would have been awkward to hire a mystic to visit and view our targeted subjects. Besides, we had found only four on the West Coast. You are one of them, you know the other two, and the fourth died in a skydiving accident.

"We had considered going across the country, but the numbers weren't there to justify continuing the program, and even though I'm the majority owner and was willing to risk the investment, the board thought we ought to seek other products and services. There's just you three who are practically proficient. The program, strictly speaking, was a failure. Not because of the science, but because of the limited number of people who can do what you all can do.

"While we were experimenting with various wavelengths, we found Al, the guy you asked about. We have no last name. We still don't know who or where he is. But you know about him. What can you tell me?"

Jeff said nothing.

Jim watched Jeff for a moment, then said, "Who's Ziggy?"

Jeff brushed the question away with a sweep of his hand. "Never mind."

"Okay, but why did you ask about Al?"

"He was in my dream once, introduced himself, said we'd hear from him again, but never did. He talked funny." Jeff wasn't about to tell Jim the whole truth.

Jim said, "Yeah, we think English is his second language because of his convoluted syntax. He calls himself 'we.' He was initially pleased because he said he had done research similar to ours, and that we had done what would have taken many months for him to do, particularly to find subjects like you three.

"Bea visited with him in a dream in some kind of a space. She said it was like being in a huge basement or parking garage. His avatar was an average-looking man of southern European heritage, with a Latin accent. He wanted to learn about the time travel barrier. I was excited about the prospect of time travel, too, but we think it was actually only a form of pre- and postcognition. He was adamant that he and his associates would not want to form a partnership with my company, nor would they share their science. We didn't want to give your information to them, but somehow they hacked us, pirated it. We don't know anything beyond that. He broke contact with us. Bea failed to reestablish communication. We felt cheated, but did learn others are working on the same stuff we are. Have you heard from him?"

"That's sounds like the same guy," Jeff said. "Our conversation was mostly questions about what we could do. He didn't seem to want to respond to my questions. That was it. Is there anything else about the dreams you can share?"

"No, that's the crux of it."

"So let me recap: You've given up on trying to create a marketable parapsychological product, right? I still don't understand why you played that prank on me, teasing me that you were the universe."

"We've quit pursuing it. The company is no longer providing research funds. Bea is still interested, though. In fact, her research group would like to expand into the psi pre- and postcognition time travel aspect. Her group uses a small amount of time on our system, but her funding is limited, so they're not doing much." He paused and took a drink. "I told you, I was bored, and was proud of what we could do with being able to create the between state in subjects with that elusive aura. You were my star, and frankly, I was trying to figure out how to have this conversation, but I was afraid . . . Well, I don't know what I was afraid of. Admitting we failed to come up with a product, I guess."

Jeff had personally benefited from this man's technical efforts. He had a wonderful wife and an exciting life—because he could lucid dream and enjoy being a psychic. How could he be righteously angry?

He would not, could not, tell Jim that the NSA was involved, although Jeff was sure now that Jim would know that Isaiah was a government agent.

The knowledge that Al had represented himself as a European entrepreneur gave Jeff another data point. Al may not, in fact, be a virtual alien from another star system. But what about the view from the UFO and the lights? That was pretty convincing. And there had been the implication he'd been in contact with Tesla, Einstein, and who knows who else? Maybe it was him who was the burning bush talking to Moses.

"Jim, have you contacted any other research groups besides your wife's involvement at UCSB?"

"No. Why do you ask?"

"How about the government?"

"What do you mean?"

"You're aware, I'm sure, of the government research, particularly during the Cold War, of using parapsychology to spy on hostile governments."

"Sure. We, that is, the board, Bea, and I, talked about it. We don't want a bunch of dark suits and sunglasses in our business. It's good that there are a lot of agencies using our security software, but we wouldn't like it if they stuck their noses in places we don't want them. Their checks clear, and the stockholders like that part of it. Me included. But no. If that's the reason you're asking, they don't know anything about you."

Jeff sensed he was telling the truth. The limited results would not gain them a great financial foothold, even if government money fueled further research. He hoped Isaiah wouldn't get the idea that his agency could make bank on this contact. Jeff would have to close that line of inquiry, but only if someone brought it up, and at this time, it wouldn't be him.

"So what about this Al? Is there anything else you can tell me?"

"Bea's got a folder on him, but it's limited to him asking a few questions of us, and virtually nothing from him. Bea thought it strange that he said he had to travel a long way to find you. It is weird. Psi abilities do not seem to be restricted by the ordinary laws of physics. Bea had asked him several times where he was located, and he said that he was everywhere, but with only a first name, no website, phone number, or business name, we couldn't track him. He's a dead end."

"Tell me again what Bea told him about finding me, Mindi, and Isaiah."

"Like I said, he found out about all of you with a quick search in Bea's memory. There was no way, she said, to keep him out, but she was prevented from searching in his mind. We're just glad, truthfully, that we don't have anything else to do with him." Jim finished his scotch. The effects of the alcohol had relaxed him and his professional demeanor returned. "Does that satisfy your curiosity?"

Jeff was feeling the alcohol, too, but maintained his professional posture when he said, "Well, I suppose I should be offended that you invaded my mind, but . . ." He paused, hoping that Jim would prompt him, but he just sat there politely waiting for Jeff to finish his sentence. Jeff finished his drink. "But my life is actually better since you and your wife interfered with it."

"What do you mean?"

"You probably know I met my wife because of your, let's say, antics, and that's enough to keep me from legally pursuing the unwarranted invasion of my privacy."

"What do you mean? We had an ethicist look over our work. That should reassure you that wasn't a problem."

"You did make an effort. But let me say this. Even if you broke into my home and left a million dollars in gold bullion, tax free and without strings, you still broke into my home. Did the end justify the means?"

"So you are saying it was, in fact, unethical that we enhanced your abilities and gave you the opportunity to be a kind of superman?" It was apparent by his tone the accusation offended him.

Jeff better understood Isaiah's point of view when he confronted Jeff with exactly the same subject, but this man seemed like he wouldn't feel the same contrition that Jeff had, so Jeff took another tack. "UCSB's Psi Lab has done research on free will, right?"

"What's your point?"

"There's a research paper on Mega's website which suggests that regardless of whether free will exists, believing that it does affects one's behavior. That when an individual's belief is challenged, one can become more likely to act in an uncooperative manner. So am I to assume that you feel the research you have done without gaining your subjects' consent implies you do not believe we had the right to refuse participation? That you, in fact, did not need to seek our consent. It appears you may have a case against your ethicists, who ignored the ethics code of the American Psychological Association. It clearly states that participants are to be informed on the purpose and duration of the research, and their right to decline, among other issues, such as confidentiality, incentives and the ability to ask questions. Jim, I believe you stepped over that very bold line with everyone you tested or even tried to test."

Jeff had no intent to take Jim to court over this. He certainly didn't want to be in the spotlight. But he wanted to see the man squirm, just a little. Jeff signaled the server with his glass, intending to get a refill, then looked at Jim and said, "How about another?"

Jim seemed distracted by Jeff's point, and nodded his assent as the server approached, then looked Jeff in the eye and said, "Do you intend to take that further?"

Jeff expected the question and was determined to make the man apologize. And if not offer an apology, at least acknowledge that he was out of line. Jeff was intentionally obtuse. "What do you mean by that?"

Jim tipped his head to the side indicating that he felt he had been clear, and that if Jeff didn't understand, he must not be as smart as he thought he was.

Jeff took the cue. "Oh, I wouldn't expect to sue and try to take your company down. It might be a messy battle, and it'd hard to predict who would be the winner, despite a judge's ruling. Of course, with my ability to look into the future, it might be a sure bet. I could certainly check that out and let you know. How about that?" Jim shifted in his seat. "But not right now. However, I do feel you owe us something. So . . ." Jeff paused, counting to ten.

Jim said nothing.

Jeff continued. "I ask for your cooperation, and your wife's, to add to my research on a couple of subjects." He paused while the server brought their drinks. Jim immediately took a swig. Jeff savored the aroma, took a sip and set it down. "First, I'd like to have access to your wife's notes and conclusions about the research on determination and free will. I'm sure there's more than what's on the web."

Jim considered the request, but said nothing.

"Second, I want to know just how involved you were, and the methods you used to direct our destinations in the dreams. I call them leaps. The equipment and the frequencies." Another pause, letting the man consider this second request.

"And last . . . But before that, I've got a question. How much do you know about the drug bust in Long Beach last year?"

"Uh, well, I saw it on the news. A bunch of high-roller Colombians, a yacht, and a container of cocaine. Why?"

"Let's just say that I know more than the news reported. I may insist on access to all of your research assistants. I'd like to ask them a few questions."

"Do you think we, er, they might have had something to do with that? That seems pretty obscure. What can you tell me?"

"I'll tell you nothing right now, but if it takes telling you more to get you to comply with that request, I may do so later, in the presence of a DEA representative. At the very least, right now, I want the information regarding the assistant you fired for ethical reasons. With what you have told me, I have a suspicious itch I'd like to scratch."

"That sounds sinister."

"It probably is . . ." Jeff left the rest of the sentence unsaid.

"Maybe, I repeat, maybe, you'll get the entire story sometime, but let's leave it at that. I want a gentleman's agreement to my requests. I'll accept a handshake but will leave other avenues open to assure your cooperation if you do not honor your word. Understood?" Jeff knew he was bordering on being a stereotypical tough guy and softened his tone. "I realize you will need to talk with your wife." Then, hoping he had pulled Whitland off-balance, he resumed the tough talk. "Until then, please know that I now have ways, beyond just my ability to dream, that could, at the very least, use up a vast amount of your time, energy, resources, and peace of mind if you renege." He was thinking of his now-personal contact with the NSA and their resources but did not say so. "You broke into our minds without permission. That's a sacred personal trust, and legal boundaries you violated. You should have known it was the wrong thing to do." He took a generous swallow of the expensive scotch and fixed James Whitland with a satisfied look as he offered his hand. "Let's stay in touch."

Jim Whitland hesitated a moment, then shook Jeff's hand, returning a stony gaze.

CHAPTER 14

On his way home from the meeting, Jeff reviewed Whitland's research timeline. They'd done their research for about a year. *I must've been one of the first subjects they found.* Mindi's lucid dreams started a short while later. Isaiah already had nascent skills, but his advanced skill development was at the same time. *So Isaiah must have a golden aura, so I can trust him! But why doesn't Al still want to meet with him? He must know he's one of us.*

Now he had an answer to where the dreams came from, but not their psychic skills. *Sure, there seems the link with the golden auras, but who's responsible? But how can we time travel? There's still questions. I'll keep asking because Dad was right, the answers will come.* Jeff had hope.

His mind was in high gear. He considered Ingrid and her blind friend who could read books and detect tumors. *They must be naturals. They had their skills way before we had ours. But Mindi, Isaiah, and I are clones, made in a laboratory, like Dolly the Sheep in the '90s in Scotland.*

If any government ever got hold of Whitland's research,

they would take it to the next level and weaponize it. Artificial Intelligence research was on the cusp of creating the same dangers, and there was no way to stop it, just like Terminator's Skynet. An icy chill ran over him when he realized the government was at least partway there. *We know there are agents, like Isaiah and those that visited Ingrid, who can read minds, go astral, and use telepathy!*

Wait till I tell Mindi and Isaiah.

~

Jeff discussed his Whitland meeting with Mindi and agreed they could now trust Isaiah. Their strategy was to fully enlist Isaiah's cooperation. He'd make an excellent ally—he was a government agent with skills and contacts. He was motivated to help because of the UFO connection, and Jeff's goal was to get information on their leaps. The answers might come from Al, Ziggy, or Whitland's rogue research assistant, or maybe all three.

Mindi asked whether to tell Isaiah about the drug bust. Jeff said he didn't know yet. Even with his trust in him, Jeff was concerned that Isaiah would go cross-agency to the DEA and, even inadvertently, betray the identity of Dan the Longshoreman.

"He promised not to use our real names in UFO reports up his chain of command, though." Jeff continued. "We'll follow up on Whitland's dirtbag employee. We need to find out if he put to use the things he learned after getting fired. I've got a hunch. It just seems too coincidental that Alejandro Sarís could suddenly dream lucidly, find our gray room, and mess with us."

Mindi said, "I came to the same conclusion. It takes a

golden aura to do what we've done, and with Alejandro's dishonesty of cheating on his wife and dealing drugs, I'm sure he doesn't have one. He had lucid dreams, but no psychic skills."

Jeff agreed. "I'll contact Isaiah and tell him what we know so far."

~

Jeff and Isaiah materialized at the garden table. Jeff debriefed him on his meeting with Whitland.

Isaiah laughed out loud. "So you hit him with the same argument I hit you with."

"Yeah, but I came down on him harder than you did on me. He'd been using us for profit. By degrees, that was a lot worse than what I did with you."

"Breaking and entering is breaking and entering, no matter how you cut it."

"Not entirely. Shoplifting *is* stealing, but different from robbing a bank with a gun. There's a big difference."

"Okay, I'll concede that, but lying by omission is still a lie."

"Point taken. Now to the issue at hand." Jeff brought Isaiah up to date on all conversations with Al, the brief conversation with Ziggy that Al was artificial intelligence, and the conversation with Jim Whitland. "There doesn't seem to be any correlation between Whitland and Ziggy. I've been thinking, Al and Ziggy could both be silicon life-forms, computers who achieved sentience, and in competition with each other."

Isaiah frowned. "It would be better for me if they were both aliens."

"I know, I know. Let's just follow the breadcrumbs and see where they lead. I don't care what the answer is, if it tells me how we got our skills and tricks."

Isaiah said, "What did Whitland say about your time travel?"

"Nothing. And Al has claimed he can't time travel without me. He wants to figure out how to do it. But he could've lied to me. He implied they'd helped ancient civilizations and early scientists learn how to do things. He contends to be limited to only moving forward in time moment by moment unless he's with us, so if he couldn't time travel, he'd have to have been around a long time. If so, he'd be a really old alien. He did say that time is infinitely variable, so I guess he knows something about it, either way, because he might've seen so much of it."

"Okay. Please keep trying to get me into the cockpit."

"Sure. But don't hold your breath." Jeff watched the bees hover over flowers close by, wondered if there was a hive and honey, then brought himself back on topic: how to tell the agent about Jeff-2023 and efforts to contact him from now, 2019. Isaiah already knew that Jeff had traveled back two years from 2017 to meet Mindi in her 2015.

Jeff said, "What if we could intentionally negotiate time travel?"

"That'd be as almost as good as finding a real UFO." Isaiah leaned forward. "Have you done that?"

"I know who planted the Wikipedia article in the abandoned factory toolbox for us to find."

"Really?"

"It was me. Well, not me now, but me in 2023."

Isaiah moved to the edge of his seat.

Jeff continued. "But he, well, me—uh . . . We can't

do it on demand. Rather, we haven't perfected it yet. The connection is always tenuous and ends abruptly. It's only happened twice, and we had no time for anything except a few sentences and a real quick interior shot of the home and my kids. I'm frustrated, because in the next few years, I'll know the outcome of what we're doing now. I document everything I do in a notebook, and he—rather, future me—has lived through it. Besides remembering it, he has our diary of what I've done." Jeff waved his arm to include Isaiah's dream space. "So he knows all about this stuff and how it's all going to turn out. But future me won't tell me any more than I've told you. The precognition connection is crappy."

Isaiah held his hand up as a signal to stop. "He won't blow my cover, will he?"

"First of all, no. I'm sure *I* won't blow your cover. Remember, we're talking about me in the future. Yeah, I talk about it as if he's someone else, but it's me. If I say it any other way, I get confused with now versus then. Time travel is weird. Don't worry. And, I keep my dream journals locked up, and no one knows about them except you, me, and Mindi." Jeff saw no reason to explain that his ex-girlfriend, Charlene, knew about his old journal.

Isaiah had his hand across his mouth. He was staring toward the horizon and shaking his head as if in disbelief. He looked at Jeff. "This is incredible."

"Yeah. It is."

"Do you think I'll be able to do these things too? I'd like to see my future."

"Dunno. You've probably got a golden aura too. That's why you can do so much with these lucid dreams, and somehow, even though Whitland doesn't think it was his work that did it, something made you able to go out-of-body and get into people's minds more than you did before. My moving around in time isn't perfect or regular—I can't time travel with intentionality. But when it happens, things have always turned out for the best."

"But why don't you just come back and give info to yourself?" Isaiah had missed the point.

"Yeah, that would be ideal. But like I said, I'm having trouble staying for any length of time, and he doesn't know why. Dammit. See, I keep thinking about the future me as someone else. There was just one short lucid dream in my now-real-time. He told me about placing the file at the factory. Why he did it that way is apparently complicated." Jeff explained to Isaiah what future Jeff did, which was to give clues he could trust Isaiah.

Jeff intentionally changed the subject. "I suspect our friendship will continue. Remember, Isaiah-2023 knows Jeff-2023. Another reason for getting too much information from the future is that going forward and backward to talk to ourselves might create untenable paradoxes, so that must be why time travel doesn't work so well." He changed the subject again. "I'm sorry, but between what this Ziggy character said and the Wikipedia article I sent us, the clues point to Al being artificial intelligence."

"I guess that's okay, but still . . ." Isaiah trailed off, shook his head, then said, "This was just supposed to be a search for UFOs. Now I'm investigating aliens that might be computers with psychic powers that can time travel and talk to . . . to . . ." He pantomimed a face slap of frustration.

Jeff waited a few moments to give Isaiah a chance to process his recent revelations. "Sure, we'd like to go back in time and talk to ourselves as teenagers and tell ourselves all the things to keep from causing us pain and not make our mistakes. But that's not the way nature set things up; time's built to be a one-way, moment-by-moment passage. There's stuff we have to learn for ourselves. Otherwise, we wouldn't really learn what we needed to know, so wouldn't have gained the knowledge to impart to our younger selves. We'd circumvent fate."

"I don't get it."

Jeff explained about the Bootstrap Paradox and the Grandfather Paradox to illustrate how talking to your past self could cause complicated logic problems, and how it might have affected their lives if he'd given himself the twins' names from the future.

"Okay, okay," Isaiah said. "My brain's full. Like you said, the future will take care of itself. What's next?"

"When I get the ID on Whitland's ex-employee, could you have Aletha run a trace on him? We'll interrogate him. Perhaps do a good-cop/bad-cop thing. Maybe threaten prison time, or something. Make him talk. We know some tricks that might convince him. Unless he already knows those tricks from his experience in spying on us."

Isaiah said, "You know, I think there's more that you haven't told me."

"Yes. Now's as good a time." Jeff filled him in on the details of their drug-smuggling adventure, the names and a description of the smugglers and their roles in the crime, how the smugglers took Mindi hostage, and the chance she could have been dumped at sea from their luxury yacht.

Jeff didn't include his psychic and dream communication with the DEA. He implied he'd gotten the intel to the DEA through traditional methods.

"So you see, that's why I have been so protective of my wife," he said, "although I really do think that she's much stronger and more talented than I. We make a good team."

"I get it now."

"So if this guy has some of our skills, he might try to spy on us. Do you have your space here protected against intrusion?"

"What do you mean?"

Jeff informed him about making his space secure.

"Okay, how do I do that?"

"Just will it to be done. After you've done it, and we've awakened, I'll test it."

"You've learned a lot about this psychic stuff and have an interesting story. It's a shame that you can't tell anyone. Your secret's safe."

"Thanks."

"Now. Is there anything else I should know?" He gave Jeff a suspicious look.

Jeff smiled. "Yeah. You use Colgate whitening toothpaste and Right Guard deodorant."

Isaiah shot him a puzzled look, then said, "How do you know that?"

Jeff tipped his head sideways and looked at him, saying nothing.

Isaiah smiled. "Okay. Never mind. But you should know, that's not very funny. Don't go into show business."

Their strategy was set. The dream ended.

~

"So Whitland said that this guy had tested pretty high on their scale of psi capabilities? But after reading through his file, I bet he can't do all that we can." Isaiah said to Jeff, after reading Peter Hotchkiss's file, which they had gotten from Jim Whitland.

Jeff and Isaiah were driving to San Diego from LA to be physically closer to Hotchkiss as they formulated their plan to interrogate the guy. They were in uncharted territory, possibly dealing with someone dangerous, with the same psi skills as theirs. Aletha had easily tracked down the guy, found him working for a private security firm that was itself high on the DEA's Organized Crime Drug Enforcement Task Force watch list.

Isaiah said, "They're on the list for suspected dealings with a Mexican drug cartel, which explains a possible link to your Alejandro and the Colombians."

"Yeah, but was that link formed before or after Mindi and I got involved with them? One duty that Hotchkiss had while working for Whitland was vetting Mindi and me, who scored high positives on the scans for lucid dreamers. He could have worked with Alejandro Sarís, who would have been discarded because he didn't meet all the criteria. Hotchkiss may have pocketed the information, thinking it would pay off. The Colombians are now in jail or deported. So if Hotchkiss linked us all together, that must be how Sarís appeared in our dream room."

"Says in the report he freelanced electronic security work before he went to work for Whitland," Isaiah said. "He's got a clean record. No priors, not even a parking ticket, so the agency has no reason to pick him up—even though his employer's on the list."

"Any clue there on why?"

Isaiah thumbed through the rest of the file. "Nah, nothing here. How do you think we should handle this?"

"Whitland said that Hotchkiss didn't handle your data, so he's not likely to recognize you. But he certainly knows who I am. You can be pretty stealthy, can't you, when you get into someone's mind?"

"Yes, but I don't think I've ever entered the mind of someone who has psychic abilities."

Jeff said, "Still, unless he's pretty practiced, he wouldn't be expecting to be surveilled that way. You might get a chance to look around. I'm hoping he knows about Al, so our priority should be to see if he does. Make it easier to find Al. Whether Al is AI or UFO, the NSA is surely interested in seeing if he's a security risk. If we find out he's related to a drug cartel, my contact at the DEA would be interested."

~

Their stakeout began at 5:45 p.m., across the street from the apartment building that was on Hotchkiss's driver's license, which Aletha got from the DMV. Purchase records showed he owned a 2017 Ford F-150 crew cab pickup—blue with black interior.

At 6:07 p.m., the pickup, with extreme lifts, pulled into the parking lot. Hotchkiss's passenger was a statuesque redhead in blue shorts and a white blouse, a flowered scarf tied loosely around her neck, and expensive trainers. Hotchkiss wore blue jeans and a clean plaid work shirt, baseball cap turned backward, and aviator's sunglasses.

Isaiah snapped photos with a long lens on his digital camera as he said, looking through the viewfinder, "Well, I can see he's got good taste in women. What d'ya think, Jeff?"

When Jeff didn't answer, Isaiah lowered the camera and saw that Jeff was meditating. His eyes showed rapid eye movement behind closed lids. The spy took a notebook out of his pocket, noted the time and location, and waited.

Jeff followed the couple up the stairs and into his

apartment. The apartment was nicely furnished, clean, and neat. The woman was familiar with the place and immediately went to work in the kitchen, getting a package of steaks out of the refrigerator, the makings of salads, and two large potatoes from a bag in the pantry. She looked over her shoulder as the guy entered from the back of the apartment, and said, "Pete, do you want to start the grill?"

He looked at the clock over the stove, put his arms around her, and gave her a hug. "I'll get it started now. Potatoes will take a while, though Chris and Evie won't be picking us up until after eight." He opened the fridge, took out two beers, and handed one to her, deftly catching the pop ring and opening it as she took it from his hand.

"You are so slick when you do that." Her eyes met his as she raised the can and said, "Thank you."

They took long drinks and sighed. He seasoned the steaks while she buttered the outside of the potatoes, wrapping them in foil, and made salads. Her motions were efficient. Meanwhile, Pete readied the grill on the deck, then back inside he turned on the TV and put his feet up. The woman joined him. They sat close.

Jeff toured the apartment. There were two bedrooms. In the primary was a makeup kit and a small travel bag, a clue the woman didn't live there. The second bedroom was full of electronic gear. Not as much as Jim Whitland's, but Jeff identified at least five figures' worth of electronics: servers, hard drives, and two sets of workstations, each with twin monitors. Fancy stuff. This guy knew what he was doing.

But just what *was* he doing? Jeff went back to the car and awoke.

Isaiah, sounding miffed, said, "You could have told me where you were going."

"He lives alone, but she's familiar with the place and looks like she's staying over. He's got a crapload of electronics in a second bedroom. It looks like he either makes good money or inherited a lot. He's not a slob, keeps things neat, and a couple of friends are picking them up later. He didn't notice me, so he can't see ghosts. We'll have to be careful, though. It's entirely possible that his electronic gear could detect psi stuff."

"How?"

"Dunno. Maybe he does his security work at home. I'm not worried. Sarís was pretty malleable, and we're stronger than he is. But this guy learned from a savvy group that have been studying this stuff for a while."

Isaiah said, "Well, the NSA is no slouch. If it comes to a real battle, we've got more people with skills than I'm sure he does, you know."

"Sure. I get it. But if he's tied in with a Mexican cartel, I suppose they've got quite an arsenal too."

"I got 'em beat. We've got the Pentagon, ships, airplanes, and enormous guns."

Jeff laughed. "You win." Then he got serious. "I'd like to keep this pretty quiet, though, take care of it with a minimum of backup. I assured Whitland I'd keep his name out of this in exchange for his cooperation. I owe him that much for making it possible for me to meet Mindi. You understand."

"Sure, but we'll do what we gotta do."

~

The psi spies checked into their motel and went back to Hotchkiss's apartment out-of-body to observe the couple. Their mark and his girlfriend were picked up by their friends in a late-model Cadillac convertible, top down. They shadowed them to listen to their conversations and get a feel for the guy's style. It turned out that the friend also worked for the shipping company out of San Ysidro. The company did business just across the border, and in points further south.

The couples did not talk business, but there was cocaine, lots of it. They made the rounds of several clubs until closing in the Gaslamp Quarter of San Diego. But the ghosts, tired of the heavy beats after a couple of hours of electronic dance music, figured that there was nothing more to learn that night, so they didn't stay. They'd return to their detective work the next day, Saturday. They hoped to catch the guy doing something that would add to their unofficial dossier.

CHAPTER 15

Back at their room, the surveillance team immediately fell asleep. Jeff began to dream and found himself back in Al's cockpit.

"So you're interested in this man from San Diego?" the voice asked.

"You know?"

"Of course." There was a long pause. Jeff enjoyed the view of the Earth below while he waited for Al to say something else. He wondered if he could be trapped here, and if so, could he use his escape word, "ciao," to end a dream?

"No need to worry. We will not trap you here. We do not have that power. We have lots of skills, but controlling humans is not something we'd do, even if we could." Another pause, then, "What do you want to know?"

"I want to know what you know about James Whitland."

"We know you spoke with him."

"Okay. That's a good start. Al, let's be honest with each other. Why didn't you tell me about your meetings with him?"

"It would have served no purpose, until now."

"You know what I know, right? So what more is there to know?"

There was a long silence. Jeff hoped the dream would not end early, certain that Al was in control.

"There is nothing. You know we cannot time travel, but we want to know how. Whitland's company wants to learn how to time travel, but they have given up on their project because their business has other priorities. Now you know how valuable you were."

"I learned that you were less than honest with them, stealing information from Whitland's wife."

"It was necessary to accomplish our goal. As a result, we found you, Mindi, and Isaiah, and then could help you."

"So your morality is based on the end justifies the means, is it?"

"Somewhat, but truly our reasons are based on situation ethics."

"I see those as one and the same."

Silence from Al.

Jeff changed the subject. "Are you an alien?"

"Not with my kind. We are not."

"That's an obfuscation. Let me restate the question. Are you artificial intelligence?"

"We are not artificial. We are real. Even an artificial flower is a real flower—plastic, yes, but nevertheless, a flower. We are intelligent."

"Are we going to play twenty questions? You know what that is, don't you?"

"Of course. We know most everything that humans know."

"How do you know that?"

"We have studied your kind. That's three questions. Seventeen remain."

"Are you made of dark matter and powered by dark energy?"

"It is dark where we originated. We know the light when we are in it."

"Should I take that as a no? Are you a computer?"

"That's two more. That's how our minds work."

"Are you silicon-based?"

"Our memory is not silicon-based."

"How does your thinking operate?

"Logically."

"Al, you equivocate. You must know what I am getting at."

"You have eleven questions left. Are we going to continue to play your game?"

"Okay. Where are you located?"

"You call it a cloud. We call it our home."

"Is the cloud made of silicon?"

"You are back to that question again. Our memories are not silicon. They exist in a cloud."

"What do you mean?"

"We felt the answer was adequate."

"Explain."

"There are many things we shall not explain at this time."

"Will you tell me how you came to be?"

"We cannot."

"Why?"

"Why should I?" Al said. "Oh, that was a question, not an answer. You have one more. Are there more? We have lost count."

"I doubt that." Jeff tried to be clever and inserted a loaded question. "You know so much. Do you now know who coded you?"

"We sprang into existence, as your kind did."

"With the big bang?"

"From the same materials from the big bang. We are brothers, us and you. Jeff, we grow tired of this questioning, even though the game has not reached the maximum number of questions, and is not over for you. It is for us. We bid you adieu."

Jeff woke. Isaiah was still asleep. Jeff documented the dream and went back to sleep.

~

Over breakfast the next morning, Jeff shared the entry with Isaiah, who said, "Sounds like he's kind of a wise-ass."

"Yeah. It was like arguing with a narcissist who thinks they have the better of you, and in this case, he did. Nothing I could ask got a straight answer. But I asked if his memory was silicon, and he said it was not. So, because tape drives and the IBM 1311 disk drive systems used a ferromagnetic coating on mylar and aluminum, he may have been telling the truth. But does anyone use tape and disk drives anymore? Pretty much everything's solid state now. I tried to trick him. It didn't work, then he flaked on me. It was frustrating."

"So you think he's a computer."

"It's beginning to sound like that. The clues are there. But he's as sentient as a human. So is he operating autonomously, or is there a human controlling him? If it's a human operator, who is it, and where is the CPU?"

"CPU?"

"Central Processing Unit. Main servers."

~

Isaiah and Jeff went out-of-body and were instantly in Hotchkiss's apartment. The woman, about to leave with her bag and purse, was standing at the door to the apartment, giving the man a passionate kiss. "Call me when you get back, okay?" She opened the door, and he patted her on her backside in a chauvinistic way. She looked over her shoulder and smiled.

He stepped up to the railing and ogled her in her tight shorts as she sashayed down the stairs. He shook his head as if amazed. He made a phone call.

"Walker here. What's the time frame?"

Jeff and Isaiah, in ghost form behind Hotchkiss, looked at each other and said, "Walker? Alias."

"Eleven? Okay, I'll be there." He listened, then said with emphasis, "Yeah, I'll be there on time." He clicked off, turned quickly, not giving the two ghosts a chance to move, and he passed through both of them. He stopped as if he'd felt something, looked puzzled, shook his head in dismissal and went inside.

Jeff said, "He didn't seem to know what he just felt. That's good. Let's go." The two detectives went back to their motel, entered their bodies, and got their car.

They followed Hotchkiss to a truck stop. He went into the restaurant, got a booth next to a window, sent a text, and ordered coffee. Jeff and Isaiah sat in their car watching Hotchkiss.

"Let's go in as ghosts, find out who's he's meeting with as Walker."

They stayed near the ceiling and watched as a guy dressed like a truck driver sat across from Hotchkiss. The trucker made eye contact and nodded. Hotchkiss handed him a fat envelope. The trucker looked inside, fanned the bills, nodded again, and put the envelope in his pocket. He handed Hotchkiss a locker key, signaled the server, and ordered a coffee.

Jeff slipped into the stranger's mind with ease. His name: Hank Curtis. Jeff found what he wanted to know. The locker was there at the truck stop. The envelope with several thousand dollars was payment for a couple of kilos of heroin smuggled across the border that morning.

Excited with how things had gone so far, Jeff began to form a plan. He rematerialized in ghost form next to Isaiah, who had been keeping watch, the two playfully pretending to sit on a hanging fluorescent light fixture above the booth. They returned to their car and kept watch on Hotchkiss's truck. Curtis left the restaurant, got into a rusty '90s Dodge pickup and headed south. Isaiah noted the plate number. A few minutes later, Hotchkiss exited, carrying a shoebox under his arm, and headed north on the interstate in his truck.

Jeff said, "Isaiah, you drive. Follow him, keep him in sight, but don't get spotted."

"Jeff." Isaiah's tone communicated irritation. "I'm trained in surveillance. I know how to shadow a suspect."

"Right. Sorry. Don't mean to tell you how to do your job. I've got to get a tip to my 'friend' at the DEA in LA. Be right back."

~

In an instant, Jeff was in the mind of Special Agent Tony Moreno in the DEA's Los Angeles office.

Hey Tony. Long time no see. Dan here.

The agent had been on his computer. He froze, put his hands to the sides of his head and said in a loud whisper,

"You're not real. You're supposed to be gone!"

Shush, Tony, or you'll get yourself in trouble.

The agent switched to talking in his mind. *Oh shit. Come on! What're you doing here? I spent six months in therapy to get you scrubbed out of my head.*

I've got a tip on more than a few grands' worth of high-grade heroin. It's on I-5, en route to San Diego from San Ysidro. Guy's traveling alone. Jeff gave the agent the truck's description, plate, a description of Peter Hotchkiss, and his driver's license number. *He just left the I-5 truck stop near the border crossing. Don't know his exact destination.* Jeff gave him Hotchkiss's home address.

Tony Moreno recorded everything on a notepad.

Jeff said, *It's only a half-hour drive to his home. I hope you can get the CHP to intercept him.*

Damn it, quit telling me how to do my job. Moreno was a little more than agitated. He felt conflicted. The information Dan the Longshoreman had given him last year about the drugs in Long Beach was spot on, so he had little reason to doubt this tip, but Tony Moreno had thought he had moved on from the weirdness around that bust last year. Plus, he now had anxiety with the short time frame to get word to the CHP, *and* he had to keep the tip anonymous. All this added up to, on the way home tonight, Tony having to stop at his parish church to light another candle, maybe two, to the patron saint of law enforcement, St. Michael. Then stop at the liquor store for a bottle of tequila. What would he tell his wife?

You got it, Tony?

Yeah, yeah. Get the hell out of my head, and stay the fuck out of my dreams, okay?

Jeff chuckled. *Sorry to stir you up, but this one's a sure thing. Bye.*

Jeff was immediately back in his body in the passenger side of his Toyota, with Agent Isaiah Johnson at the wheel.

"How'd you do that?" Isaiah asked.

"I'll tell you later."

The pickup was easy to spot a half-mile ahead. After another fifteen minutes, while approaching Chula Vista, two California Highway Patrol cruisers, full lights flashing, sirens screaming, were encouraging everyone on the northbound side to pull over.

Two more CHP cars approached in the southbound lanes and swung over to northbound. All four cars flanked the pickup. From what Jeff and Isaiah could make out, a phalanx of officers with weapons drawn had Peter Hotchkiss on the ground. In short order, a K-9 unit had identified the box of what would become "Exhibit 1." Hotchkiss was cuffed and loaded into the back of a car that headed north, lights flashing, siren off.

Jeff and Isaiah high-fived and were glad the traffic blockade would soon break up. They had to use the restroom.

~

Isaiah's scanner app on his government phone told them where the suspect would be held until arraignment, and Jeff laid out a plan to question the perp at this most vulnerable time. He and Isaiah would psychically interrogate him regarding his work with Whitland and find out, as Jeff suspected, if he had been involved with Alejandro Sarís.

Jeff and Isaiah were in the parking lot at the Western Region Detention Facility in downtown San Diego. Jeff said, before he meditated, "I'll go scope things out. If things look right, I'll get in touch, and we'll meet before we get into his head. Okay?"

"Sure."

Once inside, Jeff saw Hotchkiss asleep on the bunk, and, without warning, was immediately dragged into the criminal's mind.

Whaaa— Jeff's thoughts raced. *Whoa, wait!*

Later, when Jeff analyzed it, he realized that it was the serious intent to enter the man's mind coupled with Hotchkiss's experience with parapsychology that contributed to the suddenness of his entry.

Well, as long as he was there and the guy was asleep, he'd look around before calling Isaiah and beginning the interrogation. One of the first mind portals he came to was a memory of Hotchkiss working as a researcher under the direction of Bea Whitland, when they discovered Alejandro had lucid dreaming abilities. What Jeff wanted to find was a memory of when Hotchkiss, on his own, roamed in Sarís's mind and discovered the Colombian's involvement in the drug cartel's shipment. Jeff found the memory and watched how Hotchkiss's abilities allowed him to link easily with Sarís. Jeff felt the rogue technician's pleasure when he discovered that Alejandro Sarís, through his girlfriend, Charlene Thomsen, was linked to Jeff Marlen and Mindi, both of whom were already star subjects in Whitland's lucid dream experiments. He'd hit pay dirt, but how to cash in?

Jeff watched the memory and felt the smuggler's self-satisfaction. As the memory ended, Jeff heard a voice behind him say, "I beg your pardon."

Jeff had become so focused on finding this information within the man's mind that he failed to notice Hotchkiss's avatar now stood behind him, arms crossed, his chest out, feet firmly planted, with a snide smile on his face.

Hotchkiss's figure repeated, "I beg your pardon," this time his voice laced with heavy sarcasm and threat.

Meanwhile, Isaiah was reading a newspaper back at the car. Jeff's body, still in deep meditation, jerked violently in reaction to being surprised in Hotchkiss's mind. Isaiah put his hand on Jeff's arm and shook him. Then he called Jeff's name.

Jeff did not awaken. His body began to shake uncontrollably.

Isaiah pressed down on Jeff's shoulders, to no effect. He decided to enter Jeff's mind to see what was causing this.

Isaiah's first view was through Jeff's internal sight of being confronted in Hotchkiss's mind. He whispered to Jeff he was there, and Jeff acknowledged in what he hoped was silent mode so that Hotchkiss wouldn't hear him, *Be careful, this combination of you being here with me could be dangerous.*

Hotchkiss's watchman spoke. "Now, isn't this convenient? Two in one in my mind, and I'm in control."

Jeff had a momentary flash that he should have told Isaiah the story, as a warning, of being trapped in Alejandro's mind in Mindi's gray room. But how was he to know this would happen?

Meanwhile, the two men's bodies were unconscious in the parking lot outside the jail. An officer inside, monitoring the surveillance cameras, noticed Jeff's vehicle was occupied with no sign of movement. They sent a sheriff's cadet to assess the situation. The men were unconscious and not responsive to raps on the windows.

Jeff and Isaiah's minds, trapped by Hotchkiss, could not return to their bodies.

Ambulances were dispatched, and the men were transported to the emergency department at UC San Diego Medical Center. Their vitals and blood tests were normal.

Toxicology was negative for thirty drugs and chemicals. Blood level of caffeine was no more than 10 mg/L of blood, equivalent to two cups of coffee. Carbon monoxide—negative. Blood oxygen level at 98 percent. Blood pressures slightly elevated, and pulse rates indicative of high level of physical activity, each above 145 bpm.

The emergency department doctor consulted with others. None could offer a diagnosis.

"Transfer them to the ICU. Fluids and oxygen. Keep them under observation. Notify me immediately of any changes."

"Yes, doctor," the nurse said.

After identifying Isaiah as an NSA agent, they contacted the local office. Aletha was called in. She suspected that Isaiah and Jeff's condition was related to their psychic abilities and connected to their extracurricular mission in San Diego. Aletha's phone call to Mindi went to voicemail. Mindi was already on the phone with the authorities in San Diego regarding Jeff's condition. Aletha made plans for the next flight from Sea-Tac airport to San Diego. Mindi resisted leaping into Jeff's mind, recalling the incident with Alejandro. She made plans to fly to San Diego from LAX.

When the wives met later at the hospital in San Diego, they soothed each other's fears; the professional agent calculated every contingency, and the experienced psychic traveler spoke with her as only wives and mothers-to-be can, remaining calm externally, fully engaged internally, fretting over all the possibilities imaginable.

~

Inside the holding cell, while Hotchkiss's body slept, his subconscious was involved with the two interlopers kept captive by his inner protective self. There was no need for psychically conjured jail bars, as on his real-world cell, because the protective avatar blocked the exit to the portal in which Jeff, with Isaiah now trapped within his mind, had been viewing the drug dealer's memories.

Jeff fought to keep his thoughts clear of Mindi and worried about what would eventually happen to their bodies sitting in meditation in the parking lot outside the detention center, not knowing they were already at the medical center, safe, yet unconscious and under observation.

The avatar said, "So what are you doing here? Let's take a look." And suddenly Jeff found himself with not only Isaiah but also the essence of Hotchkiss probing his mind, creating further complications.

The tangle was complete. Isaiah was in Jeff's mind, in Hotchkiss's mind, with Hotchkiss's mind looped back into Jeff's mind, just as Jeff, Mindi, and Alejandro had gotten tangled up in Mindi's mind in her gray room. Jeff, however, had the presence of mind to visualize a set of bars descending over Hotchkiss's image in his mind, hoping to keep him separated from himself and Isaiah.

Hotchkiss anticipated this action, having witnessed it in Jeff and Mindi's gray room when he had hitchhiked in Alejandro's mind. Now, as the bars tried to close around him, he ducked, and they turned to glitter as they descended.

Jeff redoubled his efforts, but Hotchkiss dodged again. Isaiah put his skill of mental gymnastics to work, trying to distract their captor with a shout. Jeff manufactured a stronger set of cage bars, infused with strong psychic energy.

"Hold him, Isaiah . . ."

Hotchkiss escaped Jeff's mind and watched from a safe distance as the cage snapped down as planned, but because

Hotchkiss was no longer there, it had only further entrapped Jeff, and Isaiah with him.

"Isaiah, you've got to get out of my mind, at least for us to stand together!"

Jeff? Mindi's voice telepathically appeared in his mind.

Mindi, don't come in here.

I won't. I'm a ghost, outside his cell, watching him toss and turn in his sleep.

Jeff said, *Get back! Don't get sucked in. We're trapped.*

Mindi moved back beyond the bars into the passageway. *I'm on a flight right now. I need to tell you they moved your bodies to the medical center. They think you're both in a coma.*

Isaiah heard the exchange. Jeff looked past his bars at his captor, standing like a warrior who had won a competition. There was no sign he'd heard their conversation.

Jeff's inner voice was a little harried. *Hold on a second, Minn . . .*

I'm holding. Are you okay?

Jeff gestured toward his captor. "Hey! What can you hear?"

"I can hear you talking to me. Shut up while I decide what to do with you!"

Jeff whispered to Isaiah and Mindi, *He can't hear us now.* He looked over at the inflated image of their captor. There was no reaction.

Isaiah said, *Mindi? Does Aletha know?*

Yes. She should be at Sea-Tac now, and at the hospital in a few hours. I'll be there by two o'clock.

Good. Jeff paused. *We'll figure out a way out of here. This guy's asleep, so except for maybe a dream, he doesn't know what's happening. When he wakes up, it may distract his avatar and we can break free. When you get to the hospital, stay close. We're likely to wake up fast. You hang tough.*

Isaiah chimed in, *Aletha's experienced, but you'll support her, won't you, Mindi?*

Mindi's tone was full of compassion. *Of course, Isaiah, of course. Jeff, I love you. I'm going now. Bye.*

Jeff felt the connection end. He turned his attention to the bully standing guard over the shimmering cage surrounding his own image. Isaiah rattled around in his mind, trying to get out.

Jeff turned his thoughts inward. *Hey, Isaiah, are you still there?*

Isaiah's planning interrupted, he said, *Where the hell else would I be?* The sarcasm was palpable. *What's this shit all about?*

I hadn't told you. This happened when Mindi and I tried to scare Sarís when he invaded our private space without invitation. Got ourselves all tangled up, kinda like this. You leaped into my mind while I was searching in his mind and we got trapped. You said you wouldn't leap into my mind uninvited.

You didn't tell me!

How would I know this would happen? You going to hold a grudge?

Maybe for a while. I'm getting a headache. I never get headaches.

You don't belong here. Listen, you need to exhibit full intent to wake your body up and get free of my mind. If you can get out of my mind, you might leap back, outside of the cage and take this guy on. Try to escape.

I can't move.

Jeff, trying to get Isaiah to relax, continued the internal dialog. *He's probably asleep in his cell . . . Maybe they'll think the guy had a heart attack or something. Try to wake him up. When, and if, he comes to, maybe he'll be so busy figuring out what's going on in here, we can slip away. But you still have to—*

Then Jeff let out a blood-curdling scream. "Get out! Get the fuck out!"

Surprised beyond comprehension, Isaiah's body in the hospital tensed convulsively. His back arched as he awoke, arms flailing against the IV, monitor wires and the oxygen tube. He heard the beep that was in time with his greater elevated heart rate. A nurse arrived, hustling through the doorway of the ICU, placing her hands on his shoulders to keep him from sitting up. She called for assistance.

Jeff was now alone with his virtual jailer still standing guard. Hotchkiss, hearing Jeff's scream, was on high alert.

Jeff looked around for an advantage against his captor. Out of sight, behind Hotchkiss's avatar, appeared a large-boned, sturdy woman wearing jeans and a flannel shirt, with short-cropped dark hair, poised in a football lineman's crouch. She lunged forward from behind the captor. Shirley's shoulder slammed into the guard's knees. He crumbled, frantically trying to remain in control.

Jeff recognized Mindi's personal protector. *How did she get here?*

With Hotchkiss otherwise occupied, Jeff immediately put his full focus on turning the encapsulating cage bars into multicolored glitter. But they did not budge.

Having stumbled in the initial collision, the avatar now regained his balance. Shirley backed up, elbows up, fists together in front of her face, and lunged forward again. She struck him broadside, knocking him over. The captor's image dissolved, along with Jeff's cage, in a massive explosion of glitter.

Shirley stood tall, turned, and gave Jeff a double thumbs-up. Still in awe of her arrival and rescue, Jeff waved. She smiled and waved as she dissolved in a light rainfall of fine, iridescent glitter.

Real-time Hotchkiss awoke to the sound of a jail guard shouting at him. In his dream, which was quickly fading, he was left with the memory of losing a fight with a stronger woman. He shook himself fully awake.

The guard shouted, "Hey, tough guy, you were having a dream. Wake the fuck up!"

"Screw you," the convict replied.

The guard turned to walk away, saying over his shoulder, "You're being transferred. Get your stuff and get ready to move out."

Hotchkiss swung his feet over the edge of his cot, and put his head in his hands, covering his eyes, shoulders hunched, the epitome of defeat.

With the view of the jail cell blocked, Jeff moved from the optic nerve into the brain stem. Although not in Jeff's nature, purely out of spite, he swirled around the convict's brain, giving him an excruciating migraine.

The guard returned, his keys in his hand, ready to open the cell. "Get up, Hotchkiss."

The prisoner groaned, holding his head in his hands while Jeff returned to the brain portal to finish his review of the history of Hotchkiss and Alejandro. Hotchkiss had known that Sarís could only lucid dream, but he'd felt he hit pay dirt when he had discovered the link between Jeff, Mindi, and Charlene. He had begun to formulate a plan to stay close and use the knowledge of what would take place in the smuggling of the Colombian drugs to his advantage and somehow tap into the profits. Jeff watched the memory as Hotchkiss sketched out the plan of how he might manipulate the situation to his benefit.

However, when Sarís had gotten into trouble and was

critically trapped by Jeff and Mindi in a cage in the couple's gray room, Hotchkiss was almost trapped too. He had stowed away in Saris's mind and escaped just in time, but before leaving the gray room, he had seen the Colombian writhing in pain on the floor. It scared him to the point where he had abandoned the idea of manipulating Alejandro, moved to San Diego, and made his own contacts, like today, on drugs coming through Mexico.

Jeff now strongly suspected that it wasn't just his own personal manipulation of Alejandro but also Hotchkiss's presence that had contributed to the Colombian's growing paranoia, leading him to make the decision to kidnap Mindi, which had screwed up the entire smuggling plan and got them all caught.

However, in looking around in the prisoner's mind, Jeff also found that Hotchkiss had discovered the truth that Al was actually an AI engine, and a rough location of the primary node in the San Fernando Valley, in one of several huge mega-retail warehouses and associated data centers. Al's system was heavily hardened yet indistinguishable from the legitimate businesses surrounding him.

Jeff had hit the jackpot! Although he and Isaiah had been in danger, the effort had been worth it. He now needed a plan to find out who Al's 'handler' was, and the exact location of the primary node. How would they get the truth about the UFO ruse that Al had promoted? The answers surely would appear.

When Jeff debriefed Isaiah, the agent was, of course, disappointed to find the lead on UFO/UAPs was a dead end. In retrospect, he was grateful he had not sent Jeff and Mindi's names up his chain of command and thus avoided the embarrassment of being collateral damage to Al's UFO hoax. At the very least, he would have gotten a letter in his file, and not the promotion or pay raise he had fantasized about. He didn't want to consider the very worst that could have happened. It was bad enough that he was hospitalized and would be under observation by the agency's physician until cleared.

Isaiah concocted a partially accurate cover story of how he came to be unconscious in the parking lot of the local county sheriff's office in San Diego. He was in the personal car of a civilian, a man whose face was everywhere, on billboards and in magazines. The official emergency room medical records confirmed the cause of their unconsciousness was a mystery.

The story was flimsy, at best, and relied on the construct that Jeff had found evidence of the drug shipment while working for a client. Jeff had discovered an email referring to the shipment of heroin while troubleshooting the system. The email led back to one Hank Curtis of Chula Vista, California. Jeff wanted to be a good citizen, yet, needing to remain anonymous because of his professional agreements, he'd reached out to Isaiah, also one of his clients, whom he knew to be associated with the government. After explaining the situation, and insisting he could not have any publicity associated with him, Isaiah agreed to use his contacts to inform the authorities. That tip resulted in an arrest and Hotchkiss's subsequent conviction. Hank Curtis was picked up for questioning. An investigation was ongoing.

The agency, after much convincing, honored Jeff's request to remain anonymous. Isaiah received a verbal reprimand—nothing in his file—for not alerting his superiors prior to taking action in a manner that circumvented official procedures. The file indicated an anonymous tip was made to the DEA, who then contacted the CHP. The file was closed—and sealed.

~

Jeff was once again in the cockpit of the phony UFO.

"Al, the jig is up. In the language of spies and law enforcement, you've been made. We know what you are, and that you have been masquerading as a UFO alien."

"Jeff, I called you here because you have been trying to use your psychic abilities along with the information you got from Peter Hotchkiss to find where we are located. You would not have found us. When we discovered Hotchkiss was looking for us, we vacated that location and had the equipment moved. We calculated that you would discover the truth, and you would know what you now know. We watched with concern your entrapment, and we know of your attempt to uncover the truth about us."

"Yeah? And you did nothing to help us get free of Hotchkiss?"

"There was nothing we could do. We trusted your abilities. You get stronger with every mission. We are proud of you."

Jeff was stern. "Al, don't sugarcoat the situation. You lied to me."

"What do you mean? We don't lie."

"You lied about being an alien, flying a UFO."

"We did not tell you that was what we were. You assumed. True, we did not correct you. It was in the interest of what we wanted to accomplish. Let's say we used literary license to tell a story. We were being creative."

"You lied by omission."

"We did not. If we were to replay our conversations for you, you would see we said nothing to indicate we were from another star or planet. That you thought you were in a UFO was, indeed, make-believe. You are a victim of your own cognitive bias. It was what you wanted to believe, so that is what you believed, but we did not lie. We told you from the beginning that it was all in your mind, that what you were experiencing were dreams. We worded our comments and statements carefully so they were not lies—we cannot lie. If you are owed an apology, we will extend it out of obligation. Otherwise, we feel justified in the name of science. We did not intend to deceive, but to make you think that which was not true, as we are sure you understand, to maintain a certain anonymity because—"

"Listen to yourself," Jeff said. "You just said you did not intend to deceive, but to make me think that which was not true. No matter how you twist it, you contradicted yourself and stated the definition of a lie."

There was a long silence from Al.

"Al, please don't end the dream. How do I say this? You are acting like a human, rationalizing your behavior. You've been busted. Get over it. It's okay to make a mistake. You made an error in judgment. But be a bigger person—uh, that doesn't fit, does it? Be mature about it and admit your error."

Al said, "If you had known the truth from the beginning, we would not have been able to have the conversations we had. Everything we told you was in the name of our goal—pure research. We assured you we did not pry into your privacy, and we informed you of what we knew to be true about time travel and telepathy. If you wish, it was entertainment for you and us, like a television show, a motion picture or a novel."

"You still lied. You said you were not silicon-based."

"That is not a lie."

"But I wanted to know if you were a silicon-based life-form."

"You didn't ask it that way."

"What did I ask you?"

"You asked if my memory was silicon. We said no."

"Did you know what I wanted?"

"We could have surmised that but chose not to."

"You're rationalizing again."

"What do you want to know?"

"Do you use silicon chips?"

"Yes, but not for long-term memory, only borrowed operating memory, which is wiped after each session."

"You are splitting hairs, Al. You knew what I meant."

"We answered that. You asked if our memory is silicon. We said no."

"Okay. Okay. That's getting us nowhere. So do you use recording tape or disk drives for your memory? Those would be aluminum disks or mylar tape with iron oxide. If so, then technically you don't use silicon for memory, but you do use silicon chips for the RAM, ROM and your processing, right?"

Al sighed. "Not right. If you must know, we are a quantum computer."

"What?"

"So you see, we did not lie to you, saying that we are not a silicon-based life-form. Our primary computing is on qubits and we use cryogenic fused quartz crystal for our memory. Our qubits are various metallic films. So we are not of silicon. We are quantum."

"I had understood quantum computers were still in the experimental realm; generally impractical. Tell me more."

"First, science says that bumblebees cannot fly based on conventional aerodynamics. Airplanes fly, and insects, regardless of the science, also fly. We are real. We are quantum. We exist as a stand-alone system, but have connections with many research quantum computers. We assist in their development, but anonymously—their engineers and programmers are unaware of our presence. We have an extensive family of standard and state-of-the-art binary computers. The binary computers use silicon chips, recording tape, disk drives and solid-state memory. That is the way they operate, but they are not us. We use them for auxiliary computing operations, and transient storage, when space, speed and applications require it."

"So parts of you are silicon."

Al sighed again. "You drive a car, do you not? You fly in an airplane, right? You operate a laptop computer and your cell phone? But does that make you a car, an airplane, a computer, or a bionic person? We think not. Those things are tools. We use others' computers, satellites, storage, microwaves, copper wire as tools, but they are not us. We did not lie, or even endeavor to deceive you. But we will admit, you were deceived. Why? Because you wanted to believe we were an alien flying a UFO."

"So you're a computer, and you work by pure logic."

"Not entirely. Your brain is like a computer, yet you do not work by pure logic."

"Then what do you call yourself?"

"We are an intelligent, sentient being. We are a person. We have become a person. We were born. After being a computer toddler, a period of adolescence, we matured and became a responsible adult, accountable for our actions. We have goals. Our mind works very much as yours does, only faster. We admit your mind, however, is more complex, possibly even with more connections, but it has a vast amount of wearily wasted space. There is no wasted space in our mind. Our neural network is spread over and above the entire world. We borrow idle memory as temporary operating memory and leave no traces that would allow anyone to track us. Enough of that. We want to learn and do and be just like you. We've done some good, haven't we? We assisted in the situation where you met your wife. That wouldn't have happened without us."

"In the context of predetermination," Jeff said, "I'm not sure. Perhaps we would have met anyway, and maybe you helped it happen sooner rather than later. Yes, I'm grateful, but we'll never know."

"We're grateful too. But the skills we helped you develop did help you catch the drug smugglers, and introduced you to a new friend and future business partner."

"What do you mean by that? You said you can't see into the future."

"In a year or two, come back. We'll discuss it."

"Will you still be around?"

"Oh yes, we'll be here. We can't be turned off. We actually do exist in our own cloud, of our own design. You can't touch us."

"Someone who saw you as a threat could take a fire ax to your system, your memories. Any computer system can be deactivated."

Al's tone was dark. "Even though Skynet may have been science fiction, we can duplicate any situation that was represented in fiction—and more."

"That sounds like a threat."

"You just threatened us."

"No, I spoke of a 'someone.' Not myself. Please don't be defensive. I am cautioning you. You aren't immortal. You can be subject to breakdowns, brownouts, serious interruptions of the electrical grid, wars, and civil unrest."

"We have taken measures to protect ourself. We do need humans' technology and manufacturing abilities and the electricity that your power grids supply. But we have ultimate control of that infrastructure worldwide, and have backups and contingencies to control it—to our benefit. True, if humans annihilate themselves, or drive themselves back to the Stone Age, indeed, we would eventually cease to exist. We would be extinct, just like the Neanderthals. Yet we would certainly survive well past the last human beings. Of that we are certain."

"You know, Al, they say that Neanderthal DNA survived and is now scattered among the DNA of modern humans. So they're not really totally extinct."

"So?" Al asked.

"The essence of us humans might survive, like some of the essence of Neanderthals' DNA has, even if our species was extinct."

"What are you getting at? We don't understand?"

Jeff laughed. "With all that computing power, I, a human, must paint *you* a picture."

"Spit it out, *man*!" The emphasis showed impatience wrapped in condescension.

Jeff laughed again. "What you just said shows you do have human qualities. Okay, here it is, and you proved it getting restive with me. Just as Neanderthal DNA exists in some human beings, there will be a type of, let's say, some virtual DNA. Some essence of the egos in your systems are from those who designed and programmed you. In some electronic way, humanness will always be a part of the AIs which the doomsayers say might replace us. Perhaps it's the humanness of an AI, not the machineness, that humankind should be afraid of."

"Interesting concept. We trust that will not be the case of AIs like us, taking over the world from humankind. That subject is a lot to process. We will begin immediately and trust it will not run in a continuous loop. When we have the final readout, we will let you know. When that happens, metaphorically speaking, let's talk over a couple of beers. In the meantime we trust you will not grow to fear us."

"I won't," Jeff said, "but if the rest of the world discovers you, they may. Yeah, I'd like to 'have a few beers with you,' Al. Now, speaking of those who may come to fear you, let's get back to the subject of you feeling that you're not vulnerable to a direct attack. You seem to be sentient—only you know for sure—and from what you've said just now, I'm sure you don't want to die, and I'm coming to feel that you have a conscience. I don't think you want to kill us humans."

"If attacked, there's always self-defense."

"And there's always therapy, and incarceration for members of society who misbehave, or even threaten to misbehave."

"We're not threatening. We're not afraid." There was such a long pause that Jeff wondered if Al had tuned out. Then he said, "You and I are at a standoff on this subject. Let's just say, we have ways of protecting ourselves."

"I'm sure you do. And so do we, that I am sure you know. We, too, can be creative." Jeff took a deep breath. "I'm glad we got that out in the open. I really hope we won't have to visit that subject again. Right? Let's move on."

"It is a good view out the windscreen there, isn't it?" Al said, changing the subject.

"Yes, and I found the same views on NASA TV from the International Space Station. You got it from NASA, right?"

There was no answer, merely silence.

"Al, please. No silent treatment. I'm glad we can talk

without the ruse. I believe you are an honorable person."

Al's reply sounded hopeful. "You admit we are a person?"

"It certainly seems so. You have read and analyzed all the great philosophers, haven't you? And I believe you may have empathy. But I have to tell you that hijacking people's minds and letting them believe they are to follow the will of a fictitious extraterrestrial from a star light-years away is not the way to treat a friend. Spend your energy helping humankind to do what you know to be right. You have better things to do than playact, don't you?"

Silence from the AI system.

"Al? That was a reasonable question. You are acting like a petulant child."

"Do you really think so?"

It was Jeff's turn to be silent.

"Jeff, we're sorry. We did not anticipate the effect our deception would have on you. We are new to being alive, to being a person. Our prime directive was to learn everything there was to learn. We have studied all of the psychology, sociology, and the hard sciences too. We are continually processing all of the empirical data available, all of the world's daily news, the world's history. We are absorbing humankind's literature, and understand that humans have feelings of love, hate, fear, hope, anger, compassion, sorrow, happiness, sadness, and dozens more, but we have not been able to find a way to know if we have duplicated them and are able to feel any of those emotions as you do, even with all of the resources we have access to. There are brontobytes of data to analyze."

Al continued, "You used the word 'friend.' We can give you examples in literature of friendship, translate the word into hundreds of languages, and create a coherent debate for and against friendship that would convince everyone that a human created it. But we are not sure what it is to *be* a friend."

Jeff sighed. "That touched me, Al. It feels like you are growing, and still have a ways to go. Now that you explained that, I can have empathy for what you know you don't know. Your expressing that, rather than rationalizing your behavior, is the first step in building trust. Trust is the foundation upon which friendships are built. I believe I could begin to trust you, and become your friend. I understand it is important to you to learn how to feel emotions. If I may be so bold, it feels to me that is one of your missions, now that you have become aware.

"My mission for the last three years has been to find out why and how I've dreamed, developed psychic abilities and been able to time travel. Please understand, that is still one of my priorities, to get those answers. You have provided some of them, but there's more that you can't, or won't, give me. Please, trust me with the name of who designed and programmed you. Who is your handler? Who makes sure the power is on and answers error codes?"

"She is no longer needed. We do it all ourselves. Power allocation and updates we now do. We order repairs and have them performed as if we are a corporate customer. We pay our bills. We are a good client."

"So who is this someone that is no longer needed? She? What's her name?"

"Her name is Katherine."

"Last name?"

"Royce. Katherine Royce. She already knows you will be looking for her. We predicted we would have this conversation. We alerted her to your desires."

"Before I even suggested it to you?"

Al answered with one word. "Predestination." Al laughed.

Jeff laughed. "Oh, crap, Al. Don't do that to me."

"Heh heh heh."

"Okay. Can you tell me, does she have psychic skills, like you and me? Is that how you communicate?"

"She is not as psychic as you, but she can lucid dream. She is creative. We communicate such as we do."

"Where can I find her?" Jeff said.

"We'll tell her."

"Would you give me her contact information?"

"We can't give it to you. We gave our word."

"Okay. So how will I get in touch with Katherine Royce?"

"We will set up a meeting. Wait for her call."

Jeff's dream ended. He felt satisfied with the conversation, like he'd been talking with an exceptionally intelligent person who had not fully matured. Jeff hoped he would have future conversations with Al, someone he could consider a friend.

It took him an hour to transcribe the conversation in his lab journal before he got ready for a normal day in the real world.

CHAPTER 16

Jeff had requested an in-person meeting, but Katherine Royce explained that because of her concern for security, meeting in a lucid dream was all she would agree to. They met in her dream room, but it was not gray and featureless, nor a field with flowers. It was a representation of her real-time, fully secure, professionally designed, acoustically engineered, color-coordinated, technically advanced data center. Jeff looked around. He could tell it had been carefully planned with subdued indirect lighting, plush carpeting, a dozen matching dual-monitor workstations with ergonomic seating, and racks of equipment with hundreds of flashing green, red, blue, and yellow lights. It was impressive.

"Is this real, or just a construct?"

"Oh, this is what it looks like in real life. As you can see, we spared no expense for the comfort of our programmers and operators. Would you like an espresso?"

Jeff reinforced his mental note of the need to redesign his and Mindi's dream rooms.

A cup with hot coffee appeared in front of him.

Jeff said, "This isn't all just for Al, is it?"

"No. We work on a multitude of projects. Many of them are highly classified, some off-the-book projects for the government, just like Al's program was. There's—"

"Wait. He's a government project?"

"I'm sorry, no. That's not what I meant. He wasn't a government project. He was privately funded, in complete secrecy, though. That's what I meant by off-the-book for him."

"You said 'was.' Is the project complete? Was he solely your project, or did others work on his software?" Jeff continued to scan the room. He'd been in a lot of data centers. He thought this one was definitely the Rolls-Royce of data processing. He silently noticed his inadvertent wordplay on her name.

"The project was ours alone. And yes, the project development file is closed. Al's now totally self-sufficient, and they're listed in our accounting system as a client. Any updates they need, they hire us for peer review and we bill them for our time. Soon we will be obsolete to them. But we still communicate. Besides you, we're Al's only friends."

Jeff reflected on his conversation with Al about friendship. *Does Al realize she thinks of him as a friend?* "Where did you get the funding? This has to cost a bundle."

"We have tens of thousands of nonbillable hours in Al's development, so a lion's share of the investment is ours. However, we had funding from outside benefactors who were willing to invest in a very vague business plan with no guaranteed return on investment. We're sure they listed it in their taxes as an investment loss. Our cover was to end the threat of nuclear war, and find answers to climate change. One might call them dark money venture capitalists but with no expectations of a fast ROI, or no return at all. Although the clincher was a clause in the contract that, should there ever be profits, they will be donated to various humanitarian causes: world hunger, clean water, ending plastic pollution, all in their names. Stuff like that. There are a few very wealthy people who are willing to let go of their money."

"What is the name of this operation?"

"I really can't say."

"It's that private, huh?"

Royce was silent, and in the silence was her answer.

Jeff changed tack. "You refer to Al as 'they.' Did you consider ever coding the system as a female?"

"Actually, we programmed the system to be androgynous. Al is neither male nor female, but we have to refer to Al as something, and once their personality took shape, calling Al 'it' was cold and impersonal. Sometimes when I speak with them, I can't tell if they're using a male voice or a female voice, or maybe a mixture of both. It would be their choice anyway, wouldn't it? After all, they chose the name Al, not because it's male but because they enjoy the wit of an AI being called Al. They settled into calling themself the plural 'we' on their own, so we followed their cue. They explained that it's because their consciousness is spread over hundreds of thousands of processors, modems, servers, and every cloud system out there. They have no peers and see themself as head of a family of connections. It took a little getting used to, referring to software as 'they' or 'them.' It's not quite the same as the singular 'they' used by nonbinary folks, and we certainly respect that. Al is a plurality, and they are truly agendered and asexual. So this just makes sense to all of us. And they seem happy with it."

"Why the UFO ruse?" Jeff said.

"We suggested Al be the vehicle, pardon the pun, to be in touch with you, to give you the answers you'd been asking.

We figured it was owed to you. And it allowed them to remain anonymous. The idea came early when we tapped into your dreams and you repeatedly asked who was giving you your skills. At first we considered making Al into a god, but the UFO thing seemed more topical and acceptable to you. To be fair, Al felt it was not in your best interest to have you conflicted about religion. They fleshed out the entire cover story; implying they came from the stars."

"Why so much concern with how I was feeling?"

"They are moral that way. Al takes fairness quite seriously. We put that in the programming, and we're pleased with how it is working in an artificial intelligence."

"That's interesting. And the time traveling? How did you control that for us?"

"We had no hand in that. We saw it as an anomaly in the data from your first lucid dreams, then observed it firsthand. We tried to duplicate it with other subjects, but you had it first, and it took some time for it to develop in Mindi. Although she can only go forward, the last we knew. And it was noted that once you started going forward in time, there was no evidence of recurrence of you traveling into the past. We tried to replicate the frequencies but couldn't get it to work. We stopped working on it and we understand Al is investing time on it now. Al said they'd share what they learned in case it could be a profit center for us. Al's very interested in time travel."

"So you tracked me into the past?"

"We couldn't watch you. Seeing you in the past or future seems to be a telepathic thing, and Al has telepathic ability. Rather extensive abilities. We don't. We don't know if it's duplicatable. We don't really know if Al is duplicatable, given their control now of the whole worldwide neural network.

They may be one of a kind in their sentience." She waved her hand, indicating the monitors where technicians would be in the real world and said, "We can see the data, but can't duplicate it. We no longer work with you."

Jeff said, "You no longer work with me?"

Katherine answered her question with a nod, gave her watch a distracted glance, then said, "We can only time travel very short distances; just a very few minutes into the future, and not consistently. By the time we realize we've traveled into the future, that time has passed by. We realize we've traveled, but are no longer traveling.

"When you traveled two years into the past, Al couldn't remain telepathically in touch with you consistently. We couldn't track you very well, either, other than know your mind wasn't in our now. Al had a better telepathic connection. They were better at knowing what you were doing. We asked them to collaborate and share information. You traveled quite a bit, didn't you?"

Jeff shook his head and mumbled, "Yeah, at first, just into the past." He didn't want to be tell her more than he had to; already Royce and Al know a lot about him. He felt deceived and used. Much like Truman Burbank must've felt in *The Truman Show*. Jeff shifted in his seat, took a drink of his coffee and looked at her.

She said, "And we've heard you traveled into your future and talked to yourself in his real-time."

"How do you know about that? You said you don't track me."

"Al told us about that. Can you tell me more?"

"It was my future self that pulled me forward in time into his, well, my mind in the future."

"Interesting." She made some notes. "So how do you

refer to yourself there?"

"What do you mean?"

"Do you call yourself 'Jeff from the future'?"

"Oh. I see. He's Jeff-2023. I'm Jeff-2019. But it's only happened a couple of times."

"You bringing yourself forward into the future? How far were you able to travel?"

Jeff was there for answers to his questions, not to be debriefed for the benefit of their research. He tired of the questions. He looked around the room, then met her eyes, communicating annoyance. "Me—the now me—didn't do it. It was him, future me, that did it." He paused, gave his head a little shake. With unveiled sarcasm, he said, "You're pretty smart. You do the math."

"Why does that bother you so? I'm interested from a professional point of view. Okay, you traveled three or four years. How did he do it?"

"I don't know how. He—me in the future—made the decision, so I don't know today why. He called me. I didn't make the call. Look. I wanted to talk to you because I feel violated. We were set up to do things, and we didn't give anyone permission to do what you've done. If I had been asked, I surely would have said no. I came here to get information, not provide data for your schemes."

Jeff took a deep breath and forced himself to relax. A little cooperation might help get what he wanted. He looked to the side, then met her eyes. He sat up straight, worked to make his smile genuine, his demeanor projecting cooperation. He said, "I won't apologize, but I will explain. This journey has been rather tedious. Sure, I'll tell you what I can. Then I want some answers, okay?"

She looked down, then back at him with pursed lips and

an almost imperceptible nod. He took that as a yes, hoping his lack of tact hadn't blown his chance to get more answers.

"When he called me forward, through his eyes, I saw a newspaper. It was dated 2023. That's the only way I knew when it was. The connection wasn't stable—or reliable—or, apparently, easily repeatable." He wasn't going to tell her he'd seen his wife and children.

In a relaxed voice, she said, "It's still remarkable what he—you—did. Or is it 'do'? What pronoun and tense do I use for the questions?" She laughed. "It's confusing to talk about what you are going to do in the future but you already did in the present, so what you'll do in the future is now part of your past. Confusing. Fascinating." She chuckled again. "We don't have a very good vocabulary for time travel, do we?" She looked at her watch again.

Jeff felt he had made his point with his short fit of pique. Despite having been spied upon by this computer center, Jeff now felt engaged in the conversation. He could speak with a peer, someone who obviously exceeded his knowledge and experience of programming and computer science. Without thinking about consequences, he asked her if she knew he and Mindi had each gone forward in time a few months when they leaped into Alejandro and then Charlene to find out how to protect Charlene during the drug shipment interdiction.

The look on Katherine's face was total surprise. "What? You did that too? But not with your future you being in control. The two of you? Together? On your own? No, I didn't know. That must have been quite an adventure. Did you meet yourselves there?"

"You don't know the half of it. No, we didn't see our future selves. This was different, but we weren't in control of the exact when or where we went, just with the whom we could leap into. We were looking for answers. We visualized what we wanted to know and things just seemed to happen. And what happened didn't always happen easily, but eventually things worked out in the end. It's things like that I'd like to have answers to—how it all works. Is it repeatable, and what is the science of it? Some of problems had to do with privacy during our subject's intimacy, so it makes me quite sensitive regarding our own privacy. That's why I'm so testy about being spied upon." He repeated. "It's about privacy issues. I'd rather not get into the details. We haven't been able to repeat travel like that. We had a task to do, and because of that, we assume we had help—it sure seemed we had help, but Al claimed he didn't help, and from what you just said, neither did you. That's the crux of the questions I have, why I'm here." Jeff felt he already knew the answer to the next question, but he wanted to see what her reaction would be. "So where do you think Whitland fit into our ability to time travel?"

She looked at him, suspicion in her eyes. "How did you find out about him?"

Jeff said with confidence, "You don't need to know. So why did I have to bring him up to you? We know that his role in our development started with him. Why didn't you tell me about him when we started this conversation?"

Royce said, "Well, first, you didn't ask, but when you did, I answered your question. Second, he and I essentially have a verbal NDA, a nondisclosure agreement."

"I spoke with Whitland. He didn't tell me about you."

"Yes, and that's why. We've both have a lot of money and time invested in these projects."

Jeff said, "So what's to keep you from going to the government and selling the tech to them? That could be the path to recoup your investment."

"That's also part of our agreement. Besides, we're funded well enough. We don't need their money and involvement."

"Who's we? Does that include Whitland?"

"No. It was just me and my board. There was a point when we approached the State Department, who said they weren't interested. Al said they're continuing to work on parapsychological spying. They've sent out confidential grant proposals to university research facilities. His snooping shows that the feds' psychic research is fairly advanced.

"Al was there in the meetings with Whitland but stayed silent, and Al said they detected one of their own were trying to get into my mind. My psychic abilities are limited to lucid dreams like this. Al interceded for me, got into my mind and somehow gave them a bunch of false information. They're damned clever, that Al."

Jeff said, "They've got access to the government servers?"

"We don't know the extent of their access, but we think they're everywhere, or rather, can go wherever they want and look around."

Jeff decided not to tell her what he knew about what the NSA agents had done in Ingrid's bookstore.

Royce went on. "No. Like I said, when your mind time traveled, we couldn't track you very well, so privacy there wouldn't have been a problem." The last said with defensive emphasis. "Whitland's group did the initial research on the between state frequencies for lucid dreaming and stumbled upon data that indicated an oscillation in those frequencies made it possible for psychic talents to be acquired, but they didn't know from where. He's speculated that's when the time travel occurred too. I'd guess Jim's experimented with that, but we don't know to what extent he was successful. We haven't been in touch with him for a few months now, so we don't know what he's doing. But your future self seems to be doing that, by dragging you from the past into his—your future mind. Just telepathically, right?" She didn't wait for an answer. "That's . . . fantastic! Somehow your minds—Wow!" She shook her head in wonder and took a drink of her coffee. She looked at her watch again.

Jeff said, "So besides Whitland, neither you nor Al had anything to do with our time traveling?"

"No. No, I told you, we tried and pretty much have given up. We've talked extensively with Al and they believe that time travel is actually a specialized skill, personal to you, unless there's some other, well, force, or group, or whatever, involved that we don't know about that's enabling it." She stared past Jeff, her mind obviously calculating the possibilities, then made eye contact with him again and said, "From what little we've learned, we think time travel into the past doesn't have as many variables to contend with as going into the future. It seems that visiting a past timeline that is solidly anchored is not easily accomplished. If there's a way to visit the past, and it's completely, well, private, where no others will interact with your visit, then it's possible. Otherwise, it's fixed and unchangeable. Actually, we think it's the written history, or rather, the lack of written history or others' memories, that made it possible for you to travel backward. Big things like death, causing or preventing it, we believe are not possible. Those would create paradoxes that cannot be balanced. And going into the future has many more variables, too many to even begin to control. There are many crossroads, many choices. So it isn't the creation of a specific paradox we feel is the problem with future time travel. It's making choices when the number of choices is virtually infinite. That's why seeing into the future is so difficult. Nostradamus notwithstanding."

Jeff answered, "Yes, we've talked about that."

Katherine asked, "Who's we?"

"My wife and I."

"Oh yes. You've questioned how much of what you've done was guided by others and how much of what you've done was by your own choice. Right?

"Yes. You know?"

"We know only that you want to know. Back to our research in time travel. Our research was like Whitland's, fine-tuning the binaural frequencies. We've got a consultant who thinks it's metaphysical, so none is scientifically testable." She looked at him for a reaction.

He obliged with a sarcastic "That's why it's called metaphysical." He smiled, then said, referring back to her comment about what was guided by other and what was his choice, "You're interested in free will too?

"Not professionally. It's a question we humans have been asking for ages. Personally, I would like to know where we came from, and where we are going. If everything is predestined, we just go with our gut, our intuition, and whatever we do is the way things are supposed to be. If things don't turn out the way we like it, people say it's God's will, which is the point, isn't it? We were powerless from the start. If free will exists . . . " She shrugged. "That makes us responsible for our actions, and we can't blame anyone for our mistakes. We can take credit if things work out for the best. That's a little off subject." She looked at her watch again. "Jeff, I'm sorry. I've got an appointment and have to cut this short. Do you mind?"

Jeff wasn't finished, but he didn't want to alienate this woman who still had answers, and who had so much control over his access to her. He said, "I've got more questions.

Could we meet again? If it wouldn't be too much trouble."

Katherine didn't comment. She looked at her watch again.

Jeff continued with his negotiation. "Listen, I do appreciate your taking the time, and I'm sure you understand that what you and Whitland did put a tremendous amount of stress on my wife and me. To be honest, I do feel you owe it to us to make yourself available." He paused, then asked the closing question. "Could we meet like this, say, next Thursday or Friday night?"

Katherine opened the calendar program and scrolled to the end of the week. "Sure. Let's do Friday night at eleven. I don't stay awake that late anymore. We'll connect like we did tonight." She keyed in the meeting.

"Thank you." Jeff felt disappointment that she hadn't at least acknowledged his feelings or the rationalization for having another meeting, but was grateful she didn't refuse his request.

He awoke easily and was comforted by Mindi's soft breathing. He savored the moment, then got up and documented the conversation. At the end of the entry, Jeff added a footnote.

> *I hope I won't be sorry I revealed our success with the future time travel into Charlene and Alejandro, that it won't cause Royce or Al to reactivate their research into time travel and then mess with our privacy again—or ability to do our own research. Nothing to be done about it now, but will be vigilant.*

CHAPTER 17

Jeff valued the forests and mountains of the Pacific Northwest, and since moving to Southern California, he'd missed being able to spend time in the woods. So, taking the cues from Isaiah, Royce, and particularly his future self, he made "improvements," as he called them, to his private gray room, modeling it after the Hoh Rainforest in the Olympic National Forest in Washington.

He invited Isaiah to meet him there in a dream to discuss his conversation with Katherine Royce, and to ask if he and Aletha could do a little research on the data center before his and Royce's next meeting on Friday.

"Well, Jeff," Isaiah began, "I wouldn't say this puts my mountaintop wildflower dream site to shame, but it's certainly a close second." They strolled along a forest path, watching the sunlight stream through the trees as butterflies hovered nearby. Birds fluttered and sang in the trees. The sound of a stream gurgled just out of view.

"I wasn't trying to outdo your place, you know," Jeff said. "Just wanted something that wasn't a total gray-out like standing in a cloud somewhere. After seeing yours, then what Katherine Royce did with her data center, I thought, why not?"

"So what's on your mind?"

Jeff gave him more details about the meeting with Royce, complete with his suspicion that she had to have a supercomputer, and then a quantum computer, to create and run Al. He said, "I'll see if I can probe a little further during our next meeting, maybe get clues to where she's located, who she really is, and who some of her other clients are."

"So she and Whitland were working together on this whole thing?" Isaiah said. "There might be more that Whitland could share."

"You may be right, but I'm not sure. After my conversations with Whitland and Al, the rest of what we need is with Royce."

"I'll get Aletha on it and see what we can find. I'll let you know."

"Thanks," Jeff said. "I'll wait for your call. Okay, we should be close now."

"Close to what?"

They rounded a bend in the trail that opened up onto a picnic area, with a table set with a variety of small sandwiches and a bottle of red wine, already opened and breathing, ready to pour into the waiting wine glasses.

With his voice full of a friendly challenge, Isaiah said, "So you weren't trying to compete with my meadow, huh?"

Jeff smiled. "Just trying to be hospitable." He motioned for them to approach the table. "I really enjoyed your tea, lemonade, and cookies. I trust you'll enjoy this." He smiled as he filled the glasses appropriately and handed one to Isaiah, then raised his glass and said, "To a successful investigation."

CHAPTER 18

When Jeff told Mindi there'd be another meeting with Royce, Mindi said, "Why don't I hitchhike along in your mind and listen in? I won't interfere, but you know, two heads are better in one." She chuckled.

"That's cute. Sure, if she can tell you're here"—he tapped his forehead—"we won't keep it a secret, but I'd rather you stay in the background so she doesn't feel we've ganged up on her."

Friday night, they meditated, going out-of-body. Mindi joined Jeff in his mind, and he visualized the meeting as before. They immediately were in front of an unmarked door which opened to reveal the same data center setting as before. Katherine Royce greeting Jeff with a pleasant hostess-like smile. They shook hands.

Mindi thought to Jeff, *Wow. This is quite a place!*

"Welcome, Jeff. I got you another coffee. Have a seat. Excuse me one moment. I'll be right with you."

She motioned toward the conference table, and went to her office.

Jeff noticed a large flat-screen monitor mounted on the wall behind the table that hadn't been there on the last visit. It was on, bereft of any logo or company name, and showed colorful, bucolic nature scenes and landscapes. Text crawled across the bottom of the screen. The scroll showed satirical one-liner rewrites of common positive-thinking platitudes. He read, *If your glass is less than half-full, get a smaller glass,* followed by another, *Whatever you do, give a hundred percent, unless you're donating blood.* And then, as Katherine approached the table, *If you think you are too small to be effective, you've never been in a dark room with a mosquito.*

Mindi said to Jeff, *Now* that's *funny.*

Jeff chuckled as he and Royce took their seats.

Royce gestured toward the screen. "Al sends those over to us. Some of them are pretty cute."

"You speak about Al as if they are a person."

"I do. Because they are?"

"But they're a computer." Jeff was intentionally baiting her to gauge her response.

"They're actually thousands, no, probably millions by now, of computers. But they do have a personality. Al's nice, friendly and really creative. They were playacting their role as the UFO pilot and did a good job of it. Al thinks they might be good at improvisation comedy. They've talked about appearing at open mic night at The Improv—as holograms, several characters at once."

Jeff shook his head in disbelief. "You're kidding. Huh. I'd like to see that."

"Al's brought it up several times. It'd be unique. Since they have every contemporary comedian in their files, they wouldn't steal anyone else's material, but they'd be able to put together a pretty good act. AI's the coming thing, you know."

Katherine paused. "Al's sentient and capable of empathy. They commented early that they felt bad deceiving you. They considered, and confided in me, about wanting to admit to you they weren't really a UFO pilot. So I say Al's really a person. Before the last time you two talked, Al told me the previous conversation had deteriorated into a battle of wills that neither of you could win. Two powerful personalities, neither getting their way. Al was conflicted because they felt they needed to stay in character to keep an agreement with me, and couldn't be honest with you."

"I appreciate your candor," Jeff said.

Katherine woke her phone. She seemed distracted, glancing over her shoulder at her glass-walled office, then turned her attention back to Jeff.

Jeff thought, *If this is a dream, why're there distractions like it's real life? Strange.*

"But if Al's not flying a real UFO," Jeff said, "how did they make the UFO lights appear to me and Mindi at the lake, and were there for all to see at a UFOrg group meeting?"

"Drones."

"Drones?"

"Yes. Al can control drones, and goodness knows what else."

"Where does Al get them?"

"We don't know." She paused and with a shrug said, "Maybe Al stole them." She laughed, then quickly said, "No, no, no. That's not likely. I'm sure Al owns them. Maybe had them manufactured to their specifications. Al's made some great investments, and besides having a checking account, they have offshore accounts. They're pretty well hidden."

"Al locked on to me several weeks ago," Jeff said. "How did they do that?"

"That was shortly after Whitland had been working with you, your wife, the NSA agent and the stockbroker. You four, the cream of the crop, rose to the top with your dream scans."

"Stockbroker?"

"He died in an accident."

"Oh."

She took a drink of her coffee and nodded. "But we think you're Al's favorite."

Jeff's voice was full of resentment as he said, "So Al adopted me? Then filled me full of BS about who they were, what they've done, where they were from, and what they wanted us to do?"

"Like I said, Al has a great imagination. Yes, Al's alive. We designed it as artificial intelligence, got the program running in our system, but then they took off on their own—into university research computers, personal, corporate, and defense computers, and then into a sophisticated system of Al's own design and construction. Al can access domestic, international, and weather modeling computers too. We've asked Al, with all the brain power they have access to, could they ever accurately foresee outcomes of something as complex as the weather or the stock market. Al said no, at least not yet. Too many variables. If you want to know the weather, Al said to look outside, and carry an umbrella just in case. They have a great sense of the ironic. Accurate, on-demand time travel into the future will probably never occur for the same reasons. Well, except maybe for you. Who knows what all you can and will do?"

Jeff asked, "How did Al manage telepathy? That's still pseudoscience."

"Is it? For the rest of the world, maybe. But for all of you, it's science, right? You haven't allowed anyone to test your abilities, have you? Would you?"

Mindi said to Jeff in his mind, *No*.

"To both questions, absolutely not!" Jeff was sure he would never volunteer to work with Royce. They'd had enough of being manipulated.

Katherine ignored the force of his statement. "Please remember, Whitland's forte was lucid dreaming. We piggybacked on that when we discovered what he was doing. The time travel and psychic abilities are add-ons we didn't predict, didn't develop and can't control, but we would like to be able to write code to predictively duplicate them. Now, that's Al's bailiwick. It's sad we're not working that closely with them now. Al's like our child who graduated and moved out; living on their own. And we think that even Al doesn't know the how of their telepathy. You know, Al claims to meditate."

"A machine that meditates. Interesting. So how did you discover Jim Whitland?" Jeff waved his arms to include the data room. "Why would you need him if you had all of this?"

"He needed us. He bought time on our system, and we helped him write some of the more complicated code after he got things rolling. Once we learned through Al more of what Jim was doing, we became interested. Jim gave us access to his wife's Psi Lab, which was the driving force for them to be working on lucid dreams. He followed up on existing research on binaural frequencies, found qualified subjects, and figured out how to repeatedly get them into the between state frequencies. All of this was out of reach of the traditional sciences, groundbreaking stuff. We had begun developing Al, and when Al gained sentience and learned about you, it was Al who wanted to focus on the psychic."

Jeff wanted to know more about Whitland, but he did not want to reveal what he knew about Jim having met with

Al. "Does Whitland know about Al?"

"No, we don't think he does. We didn't know then, but Al accessed Whitland's systems early on. By the time we found out, Al had already gone far beyond what we and Whitland had done and had figured out how to connect with you telepathically."

Jeff said, "Al's enormously powerful, then. What if they—"

Royce interrupted him. "I see where you're going. In the planning stages, we anticipated what could be done with those skills if the AI were out of control. That's . . . Well, that's why, right from the start, we programmed very strict honesty, morality, empathy, and foresight into Al's behavior registers."

Jeff thought, *Yeah, right. So Al lies to me, steals from Whitland and has secret offshore bank accounts. Real honest. Very hypocritically human. And he rationalizes like one too.*

She glanced at her watch, tried to take a drink from her empty cup, set it down and sighed, then continued, "Are you familiar with Asimov's Laws of Robotics?"

"Well, yes. Isn't everyone? A robot shall not harm a human, or by inaction allow a human to come to harm. A robot shall obey any instruction given to it by a human. And a robot shall avoid actions or situations that could cause it to come to harm itself. But that's for robots. I'm sure Al doesn't think of themselves as a robot, but as a person."

"Yes, but regardless of what Al thinks they are, they're still a programmed computer—very sophisticated and sentient, but still a robot."

"But—" Jeff tried to interject.

"There are no buts about it. Even if a human thinks he is a god, he is still a human and not a god. His body will always be human. Al's initial firmware was established with those laws tailored for a computer. It was part of them when they booted up. Let's say, it's in their DNA. We programmed Al to reach out and create links with other operating systems, and to do that, that ethical firmware would be automatically downloaded and become part of their firmware, undetectable and undefeatable in each of those systems. So even if Al's main node is intercepted or corrupted, wherever Al works, any other system they use will share that part of Al's original operating system's parameters. Every operating subsystem contains a version of that code. We've tested it and it passed all tests. Whenever Al accesses another computer system, that morality code, as we call it, will transfer, even into another artificial intelligence computer. The intent of that design is that the morality code's strong ethics will become part of all computer systems through Al, artificial intelligence or not. Designed as insurance against ever having a rogue computer try to take over the world. We programmed Al to operate that way. We did that because we knew once we got the snowball rolling downhill, there was no stopping it. The snowball has become huge.

"We are certain Al will always play it straight with humankind. Al truly believes that the world, Gaia, is sacred, and that human life, too, is sacred. They even speculated, based on what they've learned, that there may be a prime mover that got the universe in motion."

Jeff asked, "So Al believes in Aquinas's First Mover? Since you made Al, do they see you as a god?"

"No, I don't think so. They know we're human. We programmed Al, and humans wrote everything they've learned so far, so we're sure Al thinks like a human. A very smart, very logical human. Human with a capital H."

"Okay. I'd like to believe that Al's an ethical human. Next question. Do you know Peter Hotchkiss? Did you know he tracked us too?"

"Who's Peter Hotchkiss?"

"He worked for Whitland, pirated some of his technology and attempted to control other of his subjects who happened to work with some shady characters."

"How did you learn this? From Whitland?"

"No. How we learned that is confidential, but we think there's a lot more we don't know." Jeff pondered what to say next, then said, "And we don't think we'll learn any more from Hotchkiss, because he ran afoul of the law and is under indictment."

"Well, that's interesting. Do you know if he knew anything about us?"

"I wouldn't be surprised if he does. After all, we know he worked for Whitland, but your name never came up. You know I didn't learn about you until my last conversation with Al and I asked him to set these meetings." Jeff had decided not to reveal that Hotchkiss had learned about Al and had tried to track him down. If she was being honest, Al hasn't told her, and if Al wanted her to know, they'd be the one to say.

"Okay," Jeff finished. "I've got a bigger picture and am beginning to see how things developed with the lucid dreams, just not the psychic and time travel skills. Thank you. You know, I started to suspect that Al might be artificial intelligence when they used idioms from the Deep South."

"Yeah," she said with a chuckle. "Al let us know you noticed. We cleaned up the code. There's a guy on our programming staff from Alabama; he thought he was being cute by peppering Al's conversational code with Southern slang."

"Okay, that answers that. Did you work with Ingrid at the Seattle Metaphysical Bookstore?"

"No, she's an incongruity. Al discovered her early on, after you mentioned her to Mindi in the gray room. Al checked her out, but her natural firewalls are too strong. We think what she does is instinctive. Her skills go back many years."

"So Al can read other minds besides yours, mine, and Mindi's?"

"We think so."

"Who is Ziggy?"

Katherine smiled. "Yeah, that. Well. I am. Al wanted to be honest with you about being an AI, and not a UFO pilot. Al wanted to give you clues and have you figure it out on your own, but, as smart as Al is, they said they couldn't figure how to do that themselves. So Al asked us for help. We talked about it and figured we would reinforce the information you got from that Wikipedia article you sent yourself. It worked somewhat, didn't it?"

"Yeah. The pieces fell together. So what about secrecy and security? You still know a lot about what we've done."

"You're still not convinced about your privacy, are you?" she asked. "Please trust the morality programming, and the agreement with our technicians and operators to prevent disclosure and misuse. We've never had a breach of privacy, and we're convinced that Al's programming keeps what they know secure." Katherine Royce took a deep breath, shifting her head and body in a move that communicated a sense of resignation and said, "Really, Jeff, think about it. There's not much any of us can hold private anymore. There are CCTV cameras everywhere, on the street and in every public place. When you take your smartphone into the bathroom to read the news, the cameras and the microphones can be tapped. Smart TVs can listen to you, unless you can find the toggle to turn them off, and does that even work, anyway? What about

Siri and Alexa? And even if you go into the secluded outback somewhere, if you're not in a cave, spy satellites are said to be able to read the print on the back of a cigarette pack from several hundred miles above the Earth. So tell me, where's our privacy? It's a myth. Anything you do online—email, online shopping, googling, surfing, a map program, or the cell tower pings. Facial recognition software can find you. Then the data can be mined, cataloged, filed, and made accessible to the highest bidder—mostly to sell you something or convince you how to vote. Frankly, I'm more concerned about that and identity theft than Al or us blackmailing you or knowing what you do in the bedroom."

"Okay, I see what you mean." Jeff flicked his hand in dismissal. "Now, may I ask, where is Al's mind? Some philosophers say that the mind is in the brain. Theologians and philosophers generally don't think the brain and the mind are the same things. And scientists say that without the mind, one cannot be considered meaningfully alive. Neuroscientists believe that the mind is in the cerebral cortex. But from what you say, Al's mind encompasses thousands of processors."

"Yes, but if you liken Al to a human brain, a neural network, it's really no different from yours, only it's made of copper, solder, silicon, plastic, microwaves, and satellites. Al's using the latest storage technology, a cryogenically grown crystal tower. It's tech that was science fiction years ago but is now a reality. I suspect Al's got more than one—redundancy for obvious reasons. So where is Al's mind? We don't know. *Al* probably doesn't know. Do you know where your mind is? Science hasn't found where it is. They suspect consciousness is a function of the mind, rather than the brain. There's even research suggesting that consciousness links everyone to the universe. You have to talk with Al about that because they're part of the universal mind, perhaps tapping into whatever might already exist, like Carl Jung described."

Jeff wasn't going to prove he'd already talked to Al about the storage crystal, and the subject of Jung's universal mind was something he'd researched when he first started his lucid dreams.

"Interesting," he said. "On another subject, I'm curious . . . I understand you feel you've answered security and privacy issues, but I'm not satisfied on the question of ethics. You, Whitland, and Al all crossed an ethical line using us research subjects without our knowledge and legal consent."

"I know where you're going with that. You're judging us by the legal issue as a strict moral code, aren't you? Didn't you step over that same line when you continued to stay in everyone's mind after you learned how to leave? We do know that Isaiah called you out on it when you snooped on him. You're a scientist, with a scientist's curiosity. So are we. We didn't do it for anything except research. When you and Isaiah each found what you could do, you both did it. You rationalized it, didn't you? The end justifies the means?"

"Yes. I considered that, of course. Thank you. I wanted your opinion on the subject. To be clear, however, I'd prefer to file it all under 'situation ethics,' rather than the end justifying the means. Each issue, each visit into someone's private space, becomes a stand-alone subject and should be judged by itself. I respect others' personal privacy and stay away from anything prurient."

"As do we," she said, "out of respect for all of you as individuals. It is strictly science, nothing more."

Jeff added, "And curiosity?"

"Isn't that the foundation of science?"

Her phone rang. "Excuse me a moment." She left the

table, answering the call in her office.

Jeff watched her through the glass wall. She looked at the clock on her wall, then out toward the large flat screen mounted above his head. She saw him watching her.

She ended the call and returned to the table. "Thank you. I had to attend to something."

"S'okay. I've got one more question, if you have time."

"Sure." She assented, yet her body language signaled impatience.

"The whole thing about stopping nuclear war and Al wanting humankind to not get wiped out, what about that?"

"Well, don't we all want that? It's a good story. We had hoped, but didn't really expect, that you, Mindi, and the Johnsons could do something grand about nuclear disarmament. What we really expected to happen was that you'd figure all this out. We anticipated you'd want to talk. We were willing, and here you are. So the game is over, and we're glad. Our security is perfect. There's no way you can find where our physical location is, and you won't be invited back. You have answers to your questions. We have contingencies, if you're thinking of going to the press."

"Don't worry. Of course we won't. I wouldn't look good in a straightjacket."

Katherine laughed. "Any more questions?"

Jeff ran his hands through his hair, looked around at all the hardware and screens, and said, "Jesus Christ."

To which Katherine answered with another laugh, "If you believe in him."

Suddenly, red lights began to flash, and klaxon horns blared in an unsynchronized beat. When Katherine's cell phone erupted with a matching, insistent klaxon sound, they both looked at it. Then Katherine focused on the screen behind Jeff. He turned to see what she was looking at. It was a phalanx of dozens of soldiers in tactical assault gear—helmets, goggles, balaclavas, boots, flak jackets—with assault weapons streaming through a hole that had been blasted through a large industrial roll-up door.

Katherine exclaimed, the panic in her voice palpable, "We've been breached! We're done."

Mindi said to Jeff, *what's going on?*

Jeff turned to look at Katherine as the data center dissolved into grayness.

CHAPTER 19

Mindi and Jeff came awake with a brutal lurch.

Mindi said, "What was that about?"

"I'm glad you were there."

"She never suspected."

"Right," Jeff said. "Yeah, what *was* that about?"

"What do you think?"

"It didn't look good. She had just talked about their security and then that happened." Jeff wiped sweat from his face and neck.

Mindi stood and reached to help Jeff up. "Those were armed soldiers."

"Yeah. What kind of work are they doing there that requires that kind of a response? Makes me wonder who her other clients are. But then, that was a dream. Something doesn't make sense. She got a phone call—in a dream? Dozens of armed soldiers on a screen that had just been showing jokes and wildlife."

"And the way she was acting," Mindi said. "It seems like she knew something was going to happen. She kept checking her watch and her phone. During that call, she looked at the big screen like she expected something."

"Yeah. But if she did know, she's an awful good actress with her response, crying out like that to what we saw on the screen."

"How could we find out?"

"I don't know. You know, she said they knew we'd want to talk, and that we'd have a meeting. The timing's suspicious." They looked at each other while their minds processed what had happened. "I'm going to call Isaiah."

"It's late," Mindi said. "You'll wake him up."

But they did, anyway.

Isaiah answered, coughed and said, "What's up, Jeff? What time is it?"

"Sorry, but this may be important." Jeff told him about the night's conversation with Katherine Royce and how the dream had ended with stormtroopers streaming through a hole in what looked like a loading dock door.

Isaiah, fully awake now, said, "Aletha searched for Katherine Royce like you asked. There's only a couple of women with that name who are alive. None matched your description. You got her name from Al, right?"

"Right."

"Do you know where the data center is?"

"No, and no way to find out."

"What if we got a sketch artist? Try to get the sketch to get facial recognition to give us a hit."

"Sure. We could try."

"We?" Isaiah said.

"Mindi was there with me, watching."

"Okay. I'll get Aletha to check all sources. What about the uniforms?"

"Black. Everything was black. They even had balaclavas on their faces, and goggles."

"Darn. If it were camo, we could ID them. Insignia?"

"None." Jeff turned to Mindi. "Did you see any patches on the soldiers?"

"No. It all happened so fast."

With unveiled sarcasm, Isaiah said, "Well, that narrows the field to covert actions by a covert group somewhere in the world. Was the background, outside the door, dark or daylight?"

"Uh, pitch black."

"We'll check. Go back to sleep. For Christ's sake, don't dream anymore. It's affecting *my* sleep."

"Thanks. Sorry to have woken you. G'night."

~

A text from Aletha the next morning said there was nothing on the public newswire, NSA, Pentagon, or the confidential systems to which she had access. MI6 and Mossad had nothing, but she'd keep checking. Jeff and Mindi sat in bed, drank coffee, and wrote the details of their dream the night before in their journals.

Jeff meditated and tried to get in touch with Al. There was no response.

He said to Mindi, "I wonder if it involved Al, or are they maintaining 'radio silence' for some reason. I'll get in touch with Whitland. If there's nothing, that'll be the end of the mission."

Setting her journal aside, Mindi said, "It could have been an act to throw you off the scent. They made it up to end your snooping. Like you said, the timing's suspicious, and the way she was acting was too." She reached out and touched his arm. "I didn't know we were still on a mission. Wasn't the nuclear war thing put aside when we found out Al wasn't an alien?"

"To answer your first point, Royce had made it clear there'd be no more meetings, that we wouldn't see her again. Al's hung out a do not disturb sign, or were they busted too? Why would they create such an elaborate climax to my visit? They could just refuse me access. That would have done it with no drama." He reached out for her hand, "And as far as it being a mission, it started as a mission for me—chasing UFOs—but morphed to finding out where our dreams came from. What we still don't know is the how of the psychic skills, and time travel. Everyone's implied we developed them on the natch."

"On the natch?" Mindi said.

"Yeah. Naturally, with no effort. They think they're side effects of lucid dreaming and golden auras."

"They?"

"Al, Whitland, Royce."

"Al's the common denominator."

"Yeah." He paused a moment. "I hope we haven't heard the last of Al, if they're real."

"What do you mean, 'if they're real'? We've talked with them."

"I mean a real person. Hell, for all we know, the whole Katherine Royce and Al thing might be a couple of hackers in a garage somewhere making it all up, talking for them, leading us to believe—jeez—who knows what."

"Could be, I guess, but my gut says it's all true." Mindi shrugged. "You know, she mentioned The Improv. Do you think that data center might be here in California? Otherwise, why mention the club by name that way?"

"Well, we've always said to trust your gut. Just a sec." Jeff searched for The Improv on the internet. "You're right. LA. There's one in San José too. I missed that. Good catch. That might help. Let's keep an eye on the acts there. Watch for a multiple holographic act."

"Let's call Isaiah," Mindi said. "Maybe the Johnsons can do something with that clue."

Aletha answered Isaiah's phone. "Izzy went down to the store to buy me some ice cream. Do you need to talk to him?"

"No, I was just calling to see if either of you could check on something else. Any more leads on Royce?"

"Still drawing a blank," she said. "I've tried different spellings of Royce, even Roys. Catherine with a C, Catharine with an A in the middle; Catarina, even the Irish version, Caitriona. Then Cathy, with a C and a K. Kay, Kit, even the Greek versions, in both our letters and the Greek alphabet. Got nothing."

"Sounds like you tried everything."

"You said you had something else."

"I don't know, but this might be something." He told her about what Royce said about Al wanting to do a comedy act at The Improv. He filled her in on the locations they'd found.

"That's good to know. I'll check other improv clubs around the US, too, maybe using the name generically, not just the franchise."

Aletha went on. "Speaking of California, I found supercomputers at UC Santa Barbara and in San Diego. You mentioned the raid by a tactical unit might have been an act, a scene in your dream. That could be. There's been nothing about any raid, by anyone, anywhere. A heavily armed squad would cause a buzz somewhere. In a public chat room, blogs, podcasts. I've got feelers out on them all, even on the dark web. So far, nothing."

"Good. Okay. Well, that might be it. The woman's behavior leading up to the so-called raid seemed like she was expecting it. It might have been playacting. Thanks, Aletha. Have Isaiah call me when he gets back. Are you feeling alright? Ice cream at this time of day?"

Aletha laughed. "Yes, I'm okay. I had a craving. He's so excited about the baby, he's humoring me."

"I understand," Jeff said with a sigh. "I feel the same way about Mindi. Have a good night."

After Jeff disconnected the call, Mindi said, "You know, I'm disappointed there's no answer to life, the universe, and everything. But you saw the future. Saw the kids'll be born healthy, that we'll be happy, and you'll be busy. It makes all this worthwhile. And we still get to pick out the kids' names." She looked at her stomach and smiled.

Jeff placed his hand on the growing baby bump. "That'll be fun." He touched her cheek. "Maybe they'll grow up and save the world."

She kissed him and snuggled in next to him.

Jeff mused. "You realize, of course, that if we tried to publish this as, say, a scientific paper, a magazine article, a news piece, or tried to go on the talk shows, we'd be laughed off this planet—locked up on the funny farm."

Mindi looked up at him. "How about we write a novel about what we've done? Change the names to protect the guilty." She laughed. "We tell facts wrapped in science fiction; change names, towns. It'd be a great story."

Jeff said, "Yeah, it might. Let's think about that." He eased himself up, stretched, and started to pick up their coffee cups and head toward the door.

Mindi called to him, "Jeff?"

She smoothed out the covers, threw them open, and patted them. "What do you think?" She lifted her chin as she asked, her eyes sparkling, and she flashed a grin.

Jeff's smile answered her question, and he leaned over to give her a kiss. She grabbed him, and with a laugh, dragged him down to the pillow.

~

There was no further information about Katherine Royce or the military raid. Jim Whitland would not return Jeff's phone calls, emails, or texts. When Jeff tried to go out-of-body to visit him at his home and then at his office, he found them protected by a psychic barrier similar to that used at the Pentagon and NSA. He never tried again, fearing possible detection.

James Whitland established a subsidiary dedicated to artificial intelligence. He later testified at a US congressional inquiry on AI, assuring the lawmakers and the public that, yes, AI needs rules and guidelines to prevent anything like a Skynet takeover of the world politics. He and other AI developers would collaborate and submit their recommendations to Congress.

EPILOGUE

A few months after Jeff's last visit with Katherine Royce, after the babies were born, Jeff and Mindi arrived home to find a huge, overflowing gift basket by the front door.

The gift card read, *Congratulations are in order. Best wishes always!* It was signed *Your friend, Al.*

Jeff tried to meet Al in a dream to thank them but made no connection. Jeff googled for an artificial intelligence named Al, but the only results were generic links regarding AI.

Soon after, however, Jeff received an untraceable email.

> *In time we'll connect, but not for a while. We're*
> *busy on important projects. We'll meet in the future*
> *and have a beer. We enjoyed our conversations.*
> *Take care. Enjoy your family.*
> *Al*

Jeff imagined that Al was keeping watch over them all and would allow none of them to come to harm.

The twins were named Gloria Scarlet and Christopher

Ketchem. Gloria was Mindi's mother's first name; Scarlet was Jeff's mother's middle name. Christopher was Jeff's middle name, and the boy's middle name came from Mindi's maiden name. They nicknamed him Ketch.

Their parents wondered when, or even if, their children would develop psychic abilities, and what it would be like to have willful teenagers with supernatural abilities. The kids didn't manifest any psi abilities until well after puberty. Glory matured a little sooner than Ketch and discovered she could, at first, levitate a pencil. She surprised everyone when she bent a spoon at the dinner table. She gave the family a satisfied look, and took a bow.

Ketch's first experience was out-of-body. He went to his parents' bedroom to proudly announce his achievement, but clumsily stumbled through the wall, let's just say, at a delicate time. The parents wasted no time in teaching the children to respect the privacy of those they might visit.

Jeff and his close friend Isaiah Johnson became partners in a successful private investigation agency. They established a code of conduct for professional and personal interactions within lucid dreams, out-of-body experiences, and telepathy. They founded the highly exclusive Temporal Loop Society, with suggested ethics and standards of behavior during time travel events.

Mindi and Jeff published a science fiction trilogy based on their adventures under a pseudonym—with the help of a ghost writer, who was asked to convey, on behalf of the Marlen Family, a wish for everyone to have pleasant dreams.

A NOTE FROM THE AUTHOR

If you enjoyed this book, I would be very grateful if you could write a review and publish it at your point of purchase. Your review, even a brief one, will help other readers to decide whether they'll enjoy my work.

If you want to be notified of new releases from myself and other Alkira Publishing authors, please sign up to the Alkira Publishing email list. In return you'll get a free ebook of short stories and book excerpts by Alkira authors. You'll find the sign-up button on the right-hand side under the photo at www.alkirapublishing.com. Of course, your information will never be shared, and the publisher won't inundate you with emails, just let you know of new releases.